Tasting Temptation

DYLANN CRUSH

To Whiskey ~
the more I learn about you, the more I realize I'll never learn enough.

CHAPTER 1

Miller

"SHE DID WHAT?" I slid a bowl of instant oatmeal onto the table in front of my six-year-old son, Jack. He'd been on a roll for the last fifteen minutes, telling me all about the pint-sized bully who'd been making his life a living hell.

"She pushed me at recess. You told me not to hit girls, but I wanted to, Dad." His eyebrows bunched up, looking like two fuzzy, angry caterpillars over his dark green eyes.

"Did you tell your teacher?" I emptied the pot of coffee into the travel tumbler my mom had given me for Christmas. Pictures of Jack plastered the sides. Yeah, I was the kind of dad who wanted people to know how much I loved my kid.

He talked around the bite of oatmeal he'd just shoveled into his mouth. "Mrs. Blessing says not to tattle."

"Jack,"—I unplugged my laptop and slid it into my computer bag—"if she's hurting you, it's not tattling." For the umpteenth time, I cursed myself for not holding him back a year. With a birthday at the beginning of September, he was always the youngest kid in his class. It didn't help that he'd inherited his mom's delicate bone structure. Some of the girls in his class towered over him. Girls like Bettina Calbot, the one

I'd nicknamed the Ice Princess, who'd been bullying him since last fall.

"If I tell, she'll just do it again." He continued to scoop his breakfast into his mouth. Oatmeal dribbled down his chin.

I stopped next to him on my way to add his lunchbox to his backpack and swiped my thumb across his face. "Where's your napkin, big guy?"

He reached for the hem of the long-sleeved T-shirt he had on.

"Try again." I leaned toward the middle of the table, where a single paper napkin sat in a plastic holder. "Damn, how can we be out of napkins already?"

Jack's brows shot up at my choice of words.

"Sorry. Here, use this." I pressed the last napkin into his hands as I glanced at the clock on the microwave. Late. Again.

"She called me puny and said if I worked out a hundred years, I still wouldn't have any muscles." He made a fist and flexed his tiny biceps. "Is she right, Dad? Will I always be a shrimp?"

My chest squeezed tight at the way his lips curved into a frown. I thought parenting a boy would be easy. Hell, I grew up running all over the mountains in Beaver Bluff, Tennessee, with my three older brothers. I figured my childhood had been enough training for raising a son. But thanks to the stocky European gene pool my DNA pulled from, I'd never been the small kid who got picked on by everyone. My brothers stopped teasing me by the time I'd turned ten since I outweighed them all. I had no experience with being bullied, especially by a girl.

"Come on. Clear your bowl. We've got to get going." I slid his chair in after Jack got up and shuffled to the sink, his favorite Star Wars bowl in hand.

"It's true then." Shoulders slumped, Jack let out a huge sigh.

We should have left five minutes ago if I wanted to make it to the eight o'clock meeting my brother Vaughn had scheduled at the distillery. I'd lost count of how many times I'd told him I couldn't make the early morning meetings he favored. His lack of consideration was another reason I didn't want to take him up on the job he kept offering. The sooner we found someone to take over the books at the distillery, the happier I'd be.

"Get your shoes on." Sensing Jack needed a little inspiration, I grabbed his light-up sneakers from the bin and set them on the mat. "What did I tell you about Uncle Evan?"

With all the excitement of a cow on its way to the slaughterhouse, Jack took baby steps toward where I waited by the back door. "That he used to be puny until he started working out."

"That's right. You keep eating healthy and playing hard, and I bet you'll be bench-pressing girls like Bettina Calbot by the time you get to second grade." I picked him up under the armpits and set him down on the bench so he could pull on his shoes. If things went well, he wouldn't have to worry about her next fall, anyway.

The bowl clattered in the sink. I looked up in time to see my dog prop himself up on the counter with his front paws and lean into the sink to lap the last bits of oatmeal from Jack's bowl.

"Titus, get down!" I clapped my hands together, but the beast just lifted his brows in my direction while his tongue continued to clean the bowl.

Something in my life needed to give. The past few months, I'd been busier than a cross-eyed rooster on an anthill, trying to get Jack through the second half of the school year, keep the family business afloat, and stay on top of my full-time job. I needed a change, so I'd put in for a director position at the consulting firm where I'd been working and hoped to hear something within a few weeks. It would mean relocating to Arizona, but I was ready to put some distance between my overbearing family and me.

Guilt pierced my gut as I imagined what it would feel like to cut my ties to the family business for good. There just wasn't a place for me there. I'd known it all along, and it was about time I made it clear to my brothers. They'd been holding out hope I'd step into the role my mom had managed for the past twenty-five years after she and my dad retired, but I couldn't.

Like Jack, I had demons to fight—the same ones that had followed me for as long as I could remember. Unlike my son, no one had taken the time to try to teach me how to defeat them. Instead of leaving them in my past, they'd grown with me. Now they were too big and too strong to take down. It was easier to walk away and let them win.

I'd learned my lesson, which was why I kept after Jack to figure out a way past his current issue with freaking Bettina Calbot. I wasn't sure what bothered me more... the fact that the pint-sized Ice Princess was making my son's life so miserable or that I could store so much hate inside my heart for a six-year-old girl.

"Tell you what, Jack. I saw an email from Mrs. Blessing about needing volunteers for your Valentine's Day party next Friday. I'm going to sign up to help." I didn't have time to take an afternoon off, but my kid needed me. No matter what I had going on, he came first.

"You're gonna come to my school?" His eyes lit up, reminding me how little it took to make him happy.

"Yeah." I bent down to tie his shoes. We were still working on perfecting that skill, and though he could do it, we didn't have time for the multiple attempts he'd have to make to get the job done.

"You promise?" He looked up at me, his eyes wide with hope.

The last time I'd tried to volunteer at his school had been right before the holidays. An emergency at the distillery had popped up, preventing me from being there to help him make a gingerbread house out of graham crackers. My sister Ruby had gone instead, and the masterpiece they created together won second place. I still felt the sharp pang of regret when I looked at the red ribbon on his bedroom wall.

"I promise. Now grab your backpack and coat. We've got to get." I stood and ruffled his hair before I planted a kiss on the top of his head. Nothing would prevent me from following through this time. I needed to see Miss Bettina Calbot in action so I could help Jack formulate a plan to put an end to her bullying once and for all.

CHAPTER 2
Amalie

A TODDLER SHOE flew past my head and bounced off the windshield as I pulled into a parking spot in front of Beaver Bluff Elementary. I glanced in the rearview mirror and made eye contact with the mischievous two-year-old who'd almost caused me to take out the bumper of the Mercedes next to me.

"Shoes belong on your feet, Caden." My too-bright, forced smile covered up the frustration I felt deep down inside. Caden's parents took off five days ago for a two-week conference in Switzerland, leaving me solely in charge of him and his older sister.

I loved kids. Adored them. Wanted half a dozen of my own someday. I was even putting myself through school as a full-time nanny for the Calbot family to earn my degree and teach at the elementary level. But Caden and Bettina had been pushing buttons I didn't know I had since their parents left.

I leaned over to reach the passenger-side floorboard and closed my fingers around the soft-sole shoe. What would happen when he started wearing those cowboy boots his grandpa had given him for Christmas? I might have to put up one of those acrylic barriers they had in cop cars to keep him from whomping me in the head.

Today was Bettina's first-grade Valentine's Day party, and Mrs. Calbot had signed up to help. Now that she was soaking in the hot springs in Switzerland while her husband attended board meetings, it was up to me to fill in. It wasn't the first time I'd had to cover a volunteer shift at Bettina's school, but I'd never had to bring Caden with me before.

"Are you ready to make some valentines?" I asked him as I opened the back door.

He shoved his fingers in his mouth and let out a loud toot. A loud, juicy toot. I'd changed him moments before we walked out the door, but it sounded like he'd just filled up his diaper.

"Come on, little guy. Let's get some fresh pants on you before we head inside." I unclipped him from his car seat and debated whether to take him into the school and use a bathroom with no diaper-changing facilities or lay him down in the back of the hand-me-down wagon my mom had passed onto me. A quick whiff of his backside confirmed it would be a multiple-wipe endeavor.

Caden was usually on a pretty regular schedule when it came to his BMs. Yes, one of the joys of being his nanny was tracking his bowel movements so I could report to his mom every day. As I popped the back of the wagon and laid him down for a quick change, I ran through what he'd had to eat over the past twenty-four hours. Nothing out of the ordinary. Chalking it up to his two-year-old molars coming in, I slid a clean diaper underneath him and gently pulled the tabs holding the current diaper in place.

Call it divine timing or just a wicked stroke of bad luck, but just as I opened up the dirty diaper, Caden unleashed a stream of something so foul I couldn't believe it could come from someone so tiny.

"Aw, shit!" I grabbed a handful of wipes from the travel pack, struggling to work them free from the slit in the plastic.

Loose stool flowed from underneath him, spreading onto the carpet-covered cargo area.

"Shit, shit, shit!" I bit my tongue. All I needed was for Caden to pick up on a four-letter word. No stranger to cleaning up a kiddo covered in his feces, I persevered. At least he hadn't gotten any on me.

A few minutes later, he had on a clean diaper and a fresh outfit. I wrapped the trash in one bag and his dirty clothes in another. The carpet would have to wait until we got back to the house.

I doused my hands in hand sanitizer and balanced all twenty-five pounds of baby boy on my hip. We'd already had the blowout diaper, so the odds were in my favor that we'd make it through the hour-long party without a repeat.

The women in the office cooed over Caden as we checked in, then issued me a visitor sticker so we could head to the classroom.

Mrs. Calbot wasn't a fan of sweets, so instead of signing up for something easy like sugar cookies and punch, she'd volunteered to provide a craft project for the kids to complete. I should have been studying for my physics test next week, but I'd spent the past two nights after I'd put the kids to bed cutting out hundreds of red and pink hearts. The project seemed simple enough. Each kid would get a paper heart to decorate, and when they were done, they could paste one of their extra school pictures in the center.

I'd brought red, pink, and purple ink pads so they could add their fingerprints and a collection of crayons and colored pencils. The teacher assured me I wouldn't have more than three or four kids at my station at once, so I was confident I'd be able to handle Caden and supervise the craft at the same time.

Excited voices and high-pitched laughter filled the halls as we walked through the building. I had a love-hate relationship with Valentine's Day and all the fanfare that went along with it. When I was younger, everyone got the same store-bought cards in our classroom Valentine's Day exchange. But as I got older, the Valentines got fancier. Some kids brought handmade cards, full-size candy bars, or even gift cards for ice cream cones at the Beaver Bluff Creamery.

Though my mom worked two jobs to pay the bills, we never had extra funds for something as frivolous as fancy valentines. The only ones I ever handed out were from the packages my mom picked up at the dollar store. I shook my head, dislodging the memories. Bettina and Caden would never have to worry about things like that.

I stopped outside Mrs. Blessing's first-grade classroom. The kids had just come in from recess and were putting away jackets and getting settled in their desks.

"Titsa." Caden pointed at Mrs. Blessing through the open door.

"That's right, that's the *teacher*," I replied, stressing the correct pronunciation.

"Titsa." He nodded.

Someone behind me chuckled. I turned to see a guy standing a few feet away. He wore a plaid flannel shirt that clung to his broad shoulders. His mouth spread into an amused smile, and he bit down on his lip.

Great. Miller Bishop. I hadn't seen him this close in years, but I recognized him immediately. Everyone in town knew the Bishops. They co-owned the Devil's Dance Distillery with two other families and had been part of a decades-long feud that pitted half the town against the other half, depending on which family they supported—the Bishops or the Stewarts.

I'd never given the feud much thought, but my mom was a distant relation to the Stewarts, so there was no love lost between her and the Bishop family.

"Don't encourage him. With the way my day's been going, he'll have everyone calling Mrs. Blessing 'titsa' by the time the party's over."

Caden grinned. "Titsa."

"Looks like you're the one encouraging him," Miller said.

I rolled my eyes and turned forward again. Ever since I was old enough to know the difference between girls and boys, I'd heard girls in my class talk about the Bishop brothers. They were sweet to look at but had been known to deliver some stings. I couldn't argue with the pretty-to-look-at bit. Miller stood a whole head taller than me with shoulders so broad they looked like they'd barely fit through a standard-sized doorway. He was the youngest of the brothers but was still several years older than me.

Though some women might fall for his rugged good looks, I considered myself immune. I'd worked too hard to let myself get distracted by a man, even if the man had a build that could make me drool and smelled good enough to lick from head to toe.

While we waited for Mrs. Blessing to get the kids settled down and let us in, Caden struggled in my arms. "Down. Want down."

"Not yet, bud. It's almost time to go see your sister." I shifted the straps of my tote bag further up on my shoulder. Caden needed to stop squirming, or I'd drop the arts and crafts supplies.

"Hey, want a cookie while you wait?" Miller rummaged

through the plastic grocery bag in his hands and held up a colossal chocolate chip cookie.

"He can't have that." I whipped around just as Caden brushed his fingers against the treat. It fell to the ground and broke into several pieces.

"Cookie!" Big, fat crocodile tears immediately ran down his cheeks. He pummeled my stomach with his feet, desperately trying to break free so he could get a sugar fix.

Miller frowned and bent down to pick up the pieces. "Why not? It's a Valentine's party."

"His mom doesn't want him having any extra sugar." I shouldn't have to explain myself. Miller ought to know better than to offer food to other peoples' children.

"Cookie!" Caden continued to wail. He landed a swift kick to my gut, and the tote bag slipped off my shoulder. It landed on the thin commercial carpet and sent dozens of colored pencils and markers rolling across the hallway.

"Come on, Caden. Let's pick up the markers, and I'll let you have some of that candy you like."

"So, he can have candy but not a cookie?" At least Miller had the decency to crouch down and help me gather the items that had spilled out of my bag.

"They're fruit snacks," I whispered. Caden didn't need to know they were homemade with organic fruit and sweetened with a tiny bit of agave syrup. "Caden's sensitive to gluten."

"Poor kid." Miller stood. His long, thick fingers wrapped around a bundle of runaway markers.

I held out the bag, and he dropped them in. "Thank you."

"You're welcome. By the way, I'm Miller Bishop." He held out his hand like I had no idea who he was. Everyone within a hundred miles of Beaver Bluff, Tennessee, could recognize a Bishop brother with one look.

"Amalie Rivers. I nanny for the Calbot family. This is Caden and his older sister Bettina is in Mrs. Blessing's class."

"Bettina Calbot." Miller narrowed his eyes but didn't loosen his grip. "She's the sweet little angel who's been giving my son a hard time lately."

"Oh?" I could have pulled my hand away, but I didn't want to be rude. Besides, as aggravating as the man attached to the hand was, his was the first male hand I'd held in too long to remember.

"We should talk after the party." He held my gaze for a few beats too long, then let go of my hand. His gaze shifted to a spot behind me. "Does Caden usually dig through the garbage can for snacks?"

"What?" I spun around in time to see Caden shove a hunk of crumbled cookie into his mouth. Not only had it been on the floor, but it had also just come out of the trash. "Caden, no!"

"Good cookie." He rubbed his palm over his belly like he did when we sang the growling tummy monster song.

Wonderful. In a few hours, his stomach would rebel from a gluten overload, he'd probably be too wired for a nap, and I'd have to hold off on getting any homework done until after I put him to bed. Sometimes I wondered if raising other peoples' kids was more trouble than it was worth.

The door opened, and Mrs. Blessing offered a hesitant smile. "Thanks so much for volunteering. We're ready for you now."

Miller gestured for me to go first. I swept Caden up in one arm and grabbed my bag with the other, eager to put a little distance between me and the Bishop brother with the dark green eyes.

CHAPTER 3
Miller

SEEING the smile on Jack's face as I walked into his classroom was worth whatever bullshit I'd have to endure from my older brother for walking out of another interview. My kid could barely keep his excitement under control. I could tell by the way his butt bounced up and down in his seat.

Finally, his teacher put all the kids in small groups and told them to go to their assigned station. Jack started in the hallway at the Halloween Bingo game. While a handful of kids gathered around the make-your-own sundae bar I'd set up on the designated snack table, I glanced over to where Amalie-the-nanny was trying to explain the craft she'd brought while keeping hold of Bettina's little brother.

Hell, I didn't envy her that task. I laughed as he wrapped his pudgy little fingers around an uncapped marker and swiped it over her hand. Jack hadn't gotten into too much trouble when he was that age, at least not that I could remember.

"What are we supposed to do here?" A girl with two long blonde braids stared up at me.

She looked familiar, though to be honest, most folks in

Beaver Bluff did. I'd never lived anywhere else except for the two and a half years I'd attended college in Knoxville. That all came to an end when Jack entered my life, and I transferred to online classes so I could take care of my kid.

"This is the make-your-own sweet sundae bar." I tugged the lid off a gallon-sized bucket of vanilla ice cream. "We've got vanilla or chocolate ice cream, and you can add whatever toppings you want to make it as sweet or silly as you'd like."

The girl's eyes lit up. "Can we put candy on top?"

"You bet." I pulled out the stuff I'd picked up to stock the sundae bar. Mrs. Blessing had made it clear I couldn't bring in anything with peanuts, but I'd brought in cookies, heart-shaped sprinkles, strawberry sauce, and several cans of whipped topping.

"Can we use whatever we want?" The kid asking was at least a head taller than the other boys in his class. He had to belong to the Stewart family. They were the only ones in town with black hair and that color of light blue eyes.

My gut twinged as I looked him over. I was surprised he wasn't the one bullying Jack since his family and mine had been engaged in a longstanding family feud. Maybe this next generation would be the one to put it behind them. Sure would come in handy if our families continued to run the Devil's Dance Distillery together.

"Yeah, just save some so the kids who come after you have enough." I set the ice cream scoop down and stood by while they filled little red plastic heart-shaped bowls with their favorites.

"Are you all set, Mr. Bishop?" Mrs. Blessing stopped by the table to check in. "It looks like you've got everything under control over here."

"So far, so good." I pulled a paper towel off the roll I'd

brought with me and wiped a glob of melting ice cream off the table.

"I wish you'd told me you were planning on bringing ice cream for a treat." Her hands clasped together so tightly the area around her knuckles whitened.

"Oh. I didn't know I needed to clear it with you first. Sorry about that." Jack told me most parents brought in fruit or veggies with ranch dressing. If my kid wanted to win over some of the bullies in his class, I was prepared to help him however I could. Even if that meant bribing the mean kids to be nice to him by upping the stakes at school party time.

Mrs. Blessing gave me a tight-lipped smile. "It's just that the kids can make such a mess. I hope you'll stay on top of keeping the table clean so it doesn't get out of hand."

"Of course." I glanced over at Bettina's nanny, who must have overheard the reprimand and gave me a smug smile.

"I need to run a few things down to the office. Do you think you can handle the classroom while I'm gone?" Mrs. Blessing asked.

"Absolutely. Take your time. We'll keep things under control until you get back." I nodded, emphasizing my point that I could handle a room full of six-year-olds. How hard could it be? In a few minutes, they'd switch stations, which meant I'd have Jack at the treat table next. With four groups of kids, we'd be almost halfway through the party at that point.

Mrs. Blessing stopped by the nanny's table before heading into the hall. The timer sounded, and the kids at my table tried to slurp up the rest of their sundaes before they moved on to make their arts and crafts with Amalie.

"Can I take mine with me? I'm not done yet." The girl with the braids held her heart-shaped bowl out to show me how much she had left.

One of the kids coming in from the hall bumped her arm as

he passed. Melted ice cream spilled down the front of her shirt, covering the unicorn design with silver sparkles and a dark brown stain.

"Look what you did." Tears filled her eyes. It was like someone had flipped a switch to immediately turn on the waterworks.

"Hey, it's okay. We'll get you cleaned up in no time." I grabbed a wad of red and pink napkins and pressed them into her hands. Then I crouched down to sop up the puddle of ice cream melting into the carpet.

"Are you ready to admit the make-your-own-sundae bar might not have been the wisest choice?" Nanny Amalie glanced over, eyebrows raised.

"Nothing a little water won't take care of." I pulled a handful of paper towels off the roll and forced myself to keep my cool as I walked over to the sink.

By the time I returned to the table, the next group of kids had joined the first. Jack held up one of the scoops, then thrust it into the gallon of chocolate ice cream. It had been frozen solid at the store, but since it had been sitting out for a bit, it had softened around the edges. He pulled the scoop out. All the ice cream in the bucket came with it.

"Look, Dad. Does this mean I get to eat whatever's on the scoop?" He lifted his hand high. A bucket-shaped blob of ice cream balanced precariously on top of the scooper.

"Hey, big guy. Why don't you put that back into the bucket before it"—the entire blob splattered onto the carpet—"falls."

Jack looked up at me, his eyes wide. "Oops."

"You'd better get that cleaned up." Nanny Amalie abandoned her post at the arts and crafts table to provide assistance.

I didn't need her help. Everything was under control. I reached down with my bare hand to shovel the ice cream back into the bucket. As I did, a stream of fluffy whipped cream hit me in the chest.

Amalie turned toward the offender. "Spencer Stewart, put that down right now."

I knew the tall kid was a Stewart. Instead of dropping the can, the kid doubled down by sending a blast of extra-creamy whipped topping her way. It hit her square in the face.

Her hands went up, and she sputtered. "You've got to be fucking kidding me."

A collective gasp came from the group of first graders. Amalie pulled her glasses off and looked over at me. Except for a saucer-sized area around each eye where her glasses had been, her entire face was covered in white. She looked like an owl who'd just found itself buried up to its ear feathers in snow.

I tried not to laugh. Even clamped my arm over my belly to hold it in. But as Amalie stood there, her long, dark lashes blinking in slow motion, a deep laugh ripped free from my belly.

Her cheeks flushed—at the least the little bit of them I could see. She shoved her hand into the bucket of ice cream and flung a huge glob straight at me.

I didn't expect someone who looked like a buttoned-up librarian to make that kind of move. Thankful for her terrible aim, I turned and watched the ice cream splatter onto the cabinet behind me.

"Food fight!" Leave it to a Stewart to ramp things up. The kid she'd called Spencer dipped both hands into buckets of ice cream and slung fistfuls at his classmates.

Ice cream flew. Heart sprinkles rained down on everyone. Strawberry sauce splattered over the desks, carpet, and walls. I ducked down behind a bookshelf full of easy readers and tried to locate Jack. He stood in the middle of the melee, wiping a giant glob of strawberry sauce from a girl's cheeks.

"Jack, take cover." I caught his attention and motioned for him to join me behind the bookshelf.

He grabbed the girl's hand and tugged her toward me. "Dad, Mrs. Blessing is gonna be so mad."

I peeked past him at the wild band of sugar-crazed first graders. One kid smashed chocolate-covered candies into the carpet. Another finger-painted with chocolate ice cream down the front of the whiteboard. One little girl flung chocolate syrup and whipped cream over the collection of stuffed animals in the sunken reading pit.

Clearly, someone needed to step up and take control.

"I've got this, big guy." I stood, put my fingers in my mouth, and let out a whistle that had stopped full-contact football games.

The kids didn't flinch.

That's when I knew I was in trouble. Anarchy had risen between the four walls of Mrs. Blessing's first-grade classroom, and I was helpless to stop it.

Then I saw her. Amalie dragged a chair toward the door leading to the hallway. As food flew around her, she climbed onto it and clapped her hands. If my whistle didn't interrupt the free-for-all, a gentle clap of her hands wouldn't do the trick. Lights flickered off and back on again several times.

Amalie held up her hand, her fingers stretched to the ceiling. "Give me five."

I scoffed. Like every kid in the class was going to come up and slap her hand with theirs. To my complete shock, they all stopped and put their hand in the air, copying her movement. The silence was deafening. Except for the sound of strawberry sauce dripping from the front of the cabinets at the back of the room and landing on the pile of papers on Mrs. Blessing's desk, the room was completely quiet.

Instead of looking proud of herself, Amalie stayed on the chair, her hand raised, and turned her head to survey the aftermath. When her gaze landed on me, she stopped. Her jaw tightened, and heat flashed through her eyes.

She opened her mouth like she wanted to call me out right then and there. I was used to it. As the youngest brother in a family full of overachievers, I'd been the class clown. Vaughn and Cole were the smart ones. I learned early on that I'd never live up to the standards they set when it came to grades. Evan earned his reputation on the football field. I was bigger than him, but he'd always been more coordinated and had some sixth sense that let him anticipate what would happen on the field before the plays were called.

The only thing left for me to do was make people laugh. I'd always been good at it. Based on the daggers flying at me from Amalie's eyes, it looked like my streak had ended.

A loud gasp came from the doorway behind Amalie. Thirty-plus pairs of eyes turned to find Mrs. Blessing clutching her hand to her heart.

"Wha-a-a-a—" She surveyed the trashed classroom. "Boys and girls, what happened?"

I figured we'd do what I did in high school—everyone would deny knowing anything about how the ceiling had been sprayed with whipped cream and the stuffed animals all looked like they were bleeding out. Things must have changed since I'd been a student at Beaver Bluff Elementary. Half the kids pointed at Amalie, and the other half pointed at me.

Spencer Stewart was the first one to speak. I knew I shouldn't have given him the benefit of the doubt. "Mrs. Blessing, we were eating our snack and making crafts when Jack's dad and that lady over there started a food fight."

Mrs. Blessing staggered into the room and leaned against the doorway for support. I debated on whether I needed to rush to her side or see if there was a defibrillator somewhere in the building because she looked like she was about to collapse.

In a stern voice that didn't seem possible coming from a woman of her slight stature, she pointed a finger at me, then turned it on Amalie. "The two of you . . . to the principal's office. Now."

CHAPTER 4

Amalie

DAMN MILLER BISHOP and his make-your-own sundae bar. He was at fault, yet I was being punished for his bad judgment. No one in their right mind would think to bring gallons of ice cream into a classroom for treat time. That must be it. He obviously had a few screws loose. Maybe more than a few. The man might be living on the edge, one or two incidents away from completely losing his grip on reality.

I'd never gotten in trouble at school. Thanks to one of my elementary school teachers, I realized that getting good grades and a degree would be my only way out of the future that loomed in front of me. My mom did the best she could, but after my dad left, she had to work two jobs to pay the rent and keep food in the refrigerator. I'd vowed that I'd make something of myself so I didn't have to live like that. And here I was, headed to the principal's office for the first time in my life.

"Don't worry. Let me do the talking, and I'll take care of everything." Miller looped his thumb through his belt loop and matched my stride.

I shifted Caden on my hip. He swiped his fingers across my

cheek and shoved them in his mouth. At least someone was enjoying the aftermath of the one and only food fight I'd ever taken part in.

"I'll do my own talking," I ground out. If I let Miller take charge, I'd end up tying my fate to his. While I had no doubt he'd do his best to charm Principal Masterson, she didn't strike me as the kind of woman who'd fall for Miller's blow-sunshine-up-her-butt routine.

"Suit yourself." Miller held the door to the office open for me to pass through first. "But just so you know, she's my brother's best friend."

That comment got my attention. I didn't want to give him the satisfaction of a reply, but I was curious. "What do you think she'll say?"

His shoulders rose and fell in a shrug. "She'll probably laugh her ass off then ask me to write a big check to cover the damage."

My stomach dropped. I didn't have a big check. All the money in my meager bank account went toward my tuition. "What kind of big check?"

Miller put a hand on my shoulder then pulled it away and looked at the sticky chocolate sauce covering his palm. "Don't worry about it. I've got it covered."

I'm sure he meant to offer comfort, but I didn't like the smug look in his eyes. In that moment, he became every rich kid who'd ever snubbed me for wearing clearance clothes from discount stores and not being able to afford to keep up with the Jones's. Or in this case, keep up with the Bishops.

"You think you can toss money at any situation and not have to take responsibility for your actions?" The nerve of some people.

His brow furrowed and his eyes crinkled at the edges. "Not any situation, but that's what it's going to take to get us out of this one." He said it like it was canon. Like everyone in the world knew that was how the system worked. Like he was explaining something simple to a kid Caden's age. Like I'd be an idiot not to grasp the simple concept of his money-makes-the-world-go-round society.

"Mr. Bishop, Ms. Rivers, please come in." Principal Masterson met us at the door to her office. I didn't know how she managed, but her tight-lipped grin didn't slip a bit. Not even when the receptionist's eyes rounded and the school nurse's jaw dropped open.

"Hey, Frannie." Miller nodded toward Principal Masterson.

I rolled my eyes. Surely, she could see right through him. He was trying to use his family connection to minimize the collateral damage of his actions. What really made me mad was that he'd probably get away with it.

"Under normal circumstances, I'd ask you to take a seat." The principal shut the door behind us and walked over to lean against her desk. "However, I'm sure we can all agree these aren't normal circumstances."

Miller chuckled. "The Valentine's party did get a little out of hand."

She gave him the kind of smile a patient adult might offer a petulant child. Hope that she might be the one person willing to stand up to Miller Bishop and call him out on his shit blossomed through my chest.

"That's one way of looking at it," Principal Masterson said.

Miller shifted his weight from one foot to the other. Could one of Beaver Bluff's golden boys be getting a little nervous? I hated the sheer glee the thought sent racing through my limbs.

"Look, Frannie…"

"Mr. Bishop, I'd prefer you use my professional title when speaking to me in a work environment."

Oh, snap. I bit down on my lip to keep from laughing at the wounded look on his face.

"Fine. Principal Masterson, it wasn't my intention to get the kids riled up. I was just trying to do something special for the class so that kids would stop picking on Jack. He's been bullied all year, especially by Ms. Rivers's charge." He hooked his thumb in my direction as if there was any doubt about who he might be referring to.

"Bettina's been under a lot of stress. Her parents are out of the country, and she's having a difficult time adjusting." I bounced Caden on my hip. He'd grown tired of swiping chocolate sauce off my face and struggled to get down.

"It's been going on all year." Miller turned toward me. "She's been making cracks about his size for months. It's giving my kid a complex, and I thought if I came through with something awesome for the Valentine's party, it might buy him some respect."

Part of me wanted to laugh at his reasoning. Leave it to the rich family in town to think everything could be solved with expensive grand gestures. But there was also some truth in his tone. Knowing Bettina might be causing any other kid pain hurt my heart.

"I'll talk to her about it," I promised. Caden landed a swift kick to my hip, and I let out a gruff *oof*. I didn't want to set him down when he was covered in sticky goo.

"Let me get to the point. I'm disappointed in the two of you for the way you handled yourselves at this afternoon's event. Here at Beaver Bluff Elementary, it's our goal to teach the kids how to get along."

Miller glanced over at me and then took a step closer to the desk. "I'd be happy to bring in a commercial cleaner to clean up the mess."

She put up her hand, palm out. "I'd expect nothing less, Mr. Bishop."

He nodded, his lips curving into a satisfied smile. "I'll have my assistant reach out to—"

"We're not done quite yet." She returned the grin.

My stomach twisted like someone had strung it on one of those taffy pull machines. I didn't like the twinkle in her eye or the way her brows rose a smidge. It was like she was issuing a challenge to Miller Bishop, and I didn't want to get pulled into it as collateral damage.

"What else can I do to make things right?" Miller tilted his head and studied the petite principal.

She might have been the shortest person in the room, but she held all the power. I'd do whatever she wanted if it kept me from getting in trouble with the Calbots. No doubt Bettina would be happy to fill them in on the choice words I'd uttered in front of her entire classroom. I had a good relationship with my employers, but there was no telling what kind of transgression might be the one to set them off. Mrs. Calbot's parenting style seemed to shift as quickly as the trends she followed on social media. I needed this job and the paycheck that came with it if I wanted to finally finish my degree.

Ms. Masterson reached for her phone. "Mrs. Blessing was kind enough to send me a few classroom photos. We'll have to clear it out before the carpet cleaners come in. I'm expecting the two of you to wipe down the desks and wash the collection of stuffed animals from the reading nook. Poor critters look like they suffered the brunt of the attack."

She turned the screen to face us. The giant teddy bear Bettina liked to read to had a face full of chocolate syrup. A big bunny's ears had been covered in strawberry sauce, and the school's stuffed beaver mascot's tail looked white from all the whipped cream.

"I can have someone here later this afternoon to deal with everything." Miller reached for his phone in his back pocket.

Ms. Masterson shook her head. "What kind of message are we sending the kids if we teach them adults don't have to take responsibility for their choices? Especially their bad choices?"

"I don't understand. Do you want me to clean things up or not?" Miller's forehead crunched like he couldn't comprehend what she was saying.

I understood. For once, someone was going to make him take responsibility. A vision of Miller Bishop shoving his hands into a pair of pink rubber gloves and crouching over dozens of desks with a bucket of soapy water popped into my head.

"Yes. I want *you* to clean things up. Start by taking all the stuffed animals to the laundromat. Then you can come in over the weekend and wipe down the desks. I expect your cleaning crew to handle the walls, floor, and ceiling." She sat in the padded chair behind her desk and tucked her phone into the top drawer. "Any questions?"

"I've got meetings this afternoon, and the family's getting together to talk about the distillery's anniversary party this weekend. Come on, Frannie. Is this really necessary?" His jaw clenched.

"Not only is it necessary, if you'd like your son,"—she glanced at me, her eyes softening the slightest bit at the edges—"and your clients' daughter to be able to participate in any more Fun Friday events, you'll find a way to get it done."

"Dammit." Miller clasped his hands behind his head.

Seeing his calm, cool facade slipping away gave me a little thrill. "I can take some stuffed animals to the laundromat on my way home this afternoon."

"You're just going to go along with this?" Miller turned an accusatory glare on me. "This is ridiculous. Is there anything else we can do for you, your royal highness of Beaver Bluff Elementary?"

"There is one more thing," Principal Masterson said. "We've been looking for someone to chair the spring fundraiser. Having the two of you do it together will be a great lesson for the children on how to work with someone you don't necessarily get along with."

"What makes you think I don't get along with the nanny with the bad aim?" Miller joked.

I gritted my teeth, vowing to work on my throw in case I ever had the opportunity to nail Miller Bishop in the chin with a glob of ice cream—or anything else—ever again.

"You'll be setting a good example for Jack and Bettina." Principal Masterson shifted her attention to a stack of paperwork in front of her. "And don't think about hiring that out, Miller. I'll expect a detailed proposal on your plans this time next week. You're both excused."

My feet wouldn't move. If I understood the events of the last five minutes, I'd been assigned to wash stuffed animals and clean desks with Miller Bishop over the weekend. That, I could handle. Even though I wasn't thrilled at the prospect of spending any amount of time around the cocky jackass, I could survive forty-eight hours for the sake of keeping my job.

But working with him on the spring fundraiser? Had she lost her ever-lovin' mind?

"Ms. Masterson, I don't have ties to the school beyond being Bettina's nanny. Surely, you don't expect me to take time away from my job and work on my degree to spearhead an event that benefits the school since I don't have a child in attendance?"

Now Miller rolled his eyes. I didn't care about his reaction. The only person who mattered was Principal Masterson.

"What field are you studying?" She didn't look up as she

scrawled her signature across the bottom of a page and flipped to the next one.

"Elementary education." My throat went dry as I realized the implication.

"Don't you think spending time in the school and working on our biggest fundraiser of the year will provide you with some valuable experience?" Her dark eyes found mine. In half a second, she knew she had me exactly where she wanted me.

"Yes." That one word was all I was capable of at the moment.

"Good. I can't wait to see what the two of you come up with. I'll see you back in my office next Friday at one o'clock." She didn't look up again. There was no need. She'd said what she needed to say and issued her judgment.

Whether I liked it or not, I was about to spend way too much time with the one man I never wanted to see again.

CHAPTER 5

Miller

EVERY FOUR-LETTER WORD I could think of tried to battle its way out of my mouth, but I held back. I didn't have time to sit at the laundromat and wash stuffed animals. Hell, I didn't even know Beaver Bluff had a laundromat.

"Well, that went well." I caught up to Amalie, who had already made it halfway back to the classroom.

"We must have a different definition of *well*," she said.

"It could have been worse."

She stopped in the middle of the hall. Kids flowed around us on their way to their next class. "How could that have gone any worse, Miller?"

That was the first time I'd ever heard her say my name. Despite the circumstances, I liked the way it rolled off her tongue. Liked it a little too much. I also liked the way her cheeks flushed. Miss Everything's-under-control looked kind of hot when she was flustered.

"She could have made us apologize to the class or write a note to send home with each kid."

"Is that what you had to do when you got in trouble in

grade school?" She turned the full force of her bluish-gray gaze on me.

"I didn't start getting in trouble until middle school. Back in grade school, I was too worried about pissing off my dad." I chucked Caden under the chin. "You're probably excited about taking all those big stuffed animals home for the weekend, aren't you?"

"What makes you think I'll be the one taking all of them home?" Amalie narrowed her eyes. "I said I'd take some of them. Besides, you're the one who brought the stuff for the sundae bar. That makes you the responsible party."

I leaned close to her, not wanting to start an argument in front of the kids in the hall. The scent of vanilla and chocolate mixed with strawberries tickled my nose. The urge to run my tongue over her skin came out of nowhere. I'd have to have a serious talk with my libido. It had been a long damn time since I'd been involved with anyone, and I wasn't about to make a move on the crabby nanny.

I forced any feelings of attraction toward her deep down into my gut. "Well, you're the one who flung melted ice cream at me. That makes you more responsible for the mess."

She held my gaze, the look in her eyes a combination of anger and pure disdain. "I wish I'd hit you instead of the cabinet."

Before I could reply, she stalked off toward the wing holding the first-grade classrooms. I didn't follow her immediately. Not because I didn't have plenty of comebacks. I'd spent most of my life talking back. My mouth had gotten me into more trouble over the years than I'd ever admit.

No, I stood in the middle of the hall of Beaver Bluff Elementary as she walked away because, at that moment, I realized how much I enjoyed watching her go.

She had on tight leggings that molded to her curves with a

sweatshirt that barely covered her ass. Her hair sat on top of her head in some sort of messy updo that slid to the side as she stormed off. I was used to getting a reaction from women, but not the kind Amalie had given me.

As a man who usually succeeded with the ladies, the nanny represented a challenge. The only question was, what was I willing to do about it? While I stood there weighing the pros and cons of going after her, my phone vibrated. Fucking Vaughn. My brother was like a rabid hound dog searching for someone to take over the accounting side of the family business.

I held the phone to my ear and stepped out of the continuous stream of kids in the hall. "Vaughn, what a pleasant surprise."

"Cut the bullshit. Did you make a decision on the guy we talked to this afternoon?"

"Not yet, bro. I want to check a couple of his references first." As eager as I was to step away from the distillery and return my focus to my full-time job, I wanted to make sure they hired the right person. It would be the first time in history that the Bishops didn't have a family member in charge of the numbers. We couldn't afford to make a mistake.

Vaughn groaned. I pictured him sitting behind the oversized desk in the office our dad had passed on to him. He had big shoes to fill as the general manager of Devil's Dance, but he was stubborn and bossy enough to do it.

"We need to bring someone on board ASAP. Unless you want to quit your job and come to work with us—"

"I'll call and check on them this afternoon." Every time one of my brothers suggested I join them at the distillery, I'd held my ground. It wasn't that I didn't love my family or want to see the business succeed. I just didn't want to fail them.

If I were the kind of guy who believed in talk therapy, I'm

sure some glasses-wearing, note-taking psychologist with too many expensive degrees would tell me my reluctance stemmed from my relationship with my dad. I wasn't about to give him any additional reasons to think I was a fuck-up. Not when that's how he'd viewed me my entire life.

"I'll be working on the budget for the anniversary party over the weekend. Think you could swing by for a bit on Sunday afternoon to look at it?" Vaughn asked.

"Why don't you go out this weekend? Hang out with the guys, maybe meet a girl?" Calling my oldest brother a workaholic would be a massive understatement. He lived and breathed the distillery. His twin, Cole, had been like that too. At least until a certain marketing consultant came onto the scene last year, and he lost his fucking mind over her.

"I was thinking around three. We can go over the numbers, then catch the hockey game over a few beers." Since he'd stopped seeing the last woman he'd been dating, that was Vaughn's way of socializing. Business and beers.

"Sure. See you then." It was easier to give in to him than resist. When he wanted something from someone, he'd figure out how to get it from them, one way or another.

"Oh, and why don't you stop by the distillery on your way home? I have some resumes I want you to look over."

"Can't you email them to me?"

"It won't take more than a few minutes. You're the one who wanted to be hands-on with finding a replacement."

"You're the one who asked me to help."

"Yes. Which is why I want you to stop by," Vaughn repeated.

"Fine. We'll see you in a bit." I tucked my phone back into my pocket and continued to Jack's classroom.

Before I made it there, my son rushed up to me. "Dad, we

get to take the stuffed animals home this weekend and give them a bath. Isn't that awesome?"

"Yeah, it's great." I smoothed my palm over his dark brown hair, wincing when I brushed over a crusty glob of dried whipped topping.

"Bettina gets to take some home too. She said she gets to pick which ones she wants first because she's a girl. Is that true?"

"Which stuffed animal do you really want to bring home?"

"The big beaver. It's got this awesome tail, and it's everyone's favorite." His eyes lit up, and I immediately pictured an image of me hauling a massive stuffed beaver home in the back of my truck.

"Let me tell you a little secret about women, Jack." I crouched down to put myself at his eye level. "While sometimes it's better to hold your ground, it's also good to give in every once in a while. Let them think they've got the upper hand. Does that make sense?"

"Why would I do that?" His nose crinkled, and his eyebrows knit together.

How could I explain the nuances of navigating a relationship with the fairer sex to a six-year-old? "Because it helps you get what you want in the long run. You let Bettina pick first, and maybe the next time she's about to say something mean to you, she'll remember how nice you were about it and change her mind."

Jack rolled his eyes. "As if. I tried being nice to her one time before. She still calls me names."

"You've got to do it over time. Wear her down. Kill her with kindness."

His brow furrowed. "I don't want her to die."

"Great advice." Amalie stood in the doorway, her arms wrapped around the gigantic stuffed beaver. "I really like the part about wearing women down. How do you do that, exactly?"

I put my hand on Jack's shoulder and stood. "You look like you might need some help with your beaver. Can I offer a hand?"

Her cheeks took on the color of the red napkins I'd brought in for Valentine's Day. "I can manage my beaver on my own, thank you very much."

"If you say so." I didn't know what it was about the woman, but every time I made her blush, it was like catching a slight buzz. "Come on, Jack. Let's get the rest of the animals out to the truck so we can get them cleaned up."

"Oh,"—Amalie nudged her chin toward the room—"I hope you don't mind, but I told Mrs. Blessing you'd be happy to take home the egg-ubator this weekend."

"What egg-ubator?" My joy at making her blush faded. I didn't like other people volunteering me for shit I didn't know about.

"Mrs. Blessing is worried the chemicals they use for cleaning might disturb the eggs they're incubating. Didn't Jack tell you they're going to get to watch baby chicks hatch?" The satisfied smirk stretching across her lips told me she thought she'd gotten the best of me with that trick.

"We get to bring them home?" Jack tugged his hand away from mine and ran into the room.

"And what am I supposed to do with chicken eggs?" I asked.

"Well, whatever you do, don't kill them with kindness. You'll have thirty teary-eyed first graders on your hands if you do." She turned to call back to the kids. "Bettina, Caden, come on. We've got to toss these animals in the wash."

Bettina came out of the room, dragging a teddy bear by the foot. "I need help. Brownie Bear is too heavy for me to carry."

"I'll help you." Jack picked up the bear's head. My chest swelled with pride that my son was trying to put my advice into action.

"You're not strong enough to carry him." She tugged the bear out of Jack's hands, and it dropped to the ground.

Amalie glanced up at me, her eyes full of sympathy. For the first time, I felt like we might be on the same page. "Bettina, why don't you let Jack help? He looks like he's more than strong enough to get Brownie Bear to the car. Besides, you don't want to drag him on the ground, or he might rip."

"Fine." The little girl's bottom lip stuck out in an exaggerated pout.

Thank fuck I wasn't trying to raise a girl. Being a single dad to a boy was hard enough.

"I'll grab the rest and meet you out by the truck, okay, Jack?" I waited for some sign of acknowledgment from my kid before I re-entered the classroom. All the other kids had left for the day, which meant I was alone with a frazzled Mrs. Blessing. She looked like she could use a night off—or better yet, a stiff drink. I usually had at least a bottle or two of my family's whiskey in my truck, but I'd given the last one away a few days ago and hadn't restocked. Mrs. Blessing didn't look much like a whiskey drinker, anyway, but with the popularity of whiskey continuing to rise, I was often surprised by the customers we'd been gaining.

"Oh good, you can take the egg-ubator now. I've unplugged it, but you'll want to get it set up and plugged back in as soon as possible so the temperature doesn't fall too much." She stood by the back wall next to a glass aquarium I hadn't noticed before.

"What exactly do I need to do with this?" I'd grown up on my family's acreage, but we'd never raised chickens. Except for horses and maybe a barn cat or two, I was out of my element dealing with animals. And Titus, of course. Oh shit, Titus. My hellion of a dog would probably try to eat them.

"Just keep an eye on them. The chicks shouldn't start to hatch for another two weeks. I'd take them home, but I'm heading out of town for my niece's wedding and will be gone next week."

"When can I bring them back?" If I shut them in the laundry room, I could keep Titus away. But this was one more thing I hadn't seen coming. How had I suddenly become responsible for washing stuffed animals, planning a spring fundraiser, and trying to keep a dozen eggs warm and out of my dog's jaws?

"I'll touch base when I get back in town. I hope you'll have a handle on everything by then, Mr. Bishop."

"You and me both, Mrs. Blessing. You and me both."

Amalie

AS WE APPROACHED MY PRACTICAL, compact mini-wagon in the parking lot, I wished I'd thought to drive Mrs. Calbot's super-sized SUV instead. She'd offered to let me use it while they were away, but being behind the wheel of a vehicle that cost more than my four-year education made me nervous.

Caden's car seat in the back didn't leave much room for the menagerie of stuffed animals we were charged with bathing.

"Still got everything under control?" Miller caught up to us in the parking lot. It made my heart do a little jig to see him wielding the big aquarium-turned-incubator in his arms. He headed toward a big, black pickup truck parked a few spots away.

"I'll figure it out." Something about the man got on my nerves. I hadn't figured out if it had to do more with the cocky grin he always seemed to wear or the condescending attitude that hovered around him. It was like he had a neon sign flashing over his head that read "Beaver Bluff Royalty. Untouchable." He and his brothers paraded around town like the rules didn't apply to them. Knowing he couldn't talk his way out of washing stuffed animals gave me a perverse sense of pleasure.

"I'd be happy to take all the animals to the laundromat for you. It's not like I don't have to head there myself." He balanced the egg-ubator on his hip while he opened the back door of his truck.

"Don't you have to take the eggs home first? You can't leave them sitting in the parking lot while you wash teddy bears."

"I was thinking you might be willing to keep them at your place. See, I've got this dog who'll go nuts if I bring anything living into the house." He set the aquarium down on the backseat. "Maybe we can work out a trade of some sort."

"Not interested." I pulled open the door to my backseat and began stuffing the beaver into the car, tail first.

"It wouldn't be any trouble at all. Brownie the Bear could sit in the backseat. I've got room for your beaver right up front."

I glared at him. Talking about the huge stuffed beaver like it was mine got me a little heated under the collar. Or at least it would have if I'd been wearing a shirt with a collar. As it was, hearing his deep, rich voice referring to beavers and stuffing and making room for me seemed to be affecting me a little lower than the neck area. I might carry a lifetime of grudges against men like Miller Bishop, but I still couldn't deny that the man was positively gorgeous.

If we were going to be spending any amount of time together—and unfortunately, the penance the principal had given us indicated we were—shutting down his teasing flirtations needed to be step one in negotiating the boundaries of our working relationship. Heat rolled across my chest. *Relationship* was too strong of a word. That implied intimacy and connection. *Arrangement* sounded better.

"If we're going to have a successful *arrangement*"—I drew out my chosen word—"you're going to need to stop slinging innuendos my way." Ugh. I didn't mean to utter the word innuendos. Now he'd know he'd been getting to me.

"There's nothing innuendo-ish about it. Your beaver can sit right next to me on the front seat. Sidle up close, maybe even brush against my thigh if it needs more room."

There was only one emotion stronger than the hate I felt for him at that moment, but I wasn't about to acknowledge it.

"Come on, Bettina. You and Caden climb in the back. I'll get this beaver stuffed in here if it's the last thing..." Now I was the one talking about stuffing beavers. Get a freaking grip, Amalie.

"Can we have ice cream tonight? I never got any at my party." Bettina dropped her half of Brownie Bear before she made it to the car.

"I bet my dad still has some ice cream you can have. Don't you, Dad?" Jack looked up at his dad with hope shining in his dark green eyes. Despite his relation to the man who fathered him, he seemed like a really good kid.

"Yeah. We always have tons of ice cream on hand. Tell you what—why don't I stop by my place to drop off the scrambled eggs, and I'll bring some ice cream with me when we meet you at the laundromat?" He shot me a glance over the tops of the kids' heads. "Assuming that's okay with bailiff Amalie?"

"What's a bailiff?" Jack asked.

"Don't you know anything?" Bettina snapped. "A bailiff is like a guy who works in a jail. There was one in the story Mrs. Blessing read to us before Christmas."

"Not everyone has a memory as good as yours, Bettina." I meant it as a gentle reminder to be kind, but based on the way Bettina preened, she took as an unintended compliment.

I didn't care for Miller comparing me to a jailer, but it was better than him continuing to spout not-so-innocent innuendos. "Why don't we get to the laundromat, and then we can figure out the ice cream situation, okay?"

"Sounds like a plan." Miller picked up Brownie Bear and shoved him in the back of his truck. "I'll go in for the rest of the animals since it looks like you barely have room for the one. Meet you there?"

If only Beaver Bluff had more than one laundromat to choose from. It sure would have made my life easier. Tempted to cram the big beaver into the big front loader the Calbots had at home, I almost told him I'd rather take a flying leap off a high bridge into a pothole than spend any additional time together. But, Principal Masterson had made it clear my fate was tied to the success of the spring fundraiser, at least if I wanted the chance to student teach in Beaver Bluff. There was one elementary school in town, and I couldn't afford to move away and give up my nanny job until I was done with my degree.

"I'm looking forward to it already," I lied.

Miller rubbed his hands together. "Oh, me too. Now, can you give me a hint as to where I can find the laundromat?"

———

OF COURSE, he'd never had to enter an establishment as lowly as the Beaver Bluff Fluff and Dry. He'd probably never done a load of his laundry. I'd driven by the Bishop family compound almost every day of my life. I imagined they had servants inside who were willing to pre-treat his whites, make his bed, and maybe even wipe his ass. The closer we got to the Fluff and Dry, the more bitter I became.

By the time Miller walked in, the big beaver was halfway through a hot wash, and Caden's clothes were soaked through from climbing into a commercial washing machine before it fully drained when Bettina challenged him to a game of hide and seek.

Miller had used the stop home to his advantage and had on a fresh pair of jeans and a clean, long-sleeved Henley. Based on the whiff of masculine shower gel that assaulted my nose when he passed, he'd probably even taken a quick shower. Meanwhile, I still wore the sweatshirt and leggings I'd had on during the food fight. Strawberry sauce had dried in my hair, and it looked like someone had finger-painted with poop down my thighs.

"You look annoyingly refreshed," I called out as he passed.

"It's amazing how good a hot shower and a fresh shirt can make a guy feel." He held the bear out in front of him to keep from getting his clean clothes dirty.

"I can imagine." My tone came out as icy as I'd intended. Due to the timing of the Valentine's party, I hadn't been able to put Caden down for his afternoon nap. Lack of sleep and too much sugar had him on the verge of a meltdown.

I picked him up from where he'd collapsed into a heap in front of the vending machine. He wanted candy, but there was no way I'd give in. If I let him have more sugar, I'd never get him to bed that night. I needed the time to study and work on a paper I had due next week.

Miller shoved the bear into the wash and waited for Jack to toss in a few pods of detergent. Maybe he did know how to operate a washing machine. Probably googled it before he left the house so he wouldn't look like an idiot.

"There we go. Let's turn it on and give Brownie Bear the bath of a lifetime." He lifted Jack so he could press the button to start the machine.

When Jack's feet touched the ground, he ran to where Bettina sat, scrolling through the tablet her parents had given her. They expected me to limit her screen time, but desperate times called for desperate measures. She'd had free reign of the video games after I ended the hide-and-seek game.

Miller moved over to where I stood in front of an oversized washing machine. I was trying to get Caden to take an interest in watching the bubbles go round and round inside. He was more interested in flopping around like an overcooked noodle in my arms.

"I suppose we ought to talk about ideas for the spring fundraiser while we're here." Miller drew in a deep breath and let it out with a sigh. "Do you have any suggestions?"

My eyes burned from lack of sleep. I blinked slowly, hoping it would chase the dryness away. "There hasn't been much time to think about it yet. What about a readathon?"

He leaned against the machine. "How would that raise money?"

"The kids get sponsors to pay them for every book they read. It promotes literacy and raises money at the same time. A win-win, right?" I flipped Caden around so he wouldn't bang his head. Based on previous tantrums, I had ten minutes or less before he completely lost his shit.

"I was thinking about something on a bit bigger scale. What if we bring in a mascot from one of the sports teams in Nashville and have kids pay to film a video with it?"

"How much would you charge per video?"

"Fifty bucks? It would probably cost a couple grand to hire the mascot. Then we'd need to pay for some video equipment to rent. Unless maybe I could get the company that does our promo for the distillery to come in." He cocked his head and focused on a spot on the opposite wall like he was adding up the numbers.

"That's ridiculous. No one I know has an extra fifty bucks sitting around to spend on some stupid video." While I shot down his idea, I untangled Caden's fingers from the frames of my glasses. "How about a dance party? We could have kids vote on their favorite songs, then—"

"Yeah, we can hire a band to come in and play. We're talking about bringing in a big star like Brandiss for the anniversary party we're throwing at the distillery this spring. Maybe we can have her play at the school on the same weekend."

"Brandiss is coming?" Bettina abandoned the tablet on the chair next to her. "To our school?"

"Hold on, honey. Mr. Bishop is just talking about some ideas." I gritted my teeth and glared at him... again. "Don't go getting their hopes up with big ideas that are never going to happen."

"Who says they won't happen?"

"I suppose you have people who can talk to her people?" A tic made my left eye twitch. Caden wasn't the only one about to pitch a fit.

"I'm sure Brandiss and I have some people in common. What do they call it, like six degrees of separation?" One side of his mouth lifted like he could smell the scent of victory in the air and couldn't wait to taste it.

That might be the name of the game, but when it came to connections, I was more like twenty degrees of separation from anyone who mattered. The Calbots knew people, but I'd never try to exploit my work relationship. Miller seemed like he wouldn't hesitate to exploit any kind of relationship for any reason if it might get him what he wanted.

"Jack, your dad's going to bring Brandiss to our school." Bettina skipped over to Jack, who didn't look nearly as excited about the possibility of hearing the chart-topping pop singer.

"Why can't we do hot air balloon rides instead?" Jack asked. "I've always wanted to go in a hot air balloon."

"See what you've started?" I glared at Miller.

Caden tossed his head back and banged it against the side of a dryer. The wail he let out sounded like a wounded animal who'd just been caught in a trap. All eyes in the laundromat turned on me.

"Hey, bud. You've got to be careful." I rubbed the knot forming at the base of his skull.

Miller reached out to keep Caden from launching himself out of my arms. "If you want to take the kids home, I can stay and finish the stuffed animal baths."

His offer sounded too good to be true. I turned my attention from Caden to meet Miller's gaze head-on. "Do you mean it?"

"Yeah." He backed up a step, evidently satisfied that I had a good enough grip on the flailing child in my arms.

"But we're in charge of the beaver, Amalie. It has to stay at my house, not his." Bettina folded her arms over her chest.

Before I could nip that attitude in the bud, Miller put a hand on her shoulder. "You can have the beaver. Jack and I will drop it off on our way home tonight. That will give Amalie and me a chance to settle on a fundraiser idea."

Bettina's eyes narrowed. She didn't like thinking someone was getting the best of her. "And you'll bring ice cream?"

Miller's head rolled back. "Shoot. I forgot I said I'd bring it back with me. Yep. I'll bring ice cream tonight. Sound good?"

He stared at me, waiting for a reply. All hope of getting the kids to bed early and catching up on my studying vanished. "Can't we just figure that out via text? Or phone?"

"I won't go to bed without the beaver." Bettina tapped her foot on the cracked linoleum.

She'd been a real treat lately. Knowing most of her behavior was coming from a place of hurt was the only reason I put up with it. She'd been getting better, but with her parents leaving town again, her attitude had slipped back into place.

"I'll bring pizza." Miller spread his arms wide. "Pizza, ice cream, and the big beaver. How can you say no to an offer like that?"

CHAPTER 7
Miller

WITH THE BED of my truck full of stuffed animals and two gallons of ice cream sitting in the back seat as a peace offering, I pulled into the parking lot of the main office of Devil's Dance Distillery.

"I thought we were going to Bettina's house." Jack leaned over the backseat.

"We are. I have to stop in and talk to Uncle Vaughn first. Can you grab that ice cream when you get out? We can put it in the freezer so it doesn't melt before we get there." I'd cut out of the interview he'd scheduled early today to go to the party, but Vaughn didn't understand the concept of taking an afternoon off.

Jack handed me one of the plastic bags, and we walked into the office together.

"Hey, Jack. Did your dad bring you in to get us straightened out?" Charity Devine sat behind the reception desk. Her family owned an equal partnership in the distillery. The three-way split between the Stewarts, the Devines, and us went back a hundred and fifty years.

My dad used to say that if the Devines hadn't been

involved, the Bishop and Stewart families would have done each other in a long time ago. That had been back when we were on speaking terms. He hadn't said much of anything to me lately.

"Hi, Miss Charity." Jack brightened up when he saw her. He knew she kept a jar full of candy at her desk just for him.

"What are you doing sitting out front?" I asked. As Vaughn's right hand, she had an office by his in the back of the building. When I'd been in earlier today, a woman with two high ponytails and a mouthful of chewing gum was sitting at the desk.

"The new receptionist didn't work out." Charity scooted out from behind the desk. "She was more interested in scrolling through her phone than answering ours."

"So, Vaughn's got you manning the front desk?" My older brother could be an ass sometimes. He practically lived at the office and expected his direct reports to do the same. Technically, Charity didn't work for him, but as part owner and almost as big a workaholic as my brother, they were both incredibly invested in the success of the business.

"I volunteered." She nodded at the bag in Jack's hand. "What have you got there?"

"It's ice cream. We're taking it to my friend Bettina's house tonight. Dad said I should put it in the freezer so it doesn't melt before we get there."

Charity held out a hand to take the bag from me. "How about we put this away and then check to see what kind of candy I have in the jar this week?"

"Can I?" Jack looked at me, his reluctance at stopping by the office overcome by the anticipation of more sugar.

"Yeah, just don't ruin your appetite. We're picking up pizza on the way over, remember?"

"Okay." He took off down the hall, more familiar with the

offices of the distillery than a lot of the folks who'd worked there for years.

"If you're looking for Vaughn, he's in the small conference room." Charity smiled at me. "And he's not in the greatest mood."

"Thanks for the heads-up." I took off in the opposite direction, quickly navigating through the maze of hallways to get to the conference room across from Vaughn's office.

"I'd almost given up on you." Vaughn looked up from a stack of papers in front of him.

"I said I'd be here." The soft leather chair gave up a sigh as I settled into it. "It's five-thirty on a Friday night. I bet you've got another two or three hours of work ahead of you before you leave the office."

He didn't acknowledge the jab at his lack of a personal life. Instead, he slid a resume printed on cream linen over to me. "Did you have a chance to check that guy's references yet?"

"Jesus, Vaughn. I just spent the last two hours at the Fluff and Dry watching a giant beaver go through the spin cycle. No, I haven't had a chance to call yet."

He arched a brow but didn't look up. "Do I want to know why you spent your afternoon at a laundromat?"

"No, I'm pretty sure you don't." I cradled my head in my hands as I studied the resume. "You can't hire this woman. She doesn't have experience with our accounting software."

"She spent the past five years running a whole department." Vaughn glanced up. "Can't she learn a new software system?"

"Sure. I mean, it only took me two years to become proficient, but if you want her to use Devil's Dance as a guinea pig, go ahead." I spun the paper toward him and got up from my seat.

"You know you'd make this a hell of a lot easier if you'd

take the damn job yourself." Vaughn's chair creaked as he leaned back. With his arms crossed over his chest and a dark glare on his face, he looked like a mafia don about to order a hit.

"I can't work here. You know that." I shoved my hands in the pockets of my jeans and studied the framed photographs on the walls. Most of them showed members of the Bishop and Stewart families with their arms wrapped around each other and smiling at the camera. None of us would pose for pictures like that now. The ones on the wall had to have been taken long before the feud that drove our families apart erupted.

Vaughn got up and walked toward me. He stopped next to me and looked at the same photo. "Why not? This is our history, Miller. You're part of this family, whether you want to be or not."

"That's not how Dad looks at it." It had been six years since my dad cut me out, but the pain was still as fresh as if it had happened just last week.

"What's going on in here?" Our brother, Evan, walked into the room. He had a knack for showing up at just the right moment. Tension between Vaughn and me let up a little.

"Vaughn's trying to convince me to abandon my career and come to work at Devil's Dance." I turned from the wall of photos to smile at Evan. He was the closest to me in age. After we'd survived years of trying to pummel each other into the ground, our relationship had changed from rivals to friends.

"Good luck with that, man." Evan chuckled. He knew how I felt about joining the family business. Though he had a rock-solid relationship with our parents, he'd been around during the rough years I had with my dad. By then, Vaughn and Cole were off at college, so they'd missed out on my rebellious teenage phase.

"What did you bring us?" Vaughn shifted his attention to

the bottles of caramel-colored liquid Evan set down on the table.

"First look at the fifteen-year bottle we'll be offering at the anniversary celebration." Evan wrapped his fingers around the neck of one of the glass bottles. He was in charge of production at the distillery and had been working with our sister Ruby on special packaging for our anniversary release.

"Have the Stewarts seen this yet?" Vaughn took the bottle from him and held it up.

"Not yet. I wanted to run it by you first. I'm sure they'll find something wrong with it." Evan funneled a hand through his short hair. He'd been in the service for a stint before getting injured and being shipped back to Beaver Bluff, and he still kept his hair cropped close to his head. If anyone could understand my reluctance to hop on the Bishop family gravy train, it was him.

"I like it." Vaughn nodded. "Classy with a call back to days gone by. I bet Cole will nut over this."

"That's an image I don't want in my head," I joked. Cole shared the master distiller position with one of the Stewarts. It was shocking that they'd come to an agreement on what barrels to feature in the 150th Anniversary blend. I'd only halfway paid attention to the battle that had gone on behind the scenes between the two of them.

"On that note,"—Evan grinned—"I'm heading out to Pappy's to meet Frannie for a burger. I heard you spent some time in the principal's office today, Miller."

I shot him some major side eye for bringing that up, though it was only a matter of time before he heard about my afternoon from his BFF and would start giving me shit over it.

"She said you made quite the impression on Jack's teacher and got sent home with a sticky beaver and some chicks."

Evan gave me a snide smile. He loved pouring gasoline on the fires I tended to set.

"What the fuck?" Vaughn set the bottle on the table. It landed with a loud thunk.

"It sounds worse than it was." Tension seeped up my back and tightened my shoulders.

Evan couldn't leave it alone. Sensing he'd gotten a poke in at our cranky big brother bear, he doubled down. "So, you being in charge of the school's spring fundraiser isn't going to be a shit show?"

"I've got it under control. In fact, I'm on my way to meet up with my co-chair right now." I stepped around Vaughn to head toward the door.

He reached out and grabbed my arm as I passed. "Take those resumes home with you. When we meet on Sunday, I want your top five picks."

I looked at the thick stack of papers he'd left on the table. "There's got to be at least seventy-five of them there."

"Then you'd better start looking through them tonight." Vaughn had the nerve to wink at me.

"I guess that means you're not free to join Frannie and me after your meeting," Evan joked.

"Not when I've got a gorgeous brunette and a deep-dish pizza waiting on me." The words flew out of my mouth before I realized I was speaking.

"Gorgeous brunette, huh?" Evan quirked a brow.

"The other party responsible for the food fight this afternoon," I offered. "Don't get too excited. She's just the Calbot's nanny." I didn't mean to downplay my association with Amalie, but it was a safer bet than letting on to my brothers how attractive I found her.

"Just the nanny. Sounds like one of those sappy holiday movies waiting to happen," Evan teased. He raised his voice a few octaves and batted his eyelashes. "We met when we both reached for the same piece of spicy sausage. It was lust at first sight."

"Cut it out." I gave him a playful punch in the biceps.

"You'd better stop fucking around, Miller. With the anniversary party only a few months away, get your shit together and stop dragging this family's name through the mud," Vaughn ground out.

"Believe it or not, I wasn't the instigator this time. Just got caught in the crossfire." I expected my dad to always believe the worst of me. I'd come to terms with his disappointment in me long ago. But seeing the frustration on Vaughn's face brought it all to the surface again. The sooner I got away from Beaver Bluff, the sooner I'd get out from under their crushing expectations.

"Sounds like it was more like chocolate sauce than mud," Evan offered.

"Some of us have actual work to do." Vaughn shifted his gaze to the open doorway, a clear sign that he wanted us to leave him alone.

I snagged the pile of resumes as I walked toward the door.

Evan followed me out. He slung an arm over my shoulders as we walked down the narrow hall together. "Don't let him get to you. He's just worried about the anniversary celebration. It's the first big event the distillery's planned since he took over at the helm."

"Doesn't mean he gets a free pass to start being an asshole to everyone." I shook Evan's arm off.

"What do you mean 'start being an asshole'?" Evan asked.

"Good point." I turned the corner into the lobby and spotted Jack spinning around in the receptionist's chair. "Ready to go?"

"Look what Miss Charity gave me." He held out a fist full of suckers. "She said I can take one to Bettina and Caden."

"I hope you said thank you."

"He did." Charity came down the hall with the two bags of ice cream. "Don't forget this."

"Thanks again, Miss Charity." Jack flung himself at her, wrapping his arms around her middle in a huge hug.

She looked over at me, her eyes wide, as she tucked him against her. "You're so welcome. Come back and visit anytime."

"I will." Jack pulled away and took the bags. "Ready, Dad?"

Seeing him hug Charity threw me for a loop. Not a day passed that I didn't think about what my kid was missing out on by not having a mom around. Yeah, I'd made a mistake when I knocked up a one-night stand my sophomore year of college, but I also stepped up and took responsibility for my actions. Since then, I'd been staying out of trouble and doing my best to be the kind of dad my kid needed. Still, my dad refused to see me as anything but the troublemaker I used to be.

One of these days, I'd have my shit together enough to start thinking about adding some female energy into the mix. But first, I had an accountant to hire, a job to hold onto, and a spring fundraiser that wasn't going to plan itself.

"Come on, Jack. The pizza's waiting, and we've got a challenging evening ahead of us."

"Why don't you take this with you? A little whiskey might come in handy with the nanny." Evan handed me one of the bottles he'd been holding. "Oh, and be careful handling your sausage tonight."

Jack glanced up at me as I propelled him toward the door,

his brows knit together in concern. "I thought we were getting pepperoni."

"We are. Uncle Evan's just trying to be funny." I turned to yell back over my shoulder. "And failing."

His hearty belly laugh was the last thing we heard before the door closed behind us.

CHAPTER 8
Amalie

"THEY'RE HERE!" Bettina yelled from the formal living room. She wasn't supposed to sit on the silk-covered sofa, let alone stand on it to peer out the window, but that's where I found her when I followed her voice.

"Hold on a sec, Mom." I put my hand over my phone's mic. "Hey, you know you're not supposed to be in here."

She turned to me, her hands clasped together in excitement. "It's the only place I can see the driveway."

"Out." I pointed to the glossy marble floor in the foyer.

Reluctantly, she climbed off the sofa and slunk to the front door.

"I've got to let you go, Mom. The guy I have to plan the fundraiser with just got here." I peeked into the kitchen, where I'd left Caden playing with a handful of colorful die-cast race cars. He'd disappeared.

"Don't forget my appointment next Thursday. Eleven o'clock." My mom's voice sounded strained. She'd been battling some type of long-term infection that affected her lungs. Doctors kept going back and forth between chronic asthma and inflammation. Nothing they'd tried so far had worked. She'd finally gotten an appointment with a specialist in Chattanooga, and I'd promised to go with her.

"I've got it on the calendar. Caden and I will be there." I'd arranged for Bettina to go home with a friend for a playdate after school that day, but I didn't have anyone to watch Caden. Hopefully, I could keep him busy with a video or two on the tablet. "Gotta go, Mom. Love you."

"Love you, too."

"Can I open the door?" Bettina asked.

I shoved my phone in my pocket, heading down the hall to search for Caden. Silence was never a good thing when a two-year-old was involved. "Wait until they ring the bell. Then you can open it, okay?"

The doorbell rang, a long, drawn-out sound that was supposed to mimic the chimes of Big Ben in London. It scared the crap out of me the first few times I heard it. Now, I barely noticed.

"Caden, where are you?" I tracked a trail of race cars through the kitchen and down the hall toward the guest bedroom—my bedroom. The door was usually latched with a childproof lock, but I'd asked Bettina to put my wallet in my room when we got home, and she must not have pulled the door closed all the way. I opened the door and paused as a weird noise came from the other side of the queen-sized bed.

Miller called out from the kitchen. "Pizza's here. Who's hungry?"

"I von piffa." Caden sounded like he had something in his mouth. If he'd gotten into the pantry and dragged snacks into my room, I'd be so pissed. Last time he'd done that, it took me an hour to scrub red dye from the dried beets he'd snagged out of the off-white carpet.

"Whatcha got there, bud?" I rounded the bed, but he dove underneath and crawled out the other side.

"Hey, Amalie. Do you have any paper plates?" Miller filled the doorway to my bedroom. "I should have thought to grab some, but—"

He was cut off by Caden running into his knees.

"Hey. Do you want pizza too?" Miller reached down to pick up Caden.

That's when I saw what he'd been chewing on. My heart froze. Heat and ice crawled over my cheeks at the same time. No. No. No. No. No.

"What's this?" Miller reached for the item Caden had wrapped in his pudgy little fingers.

"It's nothing." Suddenly able to move, I leaped over the bed, my arm outstretched. Instead of gracefully landing on my feet and retrieving the offensive object before Miller touched it, I landed on my stomach at his feet.

"Nothing?" Miller held the pretty pink silicon rose in his hand. "This sure looks like something to me."

"Something private." I stood and ripped it out of his grip.

"Tiffa?" Caden asked, oblivious to the fact he'd just had his mouth all over my personal pleasure provider. It was clean. I was anal about thoroughly washing it after each use. But still, knowing where it had been made my stomach roll. At least Bettina hadn't seen it. Trying to keep her from telling her parents about it would have taken some artful maneuvering.

"Are you coming?" Bettina skipped down the hall and ducked past Miller to enter my room.

I tucked the toy into the back of my leggings to keep her from seeing it. "Bettina, you've got to make sure you pull my door closed when you're done in here so your brother doesn't get into my stuff."

"What stuff?" she asked.

"Private stuff." I avoided Miller's gaze as I tried to shoo everyone out of my room.

"Yeah, Amalie has toys she doesn't want to share." Miller didn't try to hide the perverse satisfaction he was getting from finding me in such a jam.

"What kind of toys?" Bettina was intrigued at the idea that I might be holding out on her.

Ugh. I tried to come up with an explanation that wouldn't bring on more questions. "Boring stuff I need for school."

"Really?" Miller arched a brow. "What kind of degree are you working toward? I thought Frannie said you were going to be a teacher."

With the promise of pizza more appealing than finding out what boring toys I'd been hiding, Bettina twirled down the hall. "Amalie's going to teach my grade someday."

I stopped, mortified at what Miller might be thinking. His eyes drilled into me like a laser beam zeroing in on its target. I felt the weight of his stare right between my shoulder blades. He passed me in the hall, his big, bulky, built body brushing against mine.

"First graders? Will you be proposing a revolutionary type of curriculum?" His warm breath tickled my ear as he walked by.

This day needed to end. The sooner I could get him and Jack out of the house and the kids put to bed, the sooner I could close my eyes and try to forget everything that had happened in the past five hours.

"Who wants pepperoni?" Miller flipped open the lid to an extra-large pizza box. "I brought a cheese one, too, in case we've got picky eaters."

I slid a stack of paper plates onto the counter. Miller looked like a natural with Caden on one hip while he dished up over-sized slices of pizza.

"Careful, it might be hot. Blow on it before you take a bite."

He folded a piece of cheese pizza in half lengthwise and held it to his mouth.

I leaned against the counter and watched him gently blow on the steaming cheese. If he wasn't such a jerk, I might think he was kind of cute. The way he handled the kids was a plus. Still, it didn't counterbalance the cocky attitude and sense of entitlement he carried around with him everywhere he went.

I'd grown up under the shadow of Devil's Dance Distillery. Everyone in Beaver Bluff had. It was our one claim to fame and had done more for the economy of our struggling little town in the past hundred and fifty years than any plans the mayor or city council could have put together.

If I had to guesstimate, I'd say ninety percent of the population was tied to the distillery in some way or another. Half of them supported the Bishops, and half supported the Stewarts. There was almost no such thing as a neutral party in Beaver Bluff, Tennessee. I didn't give a flying flip about the stupid feud that had colored our local history. All that mattered to me was staying out of trouble so I could get my degree and eventually work my way out of Beaver Bluff.

"Plain or pepperoni?" Miller held out two paper plates.

"About earlier…" I started, unsure where I wanted to take the conversation except to bury it and never speak of it again.

"Don't worry about it. It's nice to know even a woman like you has needs."

A woman like me? What the hell was that supposed to mean? Before I could ask, Bettina tried to help herself to another slice of pizza and pulled the entire box off the counter. It fell to the ground. The pizza flipped, cheese-side down.

"Look what you made me do." She pointed a finger at Jack, who happened to be standing behind her.

"I didn't do anything."

"It's fine." Miller crouched down and scooped the pizza

back into the box. "Don't you know about the five-second rule?"

Bettina's face crumpled. "The what?"

I could have told him the Calbots didn't believe in the five-second rule. Once an edible item hit the floor, it was supposed to be disposed of as quickly as possible.

"The five-second rule." Jack slid a piece of the mangled pizza onto his plate. "Sometimes it tastes better after it hits the floor. If you save it before you count to five, it doesn't get any germs on it."

Bettina eyed him like he'd dared her to bend down and run her tongue over the floor instead of taking a slice that had barely touched the ground.

"Is that true, Amalie?" she asked.

"Sure." To prove my point, I grabbed a piece that had lost almost all its cheese.

Jack grinned, showing off his crooked front tooth. I hadn't noticed it before, but the tooth looked like it was about to fall out. Bettina had been wiggling hers, hoping the tooth fairy might come while her parents were gone. She thought she'd get extra if she lost it before they came home.

"I don't believe you." She looked past the mutilated cheese pizza and took a piece of pepperoni instead.

"Suit yourself. That just leaves more for me." Jack shrugged and carried his plate to the table.

Bettina hesitated, then traded out her slice of pepperoni for one of the messed-up cheese ones. I bit back my smile. I didn't want to give her any indication that I'd seen what she'd done.

"So about the fundraiser." Miller waited for me to get to the table before he took a seat. "Got any ideas?"

The fundraiser. My mind was blank. I thought I'd made some good suggestions with the readathon and the dance party, and I wasn't about to give into his idea of turning it into a rave for the under-four-feet-tall crowd.

"We could have the kids sell spring flower baskets." I was stretching, trying to remember what kind of fundraisers we'd done when I'd been a kid at Beaver Bluff Elementary. My mom never had any money to buy the stuff the school wanted us to peddle, so I'd never participated in the drives.

"Boring." Miller grabbed a bottle of soda from the six-pack he'd left in the center of the table. "We've got a chance to do some real good. They're going to put the money they raise toward updating the playground equipment. Wouldn't it be great if we could raise enough to get it set up while the kids are out for the summer?"

"Sure. They've been working on that for a couple of years. What makes you think we'll raise enough to meet the goal with one event?" In the short time I'd spent around Miller Bishop, I'd learned one thing about him: he didn't seem to do anything half-assed. Knowing that made my spine tingle with trepidation while I waited to hear his big idea.

"We should do a whole school carnival. They haven't done one of those in years." He raised his eyebrows at me as he bit into his pizza. Half the slice disappeared. The man certainly had a big mouth. One he loved to use for talking but might be better suited for something a little less verbal and a lot more oral.

Gah. Get ahold of yourself, Amalie. It didn't matter how his mouth looked or that he appeared capable of using it in various ways. What mattered was shooting down the idea of an all-school carnival as quickly as possible.

"They stopped doing that when I was in second grade. I heard it was too much trouble and didn't earn enough money to make it worthwhile." I wasn't lying. That's what my mom said when I asked if we could try for one of the pretty store-bought cakes for my birthday that year. When I was in kinder-garten and first grade, we'd watch the other kids walk around in a circle to see which spot they'd land on. If I'd been able to play and won, I would have chosen a layered cake with white frosting and rainbow sprinkles.

"Times have changed. We can bring in an operator who does carnival rides. I've been thinking about the concert too. I'll be talking to my brother Vaughn about the distillery's anniversary celebration we're having in a few months, and I'm going to suggest we bring in an A-lister to perform. Brandiss would be perfect. The school carnival can piggyback on that. It's guaranteed to be a win-win."

The excitement in his eyes might have been contagious if he'd been pitching his grand plan to someone else. Someone who wasn't carrying eighteen college credits while working as a full-time nanny and trying to manage her ailing mother's healthcare.

"It sounds like a ton of work." Even thinking about getting started sucked every bit of energy from my bones.

"I'll do the heavy lifting."

I blinked at him, willing him to abandon the idea and change his mind. "There's got to be something a little less complicated."

He leaned back in his chair and tossed his napkin onto his paper plate. "Okay then, Amalie. Let's hear some ideas."

"I have to clean up the kitchen and put Caden down. Then I've got three days of homework I need to catch up on. Can we talk about this tomorrow?" I was tired. The kind of tired that went beyond what a few extra hours of sleep would fix.

"Why don't I clean the kitchen while you put him to bed? I'll be tied up all day tomorrow getting caught up on some work for the distillery, and I have to meet with my brother on Sunday." He rubbed a hand over his chin. The sound of his rough palm scraping against his whiskers made my tummy twist. I wondered what it would feel like to have a man's scruff rub against certain parts of my anatomy.

"Amalie?" Miller leaned close. Close enough that I could see the flecks of gold in his eyes.

"Yeah. Give me ten minutes to get Caden down, and I'll see if I can come up with any ideas. Otherwise, we'll have to handle this via text." I pushed back from the table and released Caden from his highchair. No good would come from fantasizing about a man, especially if that man happened to be Miller Bishop.

CHAPTER 9

Miller

I WRAPPED the leftover pizza in aluminum foil and shoved it in the commercial refrigerator. I'd never been inside the Calbot's home before. Never had a reason to be before tonight. The kitchen was outfitted with state-of-the-art appliances, and the whole house looked like a shrine to some minimalist designer.

Eager to kick up my feet and relax while I waited for Amalie, I joined Jack and Bettina in the family room. It was slightly less formal than the other areas of the house. The carpet was a light gray instead of snowy white, and the couch cushions looked more comfortable than the fancy sofa in the formal living room.

"Who wants to watch a movie?" I asked.

"We're picking one now, Dad." Jack looked up from where he and Bettina leaned over a tablet.

"Don't you want to watch one on the TV instead of that tiny screen?" There was a perfectly good seventy-five-inch screen in front of us.

Bettina looked at me like I hadn't been navigating my way

around electronics since I was younger than her age. "We're picking one to play on the movie screen."

"If you say so." Tempted to pull off my shoes, I wondered if it would be rude to make myself comfortable. Aw, fuck it. It had been a hell of a long day. Putting my feet up for a few minutes wouldn't bother anyone.

"What smells?" Bettina stuck her little nose in the air like Titus had let one rip.

"It's my dad's feet." Jack pinched his nostrils together. His voice came out nasally and muted. "Dad, seriously."

"I don't know what the two of you are talking about. Everyone says my feet smell good." I lifted my foot and bent my leg so I could pretend to take a satisfying, deep inhale. "Mmm. Almost good enough to eat."

"Dessert!" Bettina jumped up and raced into the kitchen. "We almost forgot the ice cream."

Jack followed her like a little puppy dog. I sure as hell hoped my son wasn't about to get his heart broken by the Ice Princess of Beaver Bluff Elementary.

Groaning, I dragged myself off the couch and headed after them. I'd learned my lesson earlier in the day and intended to handle the scooping myself. Once they each had a mountain of ice cream in their bowl, Bettina grabbed two spoons and handed one to Jack.

"Let's eat in the theater room while we watch a movie." She cupped her hands around her bowl and swirled her tongue over the mixed mound of chocolate and vanilla.

"Are you sure that's okay with Amalie?" I couldn't imagine Bettina's mom would let anything except water beyond the boundaries of the kitchen.

"Yeah, she lets me do it all the time. Come on." She carried her bowl down another hall leading out of the kitchen. Jack followed.

I figured I'd better supervise, so I fixed myself a smaller bowl before tracking them down in the home theater room. Bettina was right. She'd picked a movie on the tablet and it started to play on a big screen that came down out of the ceiling. As the opening credits to some princess movie started, I propped my feet on the leather recliner's footrest and settled in.

Amalie found us there a few minutes later. "Bettina, you know better than to bring ice cream in here."

I cleared my throat. "She told me her mom lets her eat in here all the time."

"And you believed her?" Amalie collected the empty bowls from Bettina and Jack, then eyed the last bit of ice cream I'd been about to spoon into my mouth.

"I'll clean up any messes." So far, that seemed to be all I did around Amalie.

"It's fine. I'll get to it tomorrow. Did you want to talk about the fundraiser?" She slumped into the chair next to me.

Bettina and Jack turned around at the same time and whispered a loud "Shhh."

"Sure." I was about to get up when I caught her profile in the low light.

She looked tired. More than tired. With her shoulders hunched forward, she looked like she didn't have the strength to pick herself up out of the chair. I wanted to settle on a fundraiser idea so I could move on to other more important issues, like reviewing resumes all weekend, but Amalie looked like she needed a break.

I reached over and put my hand on her knee to get her attention. The fabric of her leggings felt soft against my palm. Her muscles twitched under my fingers, and I wondered how often she put that little toy of hers to work. My dick seemed to like the visions that conjured up. I shifted forward and adjusted myself in the dark as I leaned over to talk to her without annoying the two serious moviegoers in the front row.

"If you've got stuff you need to do tonight, we can find a time to chat over the weekend."

"I thought you were busy," she whispered back.

"I'm sure we can work something out." Or I could just decide and fill her in on the details later. If I had to be in charge of planning an event, it wasn't going to be some basic fundraiser. That wasn't my style.

"Are you sure?" She slid to the edge of her chair, sending my hand higher on her thigh.

I pulled back before she got the wrong idea. Amalie Rivers wasn't my type. Hell, I wasn't sure I had a type anymore. That's what I got for trying to be a mom and a dad to my kid. Once Jack got older, there would be plenty of time to sow any wild oats I had left. However, if I'd learned anything through my experience, it was that wild oats weren't worth sowing.

Knowing that, I still wouldn't change a thing about my past. Jack was the best thing I'd ever done. But I sure had made things damn hard for myself.

"Yeah. I can get Jack out of here so you can get stuff done."

She put her hand on top of mine where I'd moved it to the armrest. "Stay."

My body reacted like one of Pavlov's dogs. Immediately, my cock rallied. It had been years since a woman had said that one word to me. Years since I'd obliged. My gaze ran over the smooth contours of her face. She really was beautiful in a no-nonsense way. I'd always been drawn to women who refused to leave the house without applying pounds of makeup, who didn't want me to see them in the morning until they'd put their face on.

Amalie didn't seem to care about any of that. She had a natural kind of beauty that a guy might easily overlook. Now that I'd noticed it, I was afraid I might not be able to unsee it. Her eyes pinned mine as we stared at each other across the foot or two separating us.

"Ew, kissing!" Bettina made gagging noises.

"Gross!" Jack joined in.

I dragged my gaze away from Amalie to look at the giant screen where a male and female cartoon character barely brushed lips.

"Whoa, I thought this was a family-friendly theater," I teased.

Amalie snapped out of whatever exhausted trance she'd fallen into and jerked her hand away. "It's just the one scene. This is Bettina's favorite movie, and she reacts the same every time she watches it. Sorry, what I was saying before is that you should stay. Let the kids finish watching the movie if you don't have anywhere you need to be."

"No Friday night plans for us." My usual MO consisted of trying to beat Jack at one of his racing video games or grabbing a burger with Evan and Frannie before getting Jack home and in bed. I wondered what Amalie usually did on a Friday night. Did she put her flowery toy to work?

"Make yourself at home. I'm going to sit at the kitchen table and try to get some studying done if you don't mind."

"Not at all."

"Okay then. Let me know if you need anything." She crept out of the room without making a sound, taking the stack of dirty bowls with her.

I didn't want to admit it, but I was a little sad to see her go. It had to be because she was the first woman under fifty I wasn't related to or banned from that I'd spent more than a few minutes with in the past couple of years. The ban wasn't wide, but Evan made sure I knew Frannie was off-limits.

He didn't have anything to worry about there. The two of

them had been friends ever since I could remember. I thought of her more like a sister, which automatically put her in the no-fly zone for me.

I shifted my weight to the middle of the comfortable recliner. A guy could get used to a chair like this. The scene on the screen moved from night to day, and I had to squint against the bright light. When I looked away, my gaze caught on something sitting in the chair Amalie had vacated.

No fucking way.

I reached over the armrest and patted the cushion. My fingers closed around the item she'd tried to hide earlier. I held it in my lap, checking it out by the light coming from the huge screen. Yep, it sure did look like a rose to me. Except for a few toddler-sized teeth marks, it appeared to be unscathed. Last time I'd dated a woman, she hadn't mentioned a need for rubber toys. Is this what chicks were into now?

I tucked it into the waistband of my jeans so the kids wouldn't find it. I'd have paid good money to watch Amalie try to explain to Bettina exactly what kind of grown-up toy this was and how she used it for school. Even thinking about it made me chuckle to myself.

"Shhh!" Bettina turned around, her finger pressed against her lip.

"Sorry, I'll be quiet." She sure was a bossy little thing. Made me wonder why it was so important to Jack for her to like him. I doubted six-year-old Bettina Calbot was playing hard to get.

When the movie ended, Bettina tried to negotiate a double feature. Jack was on board, but it was almost nine. I wanted to head home to check on Titus and make sure he hadn't figured out how to get into the laundry room to help himself to the eggs.

We turned off the screen and theater lights, then searched

for Amalie. I found her face down on her laptop keyboard. There was a document open in her word processing software. The letter "d" filled up the screen. She must have fallen asleep with her cheek resting on the keyboard just right to send "d"s scrolling across her document.

"Amalie, the movie's over." Bettina walked over to the table and poked her nanny on the shoulder.

"Huh?" Amalie sat up. An imprint of the keys from the keyboard pressed into her cheek.

"We're heading out." I wiped at the corner of my mouth. "You've got a little drool there."

"Oh shoot." She wiped the back of her hand across her lips. "I must have fallen asleep. Sorry. Do you want to take the left-over pizza and ice cream home with you?"

I felt like we'd already overstayed our welcome and was eager to get going. "Nah. Keep it. One less meal you have to make, right?"

She got up, snugged her arms around her middle, and followed Jack and me to the front door. "Yeah. Thanks."

"You're welcome. By the way, what's your number? I'll shoot you a text tomorrow so we can talk about the fundraiser." I pulled my phone out of my back pocket. Damn. I still had her toy tucked into my waistband. There was no way I would hand it over now. Not in front of the kids.

Amalie rattled off her number as she pulled the door open for us. "I know you said you're busy all weekend, but I think the kids and I will stop by school tomorrow to work on those desks."

"I can send one of the guys from the warehouse over to help," I offered.

"It's okay. You handle the commercial cleaners next week, and we'll take care of the desk wipe-down. Does that sound fair?"

"More than fair." Maybe I'd misjudged the nanny. Or maybe she was just more pleasant when she was tired. Either way, I was glad I wouldn't have to worry about spending time at Jack's school over the weekend. We already had too many other things going on.

She leaned against the doorway and waved to Jack. "Have a good night. Sweet dreams, Jack. Don't let the bedbugs bite."

"Bye, Jack." Bettina flung her arms around Jack's slim shoulders and squeezed him tight. "Thanks for the ice cream."

She released her grip, leaving him with a dazed and glazed look in his eyes. I glanced at Amalie, who appeared to be struggling to hold back a smile.

"You're welcome?" His voice lifted at the end, making it sound like a question.

As his appointed wingman, I tugged him close to me and ruffled his hair. "See you later, alligators."

"After a while, crocodiles," Amalie answered. Then she slowly closed the door.

I breathed in the cold crisp air, feeling more alive than I had in a long, damn time. "You okay, big guy?"

Jack looked up at me, his eyes shining like two glittery gemstones. "Dad, I think I'm in love."

CHAPTER 10
Amalie

THE WEEKEND LASTED FOREVER. Forty-eight hours felt like five hundred. I usually worked a light schedule on Saturdays and Sundays, if I worked at all, so having the kids 24/7 with no break almost did me in. We spent several hours at Amalie's school on Saturday wiping down desks. By Sunday evening, I'd fallen further behind in my homework and hadn't given any thought to the fundraiser.

With the kids fed, bathed, and in bed, I sat at the kitchen table to work on my paper. I'd just flipped open my laptop when my phone rang with a local number I didn't recognize. Tempted to let it go to voicemail, I realized I hadn't heard from Miller yet.

My heart did a little stop, drop, and roll as I answered, half hoping, half fearing it might be him. "Hello?"

"Amalie, hey, it's Miller Bishop. Sorry I haven't had a chance to connect with you before tonight." He sounded just about as fried as me.

"No worries. It's been a busy weekend."

"Yeah, it has. I'm sure you've got stuff to do, so I'll cut to the point. Did you come up with any other ideas for the fundraiser? Frannie asked me to tell her what we've decided by tomorrow."

I racked my brain, trying to think of something clever that wouldn't require much work. Something he might not shoot down as soon as I made the suggestion. "A walkathon? We could use the high school track and have kids sign up to take shifts walking twenty-four hours straight."

He didn't respond right away. Great. He didn't like any of my ideas. The whole fundraiser was going to be a bust, and it would be my fault. I didn't even have a kid at the school, and if my plans to get out of Beaver Bluff came to fruition, I'd be long gone before I ever would.

"You want to convince parents to let their kids stay up all night to walk around the track?" He blew out a breath, probably in frustration.

"I'm sorry, but I don't have time to devote to some over-the-top event that's going to take tons of planning." Why did he ask me for ideas if he was going to poop all over them? "If you want to write a check for the equipment, go ahead. We can say we're doing a readathon, and you can donate a thousand dollars for every page Jack reads."

"Frannie's not going to go for that. She wants the school and the community to be involved."

"Then do whatever you want. Hire a party planner and put on the best school carnival Beaver Bluff has ever seen. Just tell me when and where to show up, and I'll do my best to be there." I was done trying to help. It was his fault we were in this stupid predicament to begin with. If he hadn't brought in ice cream for a snack…

Instead of blowing up at me, he paused for a long beat. "Are you okay, Amalie?"

Great, now he was going to tag me with the dreaded

woman-who-overreacts label. I counted to three in my head before I responded.

"Yes, I'm fine. It's been a long weekend, and I have to figure out how to survive another week before the Calbots get back."

"That's got to be rough on you and the kids. Is there anything I can do to help?"

His offer threw me. We weren't friends. We'd lived within ten miles of each other our entire lives, and the only time we'd ever spoken was two days ago.

"That's kind of you to offer, but I'll be fine."

"I'll take the lead on the fundraiser. I can rope my sister into helping. She's done a ton of events for the distillery, and I'm sure she'd be more than happy to give me a hand." He was offering me a lifeline. I should grab it and hold on for dear life.

"Yeah, that would be great."

"Are you sure?" His voice came out deep and low. He sounded like one of the late-night radio DJs my mom used to listen to. I always tried to find out what they looked like so I could see if their voice matched their looks. Ninety-nine percent of the time, it didn't. But with Miller Bishop, what you heard was what you got. And what you got was as smooth and deep as a perfectly aged Tennessee whiskey.

I yanked my mind out of the gutter. "Just make sure there's something for me to do so I don't get blacklisted by Principal Masterson when it comes time to set up my student teaching sessions."

"So you really want to be a teacher?"

Immediately, I went on the defensive. Not all of us were destined to sit behind a desk all day looking for loopholes in the system to make sure our big business clients paid as little tax as possible. That's what I wanted to say. Instead, I just said, "Yes."

"And you want to teach first grade?"

"Probably second or third."

"It's a fun age. They're starting to get some independence and figure things out on their own. Although, I'd say Bettina's already ahead of the curve with that."

"She takes after her parents in that regard." I'd been working with the Calbots since Bettina was a baby, and she'd always known her own mind. Recently, she'd been taking things a little too far.

"I wanted to ask you about her." He paused like he wasn't sure if he should keep going.

"What about her?" She wasn't my kid, and she did have her challenges, but I'd flip into mama bear mode real quick if necessary.

"The way she treats Jack. It's like she calls him out and makes fun of him, but I also get the sense that she kind of likes him. Have you noticed that?"

Yeah, I had. I struggled with how to respond. I didn't want to talk badly about someone else's child, especially one in my care. But I also wanted to let Miller know there was more going on with Bettina than the way she'd been acting.

"She's been going through a rough time lately. Her parents have been traveling together more now that Caden is a little older, and she misses them. It's just her way of acting out." It's not like I was saying anything about Bettina that someone paying attention wouldn't notice, but it felt like I was giving up her secrets or revealing something I shouldn't.

"So, it has nothing to do with Jack, then?"

"I don't know. She talks about him a lot and seems to think of him as a friend. They're only six. Didn't you ever tease the girls you liked in school?" Miller was a few years older than me, but I could remember the guy he'd been back then. His family had money, which already made him stand out against the majority of guys who had to rely on athletic prowess to make a name for themselves. He'd been cocky as hell and never thought the rules applied to him.

"I never said they were puny." He chuckled. "Jack's sensitive about his size. His mom was petite, and it looks like he'll take after her side of the family."

I'd heard stories about how Miller had gone off to college and came home with a baby boy. Rumors that he'd forced Jack's mom out of their lives abounded. Some said she was from one of the mountain towns in eastern Tennessee and that he'd paid her off to leave the baby with him. That was one of the reasons I didn't particularly like him. Anyone who could use his family's financial resources to take advantage of someone less fortunate had to be a major douchebag.

The other reason I didn't want anything to do with Miller Bishop was too deep and too painful to bring up. He obviously didn't remember the incident, and I wasn't about to remind him. Everything about him made me realize how much I hated living in a town the size of Beaver Bluff. Once I finished school, I'd be able to move my mother and me somewhere where the weather might help her lungs. Then I'd be able to leave my past, and men like Miller Bishop, behind me.

I wanted to ask about Jack's mom, but it wasn't any of my business. Unlike most of the other residents of Beaver Bluff, I preferred to keep to myself and didn't thrive on passing gossip around. "He'll probably hit a growth spurt when he goes through puberty. Seems like the girls in my grade were always taller than the boys until we all hit middle school."

"Yeah. I guess I do remember teasing a girl I liked back in elementary school. She used to wear her hair in a long ponytail. I'd grab onto it and tell everyone it wasn't nearly as pretty as my horse's tail. Getting her all riled up was one of my favorite things."

"Did you ever tell her you liked her?" Getting a glimpse at this side of Miller made me a little uncomfortable. I preferred to think of him as a rich asshole instead of someone with feelings.

"No. I was too scared. She had beautiful eyes. They were almost the color of yours."

Awkward silence hung between us. Did he just inadvertently compliment my eyes? I wasn't sure. Maybe he was just dropping a line on me. That was probably more like it. Wanting to call him on it and catch him in the act, I decided to press it.

"You've got to be kidding me."

"What?" He almost sounded like he had no idea what he'd done. Damn, he was good.

"I bet you don't even know what color my eyes are."

"Really?"

"Yeah."

"You want to place a wager along with that bet?" His voice lost its deep sultry tone. Now he sounded agitated—maybe even a little offended.

His intimidation tactics wouldn't work on me. "Such as?"

"I've got an incubator full of chicken eggs over here that I'd be happy to bring over. If I can name the color of your eyes, are you willing to take them?"

"And if you can't?" My confidence slipped. He sounded so sure of himself. That was the name of his game. I'd seen guys like him bully people into backing down by using sheer intimidation. It wouldn't work with me. Not this time.

"Hell, Amalie, if I can't, I'll give you whatever you want. See, I can promise you that because I know the color of your eyes. They're like the color of the sky right before a summer storm, when dark clouds roll in and squeeze out the sliver of bright blue sky. More gray than blue, but there's nothing cold about them. At least not when you think no one's looking."

Oh. My. God. I didn't know what color he'd just described, but clearly he'd been paying a lot more attention than I'd been giving him credit for.

"So…I'm assuming you're okay with me telling Principal Masterson that we want to move ahead with a spring carnival as our fundraiser?"

I tried to speak, but my voice was still in hiding. All I could do was utter some sort of grunty agreement.

"Great. We've got that taken care of. The only other thing I need to know is what time you'll be home tomorrow so I can drop off these chicks."

CHAPTER 11
Miller

I DIDN'T HAVE a chance to get over to the Calbot's house with the egg-ubator until late Tuesday afternoon. Jack helped me load it into the truck's backseat. He kept his eyes glued to the dozen eggs as we made the fifteen-minute trek.

"I think one's about to hatch, Dad." He tapped on the glass with his fingernail.

We were getting rid of them just in time. It had been difficult to keep Titus away. Every time we'd opened the laundry room door, he was there, eager to figure out where that new smell was coming from.

"*Mierda!*" Jack yelled.

I whipped my head around and barely missed a guardrail on the bridge we were crossing. "What the hell's going on back there?"

"I think I see a crack." He bounced up and down on the seat.

"You can't scare me like that while I'm driving down the road, Jack."

"Sorry." He shrank down in his seat.

"And where did you hear that word?" I was far from a

saint when it came to slinging four-letter words, but I tried to be careful around Jack. I'd grown up with three brothers. Watching my language had never come naturally. But I'd never cursed in Spanish.

"Why?" His eyes met mine in the rearview mirror.

"Because it's not nice to say." In middle school, we had a foreign exchange student from Mexico City stay with us for a couple of months. Vaughn and Cole had moved out by then, but he'd taught Evan and me how to curse in Spanish.

Jack looked out the window. "I thought it just meant the same as *wow*."

"It means *shit*. Don't use it again, okay?" I suppose I couldn't hold him too accountable if he didn't even know what the word meant. As long as his grandmother didn't hear him say it. The downside of learning all the curse words in Spanish was that my mom looked them up, so I got in just as much trouble cursing in a foreign language as I did in English. She wouldn't be amused if she thought I'd taught my son how to be bilingual with four-letter words.

"I wonder if Bettina knows that's what it means."

So that's where he'd heard it. My fingers tightened on the steering wheel. That little girl was turning into a real pain in the ass. I'd have to ask Amalie about it. She probably had no idea that the Calbot's daughter was sharing useful language skills.

"How's the egg looking?" We'd just pulled onto the tree-lined street where the Calbots lived. The sooner I unloaded the egg-ubator, the better I'd feel.

"I don't know. There's just one crack so far. Or maybe it's dirt."

"When's Mrs. Blessing going to be back in the classroom?" For Amalie's sake, I hoped it was soon. She didn't need the additional stress of caring for a dozen newborn chickens added to her already full plate. For a moment, I felt a twinge of guilt for dumping the eggs on her.

"I don't know. We have a cool sub, though. She plays the guitar, and we sang a song about vowels today."

"Vowels, huh?"

"Yeah. Did you know there are tall ones and short ones?"

I almost laughed. "Don't you mean long and short ones?"

"Oh yeah. Want me to sing it for you?"

"Sure."

He started jamming on a fake guitar while he covered the long and short sounds for all the vowels. I had to hand it to his sub, it was a catchy tune. I found myself humming along by the time we pulled into the Calbot's driveway.

Bettina must have been watching out the window for us. Before I could get the egg-ubator out of the backseat, she was standing next to me. Jack walked around the truck to join us.

"Look, one might be hatching," he pointed out.

"I wouldn't get too excited. It can take a long time for them to peck their way of their shells." Bettina stated it like she was suddenly the world's shortest expert in chicken husbandry.

Jack fell into step next to her as we made our way up the sidewalk to the front door. "Do you think it will be a boy or a girl?"

"I hope it's a girl because boys can be so gross."

"Not all boys are gross," Amalie said. She stood on the wide stoop and held the door open for us.

"Thanks for sticking up for us." I shot her a grin as I passed.

A light pink stain worked its way up her neck and over her cheeks. "I wasn't necessarily referring to you."

"And here I thought we'd reached a truce." I entered the foyer, my arms wrapped around the big glass box. "Where do you want me to put this?"

Amalie blew out a breath. "Back in your truck?"

"No way. If you didn't want these chicks, you shouldn't have agreed to a bet you would lose."

She looked up at me and then quickly shifted her gaze away. I might have elaborated a little on the color of her eyes, but yeah, I'd noticed them. I couldn't help it. I'd never met a woman with eyes the color of hers. Never met a woman whose eyes held such sadness, either. It made me curious about what happened to her. The thought of someone hurting her didn't sit well with me.

Though I wasn't looking forward to working with her, I suppose I felt slightly protective. The same way I felt about my other female friends. Yeah, right. I didn't have any other female friends. Unless I counted Frannie. And I'd never had the same type of thoughts about Frannie that I'd had about Amalie.

"Why don't you put them in the laundry room?" She led the way down the same hall we'd been down last night.

Knowing we were headed toward her bedroom made my jeans feel a little tight in front. I still had the toy I'd picked up the other night. Thinking about her using it on herself had inspired the long shower I'd taken last night. And maybe the quick shot of relief I'd needed after we got off the phone on Sunday. I had to chalk it up to suffering through the longest dry spell I'd ever experienced. It couldn't be because I found the Calbot's nanny attractive. She was too... I couldn't quite put my finger on it. Too much not like me, I guess.

"On the counter here." Bettina flipped on the light.

I stepped into the biggest laundry room I'd ever seen. A sparkling white matching washer and dryer sat against one wall, and a waist-high countertop stretched along the opposite side of the room.

I set the egg-ubator down and plugged the cord for the

heat lamp into a nearby socket. "There you go. Project rehoming eggs is officially complete."

"I wish I could see them hatch." Jack touched his finger to the glass. His lower lip barely jutted out in a tiny pout.

"You might miss the first one, but I'm sure you'll see others hatch when they get back to the classroom." I put a hand on his shoulder and squeezed. I figured he'd be down after dropping off the eggs, so I had something planned that might cheer him up. Since Frannie had agreed to let me—Amalie and me—move forward on the idea for the spring carnival, I'd called a place not far away that rented out inflatables. Jack didn't know yet, but we were heading over to check them out before dinner.

Bettina put her hand on Jack's shoulder. "You can come visit them whenever you want. If you give me your phone number, I can video chat with you when this one finally comes out of her shell."

Jack doesn't have a phone, but you can call me." Seeing a sign of empathy from the Ice Princess made me feel guilty for all the bad vibes I'd been sending to a six-year-old. It must have been an attempt to atone that made me open my mouth. "The two of us are headed over to check out a couple of ideas for the spring carnival. Any chance y'all might be free to come along?"

"What kind of ideas?" Amalie's eyes narrowed.

I could tell she was a little leery of agreeing without knowing the details. "If I tell you, it won't be a surprise."

"I'm not sure I'm ready for any more of your surprises." Her lips pursed.

"It's going to be fun. I promise. What do you say?"

"Can we go, Amalie? Pleeeeeeeeease? You said I got to pick what game we'd play after dinner because I got a star on my math worksheet." Bettina grabbed hold of Amalie's hand and jumped up and down.

"What math worksheet?" I glanced down at Jack.

He lifted a shoulder. "I meant to bring it home yesterday, but I forgot."

I wasn't going to give him a hard time in front of Bettina. No need to provide any additional ammunition she could use against him when the mood struck. "We'll talk about that when we get home," I muttered.

His nod let me know he'd heard me. Managing two full-time jobs made it challenging to stay on top of his homework.

"I need to talk to Miller alone for a minute." Amalie nodded toward the door to the laundry room. "Can you both take Caden to the family room for a sec?"

I'd never seen Bettina be so quick to follow directions. "Come on, Caden. Let's go see what's on the tablet."

The little boy took his sister's hand and let her lead him away. Jack went with them. When we were alone in the laundry room, she shut the door.

"If I didn't know any better, I might wonder why you wanted to get me alone so bad." Obviously, I was joking. The comment must have hit her hard, because the same pink blush I'd noticed multiple times over the past few days crept from her chest up to her neck.

"What's the surprise? You've got Bettina intrigued, and if I don't agree to go, I'll pay for it all night." She crossed her arms over her stomach, which pushed her boobs higher and made the cleft between them deeper at the v-neck of her shirt.

I ripped my gaze away and focused on the eggs. "Doesn't it get exhausting not being able to trust anyone?"

"What's that supposed to mean?"

"Nothing." I leaned down to study the egg Jack thought might be hatching. Looked like it had been smudged with dirt…or chicken poop. "We're going to check out some big bounce houses. I thought Jack would be a little down after we dropped off the chick eggs. You're welcome to come with us or not. It's up to you."

She didn't reply right away, so I pushed off the counter and headed toward the door. As my hand closed around the doorknob, she let her arms fall to her sides and faced me.

"There haven't been a whole lot of people in my life who have come through for me, okay?" Then she nudged her chin toward the door. "We'd better get a move on if you want to get them home by dinnertime."

I pulled the door open and inhaled deeply as she passed through the doorway. The scent of something sweet, like chocolate chip cookies, drifted off her. Maybe I'd misjudged her. Maybe she wasn't wound so tight because she liked to be in charge. Maybe she'd ended up that way to protect herself.

As soon as the thought entered my head, I shoved it away. I wasn't there to psychoanalyze Amalie Rivers. Whatever skeletons were in her closet wouldn't be exposed by me. The only reason we were breathing the same air right now was because she hadn't been able to keep her temper at the party last week. Still, it would be easier to work together on the carnival if she didn't look like she wanted to punch me all the time. Staying in her good graces would pay off in the long run and help lighten my load.

"Mr. Bishop's invited us on a special outing I think you're really going to like. Anyone who wants to go will need to get their shoes and jackets on in the next five minutes." Amalie scooped Caden up and set him on her hip. "I'm going to change him before we go. Do you want us to follow you?"

"Can we all ride in the big truck?" Bettina asked.

"Yeah, can they ride with us?" Jack clapped his hands together.

I looked at Amalie. She didn't seem too excited at the prospect, so I was surprised when she agreed. "I'll need to move Caden's car seat over, but sure, why not."

"I can do that while you're changing him," I offered. It hadn't been that long ago since I'd had Jack sitting in one of those big bucket seats. Not that much could have changed in the past few years.

"That would be great." Amalie started up the stairs. "My keys are hanging on a hook in the laundry room. We'll be down in a few minutes."

Bettina had shoved her feet into her glittered high tops. In her rush, she mixed up her left and right. "I can get her keys for you."

"That would be great. First, maybe we ought to switch your shoes. I don't want you to trip."

She looked down, and her eyes widened. "How did that happen?"

Jack let out a laugh. "I get mine mixed up all the time. Want me to help you tie them?"

At least the two of them seemed like they were starting to get along. Maybe Amalie and I could get some tips from the under-four-feet-tall crowd.

CHAPTER 12
Amalie

AGREEING to ride in Miller's truck had been a mistake. Sitting in the front seat of his fully-loaded half-ton pickup, I felt surrounded by him. The dark leather seat cupped my ass just right. His wallet sat on the center console between us, and a thermal mug with Jack's picture plastered all over it rattled in the cup holder. Being in his truck was too personal. Too intimate. Too something else I couldn't quite put my finger on.

I'd be lying to myself if I said I didn't enjoy having someone crawl over the backseat and snap Caden's car seat into place. Or open the door for me. Or shut it behind me once I'd propelled myself into the front seat by stepping on the running board.

The truth was, I liked it. Last time I'd been in the front seat of a guy's car, he'd been taking me out to dinner at Jackie Jay's —the best restaurant in town. It was prom night, and I'd been so excited to go with someone I really liked. My mom and I spent weeks working on my dress. She'd taken fabric from her wedding gown and added it to a dress I'd picked up at the thrift store. When we got to the restaurant, we'd barely sat down when he listed all the reasons he wouldn't be able to see me again after prom night.

We never made it to the dance. I'd called my mom, and she had to leave her shift to pick me up. I'd vowed then never to give a boy the power to hurt me.

But tonight, there was no need to stress. It's not like this was a date. We were two people working on a project together and doing some research. The side benefit would be having two tired kids who would easily go to bed. Wearing Bettina and Caden out would ensure I'd have enough time to finish my paper later. It wasn't due until Friday, but I wanted to finish it as quickly as possible. I didn't know what my mom's doctor visit on Thursday might bring up, so it would be best if I checked as many things as possible off my to-do list before then.

"What do you think is fair, Amalie?" Miller glanced over at me, a smile stretched across his mouth.

"Fair about what?" I didn't want to let on that I hadn't been paying close attention.

"Naming the new chickens," Bettina shouted from the backseat.

"I should get to name the boys, and she can name the girls," Jack said. "If the first one's a boy, I'm going to name him Gruda."

Bettina shook her head. "That's a dumb name."

"Hey, be nice." I turned around to look at the three kids sitting in a row across the backseat. "That's an interesting name. How did you come up with that?"

Jack's eyes lit up. He was so different from his dad. If I didn't know they were related, I would never have guessed it. While his dad had the bulk and build of a professional wrestler, Jack had slim limbs. He struck me as being more tuned into his sensitive side—not that Miller might not have a soft spot or two hiding behind the class clown persona he projected. Jack seemed to really care about people. Especially Bettina, which I couldn't figure out.

"He likes Yoda and Groot." Bettina rolled her eyes. "I told him the combo name thing only works when it's a couple, not when it's two guys."

"Two guys can be a couple," Miller said.

"Like Spencer Stewart's family. He has two dads." Jack sat back in his seat, a satisfied grin on his face.

"Yeah, but they don't have a couple's name. Like Brangelina. Or Bennifer," Bettina added. "If you go with Gruda, then people will assume you're putting Groot and Yoda together. They're not a good match."

A tiny muscle ticked along Miller's scruffy jawline. I didn't want Jack and Bettina to get into a full-fledged argument any more than I wanted Jack to feel like his name idea had been shut down.

"If the first chick is a boy, Jack can name it whatever he wants. If it's a girl, you can pick. That sounds fair to me. Don't you think so, Bettina?" With her in the seat behind me, I had to twist entirely around to catch a look at her face.

"Fine." She crossed her arms and stared out the window.

I was willing to take that as a win. They'd been coming few and far between since the Calbots had been overseas. We rode the rest of the way in relative silence except for the occasional "vroom" coming from the backseat. Jack zoomed race cars over Caden's car seat to keep him entertained while Bettina continued to pout.

When Miller slowed down to turn off the divided four-lane road, I wasn't sure what I expected. A massive warehouse sat a hundred yards back. Wavy, air-inflated tubes that looked like a guy with long hair waving his arms in the air lined the edge of the parking lot. A sign was plastered against the side of the building that read *Blown Inflatables*.

"We're here." Miller slipped the gearshift into park, and I gathered the canvas tote I always carried with us.

Before I had a chance to get Bettina to move so I could reach in for her brother, Miller had unclipped Caden from his car seat and lifted him onto his big, broad shoulders.

"Be careful with him," I warned. The last thing we needed was a trip to the ER because Miller Bishop had been roughhousing with a toddler.

Caden giggled and grabbed hold of Miller's ears, knocking his sunglasses off in the process. They fell onto the gravel parking lot and cracked.

"I'm so sorry." I bent down to pick them up, then held them out to Miller.

"It's my fault. I should have left them in the truck." He kept one hand on Caden's waist and tucked the glasses into his pocket with the other. "Should we go wear these kids out?"

"Yes, please." I followed him into the office area, where he stopped to check in with the guy he'd talked to on the phone.

A few minutes later, the man took us to the back of the office and opened a door. Dozens of inflatable structures filled the space, some stretching almost the entire length of the warehouse.

Bettina's lips split into the biggest smile I'd ever seen. "Do we get to play on one of them?" she asked.

"You get to play on all of them," Miller said.

She stared at him like he'd just told her she could drive the truck home. "For reals?"

"For reals." He lifted Caden over his head and set him on the ground.

Even Caden seemed to be frozen in place.

"Which one are you going to try, Amalie?" Miller cocked

his head. He probably figured I'd attempt to get out of jumping in one of the bounce houses or flinging my body down a tall inflatable slide. He couldn't have known that I'd never been inside a bounce house. That I'd spent too many hours to count watching the other kids at the Shellacky County Fair trading their parents' hard-earned cash for tickets so they could spend five minutes inside an inflatable castle or air-filled jungle gym.

I looked over the choices. There were too many options. It was like staring down at the case of ice cream flavors at a Baskin Robbins and having to choose just one. But unlike ice cream, which would fill me up, I didn't have to limit myself. I reached for Caden's hand and turned back to Miller.

"I don't know about you, but I'm going to try all of them."

His brows shot up, proving he'd underestimated how much I'd enjoy our field trip. I didn't wait for him to reply.

"Come on, Caden. Have you ever bounced inside a fire engine before?" I tugged him toward the bounce house next to me. When we got to the entrance, I helped him pull off his shoes then hoisted him up so he could get through the flaps.

Once we started, the kids didn't want to stop. Jack and Bettina moved from one inflatable to the next. I stopped trying to keep up with them. Caden was too scared to go down the tall slide by himself, so Miller pulled him onto his lap and held him close as they raced toward the bottom.

I didn't mean to, but I started to see him in a new light. He was good with the kids. When Caden seemed too scared to try something, he didn't force him or get impatient. He took his time, easing Caden into giving things a shot. The amount of patience he had for a cranky two-year-old surprised me.

Bettina was in her element. She and Jack were evenly matched when it came to racing up and down the side-by-side slides. Then they found an obstacle course. It looked like it was made for older kids, but they wanted to try it.

"I don't think you two are tall enough to get up some of those walls." I didn't want to discourage them, but I also didn't want to have to climb in after them if they got stuck in the middle.

"Then you try," Bettina said. "You and Miller can race against each other, and we'll watch."

"That's okay." Miller shook his head, slightly out of breath from having just carried Caden to the top of the big slide before traveling down together. "I don't want to embarrass Amalie by beating her."

"What makes you think you'd beat me?" With my hands clamped to my hips, I tried not to glare at him. We'd been having fun, and he had to go and insult my . . . my what? Athletic prowess? Yeah, that wasn't much of a jab. I had no athletic prowess at all. I wasn't sure I had any kind of prowess, but if I did, it definitely didn't involve anything that had to do with running or jumping or lifting my own body weight.

"Come on, Amalie." Miller's eyes danced over me, burning their way up my calves to my thighs to my middle. "I didn't mean that as an insult. I just didn't get the impression you had a lot of time to work out."

Nothing like stating the obvious. It's not only that I didn't have the time, but I hated exercising just for the sake of it. Give me a half-day bike trip, and I'd be all over it. Hiking a few trails in one of the national forests around Beaver Bluff was a perfect way to spend a Sunday afternoon. But plodding along on a treadmill for forty-five minutes or harnessing myself to a weight machine held no appeal.

Still, something about the way he brushed me off made me want to beat him. He didn't look like he lost often, if ever. I'd have to be smart about it. There was no way I could be him fair and square. But maybe if I could find a weakness . . .

"Fine. You're on. As long as Bettina and Jack keep an eye on Caden for a couple of minutes."

"We will." Bettina rubbed her hands together like she was ready to watch Evander Holyfield take on Mike Tyson. Not that she'd know who either one of them were. The only reason I did was because my mom's neighbor liked to watch the recording over and over again.

"Jack, you want to count us down from three?" Miller pushed his long sleeves up, drawing my attention to his forearms.

I handed Bettina my glasses and lined up next to him at the entrance to the first inflatable obstacle. We'd have to push through some tall posts and climb up a steep wall. There had to be some point during the course when I could slow him down. With my fingers crossed that I wasn't about to get my butt completely kicked, I crouched into what I hoped looked like a fierce starting position.

"On your mark," Jack yelled. "Get set, go!"

CHAPTER 13
Miller

I HADN'T COUNTED on Amalie being such a good sport about trying out the inflatables. She seemed to be enjoying herself almost more than the kids. I was tempted to give her a head start on the obstacle course, but I had a reputation to keep up in front of my kid.

Actually, I just wanted to see the look on her face when I beat her. Since we'd been talking on the phone when we placed our last bet, I'd missed out on getting a good look at her when I told her what color her eyes were. Now was my chance to see what kind of expression she might have worn that night.

She was smaller than me and made her way through the uprights faster. I caught up to her before she cleared the last one and grabbed hold of her arm.

"Not so fast." I laughed as I shot past her and catapulted myself toward the steep wall. Small square footholds had been sewn into the material, but my big hands made it difficult to get a good grip.

Amalie grabbed my foot and tugged me down a few steps. "You cheated back there."

"We didn't establish any rules. As far as I'm concerned, everything's fair game out here." I shook my foot, broke free, then scrambled up the rest of the wall. At the top, I scanned the rest of the course to see what came next. Looked like I'd drop down the wall, have to scale another one the same height, then squeeze myself through a series of round holes to get to the next section.

Her slimmer frame gave her the advantage, so I needed to bank as much time as possible before we got to that part. I dropped down to the low point between the walls and started up the next one. The structure shook as Amalie landed behind me. She was moving faster than I'd expected.

I didn't stop at the top of the next wall, just flew over it and slid down to the spot where I had to squeeze through the first hole. Amalie was right behind me and flew through the hole first. We both ended up in a dark, enclosed area. The only light filtered in through thin spots of the vinyl fabric and a small mesh area that allowed the air to circulate.

"Oh, crap." Amalie's voice came from the inflatable floor.

She sounded hurt. I stopped before I moved on to the next barrier. A challenge was a challenge, but I wasn't going to be a dick about it and leave her behind if she'd sprained her ankle or something.

"You okay?" I reached out, trying to find her in the dark.

"Yeah. It's just . . ." She moved. The air in the inflatable shifted, sending me off balance.

As I fell into her, I put my hands out, trying to make sure I didn't hurt her. My palm brushed something soft. Something lacy. Something that felt a hell of a lot like something I hadn't felt in a long fucking time.

She sucked in a breath and froze.

I pulled my hand away. Jesus, had I palmed her tit? "Uh, Amalie?"

"What are you doing?" she hissed out. Then she scrambled away from me.

"I thought you were hurt."

"My shirt got caught on my necklace when I squeezed through the hole."

Knowing I'd just had my palm on her breast sent blood to my cock. Thank fuck she couldn't see my face. A mixture of horror, regret, and something else filled my chest. "I'm sorry. I was just trying to see if you were okay."

"I was until . . . Oh, never mind." Her arm brushed against mine. It sounded like she'd tugged her shirt back down. Then she took off toward the next section of the course.

"There's Amalie! Go, Amalie, go!" Bettina called out.

"Dad? Where are you?" Jack asked.

"I'm here. I just need a minute." This wasn't the first time my cock had rallied around Amalie Rivers, but I sure as hell was going to make sure it was the last. There wasn't room in my life for a woman, much less a woman who had the ability to piss me off with just a look. So what if she had gorgeous eyes and lacy lingerie and the kind of hips I wouldn't mind sinking into?

Fuck. Thoughts like that were doing nothing to help with my growing issue. I dragged myself through the rest of the course while willing my cock to back down. Amalie waited for me at the end of the slide under a black and white checkered flag.

"What happened in there, Dad?" Jack's forehead creased with concern. "Did you choke?"

Amalie picked Caden up and held him on her hip. Her gaze drilled into me while she waited for me to respond.

"Sometimes you come out ahead. Sometimes you do your best and still come out behind." I slung my arm over his shoulders.

"Good race." Amalie held out a hand.

I didn't want to touch her. Not when my fingers still tingled from her skin. I didn't want to be rude, either. Or worse yet, let her think what happened in the darkness of an inflatable obstacle course affected me. So I slid my palm against hers and tried to keep my expression neutral.

"Congratulations. You got me this time." A shiver ran up my arm. I ignored it and squeezed her hand tighter before letting it go.

The guy I'd talked to on the phone and who'd met us in the office came through the door. "We're closing up soon. Did you have a chance to try everything out?"

Grateful for the interruption, I headed his way. "Yeah. I think any of these would be a great addition to the carnival. Did you have a chance to check the dates?"

"I did. We have everything available that weekend except for the firetruck bounce house. The fire department a few counties over has it rented for an event."

"Great. We'll take them."

Amalie stopped next to me and turned to get my attention. "Wait. What do you mean by 'weekend'? The carnival's happening on a Saturday afternoon, right?"

"Take which one?" the guy asked.

"All of them. We can sell wristbands so kids can have unlimited turns on both days. We might even be able to start Friday night if we get that concert set up."

"Miller,"—Amalie's hand landed on my arm—"don't you think you're going a little overboard? We haven't had a chance to talk about this yet."

I ignored the heat radiating out from where her slim fingers rested on my forearm. "You said you were okay with me taking the lead. Frannie's on board with making it a weekend event."

Her lips parted like she was about to say something. Then she closed her mouth like she'd thought better of it. "I need to get the kids back for dinner. Can we head out soon?"

"Sure." I turned back to the guy who was busy scribbling notes down on a small pad he'd pulled out of his pocket. "Do you want to get the contracts drawn up, and I'll stop by in the next few days to sign them? Or you can send them over email, and I'll scan in a signature page to get everything booked."

The guy took my business card. "Thanks, Mr. Bishop. We're looking forward to making it a great weekend for you and your family."

"My family . . ." I wasn't sure what he meant by that. Then I looked to where Amalie was bent down, helping Caden get his shoes back on his feet. Jack and Bettina sat on the ground, bumping shoulders and laughing.

"They're a good-looking bunch. We'll make sure they have fun." He tucked my business card into his notebook and slid both items into his pocket.

I didn't correct him. I was too busy looking at the scene in front of me through fresh eyes. Eyes that saw a mom and three kids. Eyes that saw a happy family of five. Of course, it made sense for him to assume Amalie and I were a couple. I hadn't given him any reason to think otherwise.

But I wasn't that kind of guy. I could barely keep up with Jack and my full-time job. When I added in the work I'd been doing at the distillery and taking the lead on planning the carnival, I didn't have anything left. Yeah, I wanted my kid to have a mom. I wanted to have someone to grow old with, maybe even make more babies with. Someone who'd have my back no matter what.

That woman wouldn't be Amalie Rivers, no matter how good she smelled or how my cock went rigid anytime we touched. She was off limits. My brain grasped that concept. It was just taking the rest of my body too damn long to catch up.

"Are you ready?" Amalie looked up at me, her eyes more gray than blue under the lights in the warehouse.

"Yeah, let's get everyone home." I held the door for the motley crew as they filed out. While Amalie got Caden buckled into his car seat, I checked my phone. Vaughn had called twice and followed up his voicemails with a few texts.

I needed to get my brother off my back. When we'd met Sunday afternoon, I'd given him my top five picks for potential hires. None of them had all the qualifications I'd been looking for, but there were a couple who might be a decent fit. I flipped through his texts, my stomach twisting tighter and tighter as I skimmed over his messages.

"Everything okay?" Amalie climbed into the passenger seat and pulled her seatbelt across her middle.

"Yeah. My brother's been texting. He needs me to swing by the distillery to interview a potential candidate tonight."

"Can I go to grandma and grandpa's?" Jack asked from the backseat.

"They're still out of town, big guy. You'll have to go with me." I caught a glimpse of him in the rearview mirror. He cupped his chin in his hands and let out a deep sigh.

"Can't he come to our house?" Bettina asked.

"Oh, um, how long is your meeting going to take?" Amalie brushed her palm along her thigh where a few of Titus's dog hairs had caught on her leggings.

"Shouldn't be more than an hour. Vaughn's got one of our top picks coming in tonight. The guy's in town for a family thing and is willing to meet with us outside of business hours."

"It's fine with me if Jack wants to hang out with us for a bit.

We can grab a bite and finish any homework they might have."

I glanced over, making eye contact for a brief moment before she looked away. "Are you sure you don't mind?"

"Can I, Dad? Please?" Jack grabbed hold of the back of my seat and leaned forward.

"It's not a problem at all." Amalie twisted around. "Are you okay with zoodles and sausage for dinner?"

"What are zoodles?" Jack's nose scrunched up. He wasn't an adventurous eater.

"They're spiraled zucchini noodles. Like spaghetti but healthier," Amalie said.

"They're an acquired taste but a good choice for low-carb diets," Bettina added.

Amalie leaned across the console. "She's been listening to her mom's keto podcasts."

I let out a chuckle. "You should try it, Jack. It would be good for you to eat more veggies."

"It would be good for you to eat more veggies, too, Dad," Jack mumbled.

"Sounds like we should plan on saving you some." Amalie's smile had me grinning back in return. I was a meat and potatoes guy. That's how my mom raised us. I'd never been a fan of vegetables unless they were slathered in butter or deep-fried to perfection.

"I'll grab dinner when I get home. No sense wasting your zoodles on me." I caught Jack's eye in the mirror again. "It's okay with me if you want to hang out at the Calbot's while I meet Uncle Vaughn. Just make sure you use your manners."

"Yes, sir." He leaned around Caden's car seat to grin at Bettina. "Maybe we can watch another movie after dinner."

"It's my house, so I get to pick," Bettina shot back.

As I pulled into the driveway, I wondered where Bettina

learned how to negotiate. Seemed like she and Amalie were cut from the same cloth when it came to making concessions— meaning they didn't.

Jack might be willing to be steamrolled by his crush, but I wasn't about to let Amalie get the best of me.

CHAPTER 14
Amalie

HAVING Jack around made things both easier and more difficult. He kept Bettina out of my hair, but he was also a constant reminder of Miller. While they didn't look much alike except for the deep green shade of their eyes, they had the same mannerisms. He also had the same smile. I tried to overlook their similarities, but it was unnerving how much he made me think about his dad.

The kids grumbled through dinner, then cheered up when they found out we still had ice cream in the freezer from last weekend. While I bathed Caden and got him to bed, Bettina and Jack took turns reading to each other. At least, that's what they said they were doing.

By the time I came downstairs, they'd moved on to watching a movie on the big screen. Bettina must have let him pick because I knew she wasn't a fan of the Star Wars franchise. But there she was in the front row, her feet tucked under her, her eyes wide as Yoda spouted his brand of wisdom on the screen.

Miller texted to say his meeting was wrapping up and he was on his way. He didn't seem interested in trying my zesty zoodles, but I'd saved some for him, anyway, along with a link of the organic Italian turkey sausage we'd had with them.

I couldn't believe he'd committed to running a weekend-long carnival. His sister was going to have to step in and help. By then, I'd be studying for finals and wouldn't have any available bandwidth to help beyond manning a shift or two. The way he had to make everything bigger than life irritated me. What was wrong with a readathon or walkathon, anyway?

He obviously didn't appreciate the simple things. Either that, or he took it for granted that everyone wanted to make as big of a splash as he did when given an opportunity. Not everyone wanted to be in the limelight. Some of us actively tried to avoid it.

I was more than happy to let him run with the carnival plans, but I didn't want Principal Masterson to think he was doing all the work. That wouldn't reflect well on me when it came time to apply for student teaching positions. Maybe I could carve out a tiny piece of the carnival that I could be fully responsible for. Something that would appeal to the kids and their parents. Something beyond splashy inflatables and carnival rides.

While I tried to come up with the perfect idea, my phone buzzed. Miller was at the front door but hadn't wanted to knock or ring the bell in case it would wake Caden. I got up and headed that way. The kids only had a few minutes left in their movie. It would be easier to let them finish than try to turn it off now.

I tugged the door open, my eyes on my phone. "Hey, how was your meeting?"

"It was fine."

The toe of a leather dress shoe caught my eye. I dragged my gaze up his pants leg, trying not to pause at the slight bulge behind his zipper. He had on a crisp white dress shirt with a dark orange tie. His charcoal suit jacket clung to his shoulders, and the five o'clock shadow on his cheeks only added to his appeal. Miller Bishop in a pair of jeans was easy on the eyes. Miller Bishop in a suit tailored to his build was a sight to behold.

"You're all dressed up." I stated the obvious, then felt like a complete idiot for doing so. He was a CPA, so it made sense for him to own a suit. I just wasn't expecting to ever see him in one.

"Yeah." He ran a hand over his short hair as he stepped inside the house. "I ran home and changed before I met up with Vaughn. Devil's Dance is more or less a family business, but we like to make a good impression."

"You do."

"Do what?" He followed me into the kitchen, the soles of his shoes tapping on the marble tile floor.

"Um, make a good impression." My cheeks flamed while I tried to figure out a way to save face. "The distillery, I mean. I've always been impressed when I've visited."

He leaned against the granite countertop, his lips splitting into an amused grin. "Have you visited often?"

Once. I'd only ever been to the distillery once, and that was when my mom had to run in to pick up an item they'd donated to a silent auction at my school. I wasn't lying—my one visit had made a good impression.

What held my attention the most was the gallery of photographs lining the walls of the front office. My mom said they took those pictures way back when the distillery was no more than a few stills in the woods. That was when the Bishop, Stewart, and Devine families were all good friends. Before the feud took hold and the Beaver Bluff's economy had almost gone down the drain with the distillery.

"Hasn't everyone in Beaver Bluff been to the distillery at least a few times?" Avoiding the question was the best choice.

"I'd like to think so, but not everyone loves having the oldest distillery in Tennessee right in their backyard." He pushed off the counter. "Where's Jack? I should get him home."

"They're finishing up a movie. I'll go get him." I turned to go, but there was something I'd been meaning to ask Miller. Now might be my only chance. "Hey, can I ask you a question?"

"Sure."

"The other night, when Caden got ahold of my, um, massager . . ."

Miller's eyebrows shot up.

I closed my eyes and pretended my cheeks weren't on fire. When I opened my eyes, he was still staring at me. "Did you happen to see it after that? I can't find it, and I don't want Caden or Bettina to get their hands on it."

It couldn't be in the house. I'd torn the place apart. The last time I remembered having it was when I sat by Miller in the theater room.

"I found it on the seat you were sitting in during the movie." His expression had relaxed, and he crossed his arms over his chest. "I tossed it for you."

"You tossed it?"

"Well, yeah. I mean, it had bite marks on it. You weren't planning on using it after that, were you?"

"No, of course not." Goodbye orgasms. That little contraption had cost me fifty bucks. I would have been willing to overlook a bite mark or two. Instead, I'd just suffered the feminine version of being cock-blocked by an overbearing Bishop. "Thanks for looking out for me."

"Any time."

I left Miller standing by the refrigerator while I went to check on the kids. The movie had just wrapped up, and Bettina stifled a yawn.

"Is my dad here?" Jack asked.

"He sure is. Time to go." I flipped the lights on and the screen off before following the two of them back out to the kitchen.

Miller held out his arm and pulled Jack in for a hug. I couldn't figure out how he could be everything the town said he was and still act like such a good dad. Either people had made broad assumptions about him, or he was putting on quite a show. Even though I'd formed opinions about Miller from our brief interaction as kids, he didn't seem like a man who'd stolen his son from his mother. The Bishops had been in the public eye for generations. They knew how to put up a front. It was possible that Miller paid her off for Jack's own good.

"How were the zoodles?" Miller asked.

Jack lifted a shoulder. "They were okay."

"Oh, we saved you some." I pulled the refrigerator open and took out a glass container. "I know you said you weren't a fan of veggies but try them. They won't get as soggy if you heat them in an air fryer."

"What's an air fryer?" He reluctantly took the container I pushed toward him.

I nudged my chin toward the large appliance sitting on the counter. The rest of the house might embrace a minimalist design, but Mrs. Calbot believed in keeping the appliances she used daily out on the counters. "It cooks with air and makes things seem deep-fried but healthier, I guess."

"Another gadget, huh?" Miller shook his head. "I can barely run a toaster oven. I'm pretty sure figuring out an air fryer is above my pay grade."

"Well, if you ever want to try it, I can show you how it works."

"Thanks, Amalie." He held up the container of noodles. "I'll get this back to you in the next few days."

The kids said goodbye, and I walked Miller and Jack to the door. Jack went out to the truck, but Miller lingered on the stoop.

"Thanks for having him over tonight. I really appreciate it." He held my gaze for a long beat. "If I can ever return the favor . . ."

"It was no trouble at all." I didn't want him to think he was on the hook or owed me.

"Still, if you need anything . . ."

"Sometimes people do things just to be nice and don't expect or need anything in return." I swung my hand out and bumped his elbow. "I think they're called friends."

His warm laugh rolled through me. "Is that what we are, Amalie? Friends?"

My breath caught at the way his tone dipped low. Just when I thought I had a handle on the way my body reacted to Miller Bishop, he'd do or say something that tested my theory. Was it possible he'd changed over the years?

I wasn't sure where a conversation like this would lead, but that didn't stop me from wanting to find out. "We can be if you want to."

He didn't look like he was too sure, either. His eyelids fluttered closed in a long blink, and I couldn't help but notice his long dark lashes. Even with three coats of mascara, my eyelashes didn't come close to being as thick and long as his.

"Friends. Yeah, okay. Let's try it out and see what happens." He pushed off from where he'd been leaning against the door frame. "See you around, friend."

The way the word rolled off his tongue made being friends

sound a little dirty. It also made me wonder what kind of friends he wanted to be.

I closed the door and leaned up against it. His truck started, and he backed down the driveway. My chest rose and fell as I drew in deep breaths. Miller had to be one of the most aggravating men I'd ever met. His need to go all out and make the most out of everything directly opposed my tendency to fly under the radar.

I hated the fact that he took control. He didn't listen to my opinions or put much weight behind my suggestions. I was sure I'd catch him trying to mansplain something to me before too long if we kept spending time together.

Yet as much as those things annoyed me, there was an underlying feeling that was growing stronger. I needed to keep reminding myself of all his faults. Especially if he ever showed up in a suit again.

CHAPTER 15

Miller

THE ZOODLES WEREN'T BAD. They weren't great, but they were better than I thought they'd be. I'd eaten half of them last night and brought the rest to the office so I didn't have to leave for lunch. I'd been spending so much time working on stuff at the distillery lately that I needed to get caught up on a few projects. Vaughn had interviews lined up later in the week with two more candidates from the top five we'd agreed on. I hoped one of them would work out so I'd be off the hook.

I slid another bite of fake spaghetti into my mouth and opened a browser window on my computer. I'd booked the inflatables for the carnival but felt like we still needed something else for entertainment. Amalie would probably disagree.

She seemed to have fun when we tested out the different inflatable options. At least until the point where I'd accidentally manhandled her. I didn't want to think about that again. I'd already devoted way too much time to reliving that moment. Though every time I did, somehow we ended up rolling all over the inflatable floor and peeling off each other's clothes as quickly as possible.

She'd gotten under my skin, and I needed to find a way to dig her out of there. As I scrolled through page after page of carnival games, looking for inspiration, a shadow fell over my desk.

"Hey, Miller. I wanted to stop by and show you the label we came up with for the 150th-anniversary bottle. Do you have a sec?" My brother Evan didn't wait for me to respond.

"Sure, come on in." It was unusual for him to stop by my office at the consulting firm. "What are you doing downtown?"

"Had to run some errands, so I figured I'd pop in."

I gestured to the chair in front of my desk. "Have you shown Vaughn yet?"

"Yeah." Evan set his bag on the floor and pulled out a few papers.

"If y'all have made a decision, you don't need my opinion." Even when I tried to make it clear that I wasn't part of the family business, it didn't seem to matter. They didn't want to hurt my feelings by leaving me out of discussions. No matter how often I told them to handle decisions, they still liked to keep me informed about what was happening.

Family dinners were the worst. My dad either didn't acknowledge me at all or pretended like there wasn't a rift as wide as the Mississippi between us. I'd stopped going for a while. Then mom got all teary-eyed and begged me to come back. She also made everyone promise to leave the business at the office when we got together outside of work. For a while, things got better. With me taking over the bookkeeping for her until they found someone to hire full-time, my siblings seemed to have forgotten that I didn't deserve to have an official opinion.

"I have a question about the numbers." Evan spread the concepts out on my desk. "Vaughn likes this one but wants to find out if we can have them do an embossed gold label. That's going to drive the price up, and I don't know how much wiggle room we've got in the budget."

"I'll have to look that up later. My personal laptop is at home."

"You know I wouldn't have stopped by if it wasn't important." Evan shuffled the papers back into a stack.

"When do you need to know?"

His lips cracked into a teasing smile. "Yesterday, according to our big brother."

"Doesn't he know there are some things he can't bend to his will? Like time?" I matched his grin, our shared frustration with Vaughn providing a moment of levity.

"You should be the one to tell him." Evan nodded with a little too much enthusiasm. "I hear he takes constructive criticism well."

Evan had always been able to make me laugh. He had such a different perspective on life than the rest of us. His time in the military, especially in a war zone, had taught him not to take himself, or anything else, too seriously.

"I'll check when I get home and shoot you a text. If it's something Vaughn wants, I'm sure we'll find a way to make it happen."

"He still has to get it past Davis," Evan said. The Stewarts didn't trust us just about as much as we didn't trust them. To ensure neither family screwed the other over, most positions at the distillery were duplicates. Vaughn shared the title of General Manager with Davis. Cole had to work with Harper as a Co-Master Distiller, and Ruby kept an eye on Sawyer in the marketing department. Lucky for me, the Stewarts didn't have anyone on their side who was interested in running the numbers. They'd hired a CPA at a local rival firm to audit the books every year. That was their way of keeping tabs on us.

The feud between our families wasn't just a ridiculous waste of time. It was also a waste of assets. The distillery could have been pulling in a much bigger profit if we didn't have two employees covering the same position.

"How's everything going at the office?" I could count on Evan to tell it to me straight. He'd always been honest with me.

"It's fine. Cole's been fighting with Harper to finalize the 150th-anniversary batch blend. Vaughn's being Vaughn, and Ruby's been trying to convince us to do a big concert for the anniversary celebration."

"Oh yeah? Who's she thinking about bringing in?" I hadn't had a chance to talk to her about my idea for the school carnival to piggyback off the anniversary party. Hopefully, she hadn't settled on a performer yet.

"She said she put some feelers out to Knox Shepler. Rumor has it he's a fan of our whiskey."

"You can't tell me he'd spend a weekend performing in Beaver Bluff just because he likes what we pull out of a barrel." Knox would be a big name. He'd won an award for best mew artist of the year the last year and was a hot commodity right now. He didn't have the same appeal for the kids as Brandiss, but the kids weren't the ones who'd be opening up their wallets.

"Hey, stranger things have happened." Evan's brows rose. "Remember when the adult film director wanted to film at the distillery because he loved how our whiskey smelled?"

"Yeah, he offered to name one of his feature films after us. I know they say no publicity is bad publicity, but I'm not sure I agree."

"Do you think Vaughn would have let him if he'd been in charge instead of Dad?" Evan lifted his leg and propped a hiking boot on his knee.

"Nah. I know Vaughn's trying to take the business to the next level, but even he probably has limits." Out of my three brothers, Vaughn was the one who reminded me most of my dad. They had the same unwavering high standards and expected everyone to give one-hundred-fifty percent all the time. They also had the same tolerance for bullshit, which was a big, fat zero. If Vaughn ever did have kids, I hoped he wouldn't fuck them up like our dad had done to me.

Vaughn having kids . . . now there was something I wasn't sure I'd ever see. Odds weren't in his favor since he must have missed the memo that there was more to life than work.

"Hey, do you think Vaughn will ever have kids?"

"Where's that coming from?" Evan asked.

"I don't know. Just popped into my head a minute ago." I put the lid back on the container that had been full of Amalie's zoodles and sausage a little bit ago.

"This wouldn't have anything to do with the dark-haired bombshell you've been hanging out with lately, would it?" The chair squeaked as Evan leaned forward.

"Excuse me?" I tried to play it off, but suddenly my office seemed too hot. Beads of perspiration formed at my hairline.

Evan shook his head. "Don't try to play dumb with me. Frannie told me all about how you and the Calbot's nanny are planning some big spring carnival for the school. First, you had pizza with her, then Frannie said you took them all to try out bounce houses together earlier this week. Anything going on there?"

"Hell no." I shook my head, unwilling to admit the thought had crossed my mind. Repeatedly.

Evan shrugged. "It's been a long time, man. Might be worth considering…"

"Did she also tell you Amalie's working a full-time job while putting herself through school? You think you're busy…

you should see the grid she has posted on the refrigerator to keep everybody on track. That's so not my style." Not my style, but that didn't mean I didn't appreciate her methods. I'd even snapped a picture of the grid to see if I could pick up any pointers on how to get Jack into some sort of routine.

"What do you mean? You've got a lot on your plate, and you seem to be handling it just fine." Evan cocked his head. "How long has it been since you've been out with a woman?"

"You just said you heard I took Amalie and the kids to try out bounce houses. I've been looking at other ideas for the carnival. What do you think about one of those cranes you can bungee jump from?" I glanced back at the screen and read off the specs. "Says here they take customers up in a bucket then let them freefall a hundred and fifty feet."

"Are you trying to change the subject?" Evan asked.

"No. When's the last time *you* went out with a woman?"

His lips curled into a lopsided smile. "Easy. I met up with Frannie for a burger on Friday night."

"Not Frannie. I mean a real woman. Someone you like, someone you might want to bang, Evan. Not your best friend from high school." I shook my head and bit back a laugh.

Evan didn't move. His smile faded and a crease formed between his eyebrows.

"Oh fuck. You like her, don't you?" How did I not see it before?

"No. Nothing like that." He tried to brush me off, but I'd seen the way the light had gone out of his eyes when I implied Frannie didn't count.

"Does she know?" The papers I'd been reviewing earlier scattered as I leaned forward.

Evan held my gaze a few seconds too long, probably hoping I'd get tired of waiting for him to say something and change the subject. This was one of the rare times in my life when I held my ground. No matter what he said now, I knew the truth.

"No, she doesn't know, and we're going to keep it that way." Any trace of humor had disappeared. His jaw tensed. He pinned me in place with an icy look that had earned him the nickname "SubZero" from his fellow soldiers.

"You got it. My lips are sealed."

Evan rolled his eyes. "What about the nanny?"

"Amalie?" I didn't like the way my chest warmed when I said her name. Pressing my palm to the spot between my pecs, I rubbed a small circle. "There's nothing to share."

"That's too bad, man. If she's a nanny, you already know she likes kids. Not like—"

"That's enough." He didn't know what he was talking about. I hadn't told anyone, including Evan, the whole story about what happened between Jack's mom and me. I'd let them assume what they wanted. Sooner or later, I'd have to tell them something.

"Sorry." Evan held up his hands in apology. "I'd better get going. Let me know about those numbers when you get home, will you?"

I nodded and rose from my seat. With lunch done, I needed to get back to work anyway. "No hard feelings at all."

Evan thrust his hand out, but I walked around the desk and pulled him into a hug instead. As much as we aggravated each other, he was still family. He was also my best friend and Jack's only godparent. He'd have to do a hell of a lot more than make an offhand comment for me to get pissed at him.

"Just think about the nanny, will you?" Evan pulled away and picked up the label mockups he'd left on the edge of my desk.

I wasn't about to admit just how often I thought about

Amalie. And I sure as hell wasn't going to tell anyone exactly what my thoughts entailed.

"Don't worry about me. Amalie and I have well-defined boundaries between us."

"Really?" Evan smirked. "What does that look like?"

"It's the strangest thing." I shrugged. "We're friends."

CHAPTER 16

Amalie

NO, no, no. I banged my palms against the steering wheel of my car as it coasted to a stop on the side of the four-lane road just outside of town. I knew things were going too well this morning. Bettina only went through two outfits before coming down for breakfast, and Caden had his morning poop before we left the house for a change.

Today was the day of my mom's doctor's appointment in Chattanooga. I'd just picked her up and gotten on the highway when the back tire blew out. I should have driven Mrs. Calbot's SUV today, but I would have felt pretentious pulling up in front of the trailer I grew up in behind the wheel of a vehicle that cost more than my mother's home.

"Do you have a spare?" Mom asked.

"No. I was going to replace it when I got new tires this spring." I'd been holding out, trying to get through one more winter and pay for my next semester of tuition before I shelled out money for tires.

I grabbed my phone from my purse and tried to think of who to call. At some point, I'd need to get a tow truck out here, but at the moment, I had a more immediate need. I had to find a way to get my mom to the appointment we'd scheduled months ago. If she missed it, there was no telling how long we'd have to wait to reschedule with the pulmonary specialist.

"Faster," Caden sputtered from the backseat.

"I wish we were." Sitting behind the wheel wasn't doing any good, so I got out to see how bad it was. "You stay here, Caden. I'll be right back."

I left him chilling in his car seat while I walked around the back of my car to assess the damage. The tire was completely flat. I didn't know much about cars, but I could tell we weren't going anywhere in this one until it got a new tire.

I'd just pulled my phone out of my pocket when a big black truck pulled to a stop behind my car. It was broad daylight, and I was parked on the side of one of the busiest roads around town. Still, a sense of uneasiness spread through me. I'd watched too many true crime shows. It wasn't like some madman was going to knock me out with chloroform, shove me in his backseat, take me back to his creepy old house, and bury me alive.

I mean, it did happen to Sandra Bullock in *The Vanishing*. I suppose it could happen to me.

My chest relaxed when I realized it was Miller getting out of the truck. He had on another one of his form-fitting suits. This one was dark, with the faintest hint of a pinstripe running through it. Today's shirt was blue, and the tie was a deep purple.

"Hey, Amalie. I thought I recognized your car. What happened?" He slid his shades off as he came closer. The purple of his tie made his eyes look greener.

If I hadn't been so stressed, I might have paused to enjoy the view. Now wasn't the time.

"I got a flat. I'm supposed to be taking my mom to a

specialist appointment right now. I must have run over something on the road. We were cruising along, then all of a sudden, we started losing speed while cars zoomed around us."

"Zoom," Caden yelled through the window.

Miller glanced at Caden in the backseat and smiled at him. "Hey, little man."

Caden waved, pulled off his shoe, and tossed it through the cracked window.

"Caden!" I went to retrieve it, but Miller grabbed me around the waist just as a huge truck whooshed by. The horn sounded, and my pulse skyrocketed. I'd been so distracted, I'd almost been taken out by a port-a-potty truck. What a way to go.

My breath didn't just catch in my chest; it got lost somewhere between my lungs my throat. I wheezed, trying to draw in some air. "I almost . . . oh my gosh . . ."

"It's okay, I've got you." Miller pulled me into his arms and hugged me tight against him.

My brush with death made me feel so alive. The strength of my senses multiplied by hundreds. I noticed everything... from the feel of fine wool under my cheek to the intoxicating, masculine cologne that filled my nose. I clung to him, sliding my hands under his jacket and grabbing two fistfuls of his soft shirt.

I gasped, trying to get my breath to slow, to get my heart to stop beating five hundred times a minute. Miller whispered words against the shell of my ear. I couldn't tell what he was saying, but his low, steady tone brought me back. In his arms, I felt safe. I felt protected. I felt... something not so soft pressing against my belly.

I pulled back, wanting to see his face. I needed to see his reaction to what was happening between us.

His eyes met mine. He didn't crack a joke. He didn't turn away. He held my gaze, his eyes searching mine. Then he shifted his hand up to cradle the back of my head. As I stared at him, knowing it was inevitable, knowing there was no way to stop what was about to happen, my entire body relaxed.

His lips brushed mine so softly that I thought I might have imagined it. Then he kissed me again, leaving no doubt that's what he intended. I couldn't move, couldn't think, couldn't focus on anything except the way the mid-morning light brought out the gold flecks in his eyes.

"Shoe. Caden shoe." Caden's shrill cry brought me back. Reluctantly, I pulled away from Miller.

"Your shoe is gone, Caden. A big truck ran over it." What was left of his shoe had landed halfway across the two-lane road.

"Your car,"—Miller loosened his grip but didn't take his hands off me—"I think we're going to need to call for a tow truck."

"My mom's up front." I was a horrible daughter. My poor mom had an important appointment this morning... an appointment I'd promised to take her to... and instead of figuring out a solution, I was kissing a relative stranger on the side of the highway. I hoped she hadn't seen us.

"I'll drive you." Miller let go of my hand and walked over to the back door. "Let me move Caden's car seat over to my truck. Lock your car, and I'll call for a tow truck on the way to where we're going."

"I can't let you do that. Her appointment is in Chattanooga. She's going to see a specialist, and—"

"I've got it, Amalie." He rested his hand on my shoulder, then nudged my chin up to make eye contact. "You don't have to do everything by yourself. Let me help you with this."

A warm feeling spread out from the middle of my belly.

Like I'd just chugged a peppermint latte, and the yummy goodness radiated out from my tummy.

"Okay." Saying that word caused physical pain. My eye twitched, and I got a cramp in my lower right abdomen. I hated asking people for help. Even when they were more than willing to pitch in, I couldn't stand to burden others with problems I should be able to handle.

Repairing a flat tire wasn't exactly in my wheelhouse of knowledge. But still… letting Miller take the lead was both comforting and panic-inducing.

Within minutes, he had Caden buckled in the back of his truck.

"Are you sure you have time to take us all the way to Chattanooga and back? You've probably got a ton to do for work, and I don't think we'll be back before school lets out. What are you going to do about Jack?"

He stepped closer as my mom approached. "It's fine. I sent a couple of texts and shifted my schedule around."

"Are you sure?" The sight of him in his suit sent heat rushing up my cheeks. He looked so out of place standing on the side of the highway. Like he was from another world. A world where people didn't have balding tires or twenty-five-year-old cars with almost three hundred thousand miles on them. He'd probably never changed a tire. I bet the Bishop family could afford twenty-four-hour priority roadside assistance if one of their shiny new cars had any issues.

His eyes softened. "I'm sure. And Jack's staying after school today for some new robotics program he wanted to join."

"Thank you." I held his gaze longer than necessary, hoping he'd be able to tell how much his help meant to me. I didn't want it and hated having to ask for it, but I was grateful he was there to give it.

"You're welcome. Now, are you going to introduce me to your mom?" He pulled himself to his full height and opened the door to the backseat as my mom got close to the truck.

"Mom, hey, this is my friend Miller." I waited for her to make a crack about the Bishop family or say something about the feud.

"Mrs. Rivers, it's nice to meet you." Miller held out his hand. To my surprise, my mom took it.

Either she didn't know who he was or must have realized he was our only option for getting her to her appointment on time. "It's nice to meet you too, Miller."

She stumbled over his name like it physically pained her to say it out loud. I'd never understood exactly what happened to turn her so against the Bishop family, but she'd held a grudge for as long as I could remember.

"It's a bit of a step up. Can I help you into the back?" he asked.

Mom didn't like anyone feeling sorry for her or seeing her as weak. She could be dying of thirst and refuse to ask someone for a drink of water. Yet she held tight to Miller's big hand and let him help her into the truck. Either my eyes were playing tricks on me, or my mother was letting a Bishop help her.

"Well, hello there, Caden." Mom settled into the seat next to Caden's car seat.

"JaJa." Caden grinned from ear to ear. He'd always loved spending time around my mom. "Gum?"

"Oh, I probably have a piece of Juicy Fruit somewhere in my purse." She smiled at Miller as she reached back to grab her seatbelt. "He has such a good memory for a two-year-old."

Miller smiled back. Then he gently closed the door, sealing my mom into the back of his truck. That had gone better than I expected. Tension seeped from my shoulders, and I took in a deep breath.

"Everything's going to be fine, Amalie." Miller reached for my hand and gave it a brief squeeze.

Easy for him to say. He didn't know that the woman sitting in his back seat held years of hate in her heart toward his family. I didn't understand it, and I never would unless my mother wanted to break her tight-mouthed silence about the topic. She could be so stubborn sometimes. I almost laughed when I realized she said the same thing about me.

I rounded the front of the truck and climbed up into the cab.

"You've got to tell me where to go now." Miller handed me his phone.

I entered the address for the doctor's office.

"Thanks." His thumb swept over the sensitive skin on my inner wrist, and he lowered his voice so that only I could hear him. "What are you thinking about, Amalie?"

"Nothing, really." I didn't know what to think about what had just happened. Neither one of us had said anything about the kiss. God, the kiss. I'd never been kissed like that before in my life. It was like he'd breached whatever walls I'd put up around my heart with one swipe of his tongue. I was still reeling.

"I know now isn't a good time, but I'd like to talk about what happened earlier. Maybe over a beer or pizza when you have a free evening?"

"I don't know, Miller." He'd never be interested in me when he realized where I came from. That was one thing I was sure of.

It's not that I was embarrassed by my mom or the home she'd created for the two of us. It was just a completely different world than the one Miller lived in. I didn't want to see the same look in his eyes I'd seen the one other time I'd invited someone from his world to spend an afternoon in mine.

I'd been working on a team project in middle school with a boy I liked. We couldn't meet in the library that day, so I'd invited him to ride my bus home with me and work at my house. He'd only been there about ten minutes when he'd called his mom to pick him up. When she pulled into the drive, the look in her eyes said it all. I wasn't good enough. My home wasn't good enough. My life wasn't good enough. After that, I never invited another person over again.

"What's not to know? We need to talk about the carnival, anyway."

The carnival. Until we got past the spring fundraiser, I wouldn't be able to shut Miller out of my life.

"Fine. We'll talk about the carnival. But no pizza, and for sure no beer." I was already close to changing my opinion of Miller Bishop. Alcohol would cloud my judgment, and I wasn't ready to forgive and forget so easily.

"It's a date, then." He grinned, obviously pretty proud of himself.

"Not a date. A meeting," I whispered back. No way was my first date in two years going to be with Miller Bishop. No way in hell.

For the next two hours, I gazed out the window at the scenery flashing by while my mom and Caden sang songs, played games, and held bubble-blowing contests. It would be a while before Caden mastered the art of blowing bubbles. He tended to just spit the glob of gum out of his mouth, then laughed while Mom picked it up with a tissue.

Miller even got in on the fun. Before we turned off the highway, he blew a big bubble that blocked him from seeing where he was going. I had to take the wheel for a few moments while he filled it with more and more air. The bubble finally burst, sending wisps of gum all over his face.

Caden clapped until his hands hurt and asked for more, more, more. Finally, right as we got to our exit, he gave up trying to fight the lull of being in the car. His eyes drifted closed. I'd hoped he'd fall asleep when we first got into the truck so he'd be well-rested by the time we arrived. If I woke him up now, he'd be a total grump.

Miller pulled up in front of the brick office building. "Do you want me to park, or should I let you off here?"

"Here's fine. I don't know how long we'll be. You're welcome to go grab a bite to eat or something while we're inside." I gathered the tote bag with Caden's things and shoved my notebook inside so I could write down everything the doctor said.

"Why don't you leave Caden in the car with me?" Miller's hand brushed along my arm. "I'm just going to sit in the parking lot and catch up on email."

I glanced back and forth from Caden's peaceful and quiet form to Miller. It's not that I didn't trust him, but I was in charge of Caden. If something happened while I was inside with my mom, how would I explain that to the Calbots?

"Nothing's going to happen," Miller said, completely reading my mind. "I'll call you if he wakes up. Or if you'd feel more comfortable, I can come in with you and keep an eye on him while you help your mom."

I wasn't going to ask him to come into the doctor's office with me. My mother would never forgive me if I let a Bishop get insider information on her private health concerns. And Caden looked so sweet, with his bottom lip sticking out in a tiny pout while he was asleep. I'd learned from experience that waking him up from a nap, especially just after he'd fallen asleep, would only make all of us miserable.

I looked Miller right in the eye. "If you're sure it's no trouble."

"No trouble at all."

"Okay then. Thank you." I grabbed the notebook out of the bag and shut the door before I changed my mind. Maybe it was okay to let someone else help me every once in a while. I just hoped I hadn't made a mistake by putting my trust in Miller.

CHAPTER 17
Miller

I GOT out of the truck to help Amalie's mom. Something was bothering Amalie. She had her jaw clenched tight and her mouth turned down at the corners. I assumed she hadn't been too thrilled at having me drive her to her mom's appointment. "Everything okay, Amalie?"

"It will be." She tucked her mom's hand into the crook of her arm.

I watched the two of them disappear through the sliding glass doors. Then I got back in the truck and moved it to a proper parking spot. A glance at the rear-view mirror confirmed Caden was still passed out. I figured I'd check in with Vaughn and let him know I wouldn't make it to the interview he'd scheduled with the last of his top picks.

He picked up on the first ring. "Vaughn. Talk to me."

"Hey, bro. Bad news. Something came up, and I'm not going to make it to that interview today." My gut clenched while I waited for him to unload his frustration on me.

"What the fuck, Miller? I thought you were just as eager as I am to get this wrapped up." I pictured him launching himself out of our dad's old leather chair and pacing the office. He always did that when he was pissed off.

"I'm sorry. I couldn't get out of something that came up at the last minute." He didn't need to know I was in Chattanooga with Amalie and her mom. If I told him that, he'd really lose his shit.

"Can you call in or join us via video?"

I glanced at my watch. The drive back home would take about two hours. Even if we left in the next ten minutes, I wouldn't be able to make it there in time to join in on the call. "It's not going to work out for this afternoon. Sorry, I'm doing my best."

"Your best hasn't been worth shit lately. You know that, don't you?" He sounded more tired than mad. I suppose he'd been putting in a lot more time than usual trying to get ready for the anniversary celebration. If my dad had a soul at all, he would have waited to retire until after we got through the anniversary.

"Thanks for that very gentle reminder," I snapped back.

"Fuck. I'm sorry. There's a lot of pressure right now to make sure everything goes well through the end of the year. Everyone's counting on me and—"

"You're not alone in this. You've got Cole, Evan, and Ruby right there. Any of them would be happy to pick up some slack if you need help." The problem wasn't that he didn't have anyone to help him. He just hated asking for it. Reminded me of Amalie, in a way. The realization caught me off guard. That was exactly it. Neither one of them wanted to let anyone in. They both thought that asking for help was a sign of weakness. What a load of bullshit.

"I don't need help. All I need is for people to do what they fucking say they're going to do." Now he was mad.

"Point taken. You know I have a full-time job already,

right? And a son to raise? I didn't ask to take over Mom's spot at the distillery." He acted like it was my responsibility to find her replacement. I told him I'd help, but I was getting sick of everyone treating me like I was the one not coming through.

"I know. Let's just get someone hired so we both can move on. Sound good?"

My breath whooshed out on a long exhale. "Fuck yeah, that sounds good."

"Fuck yeah," a little voice said from the backseat.

"What was that?" Vaughn asked.

"Nothing." I turned around and put my finger over my lip, hoping Caden knew the international sign for shut the fuck up.

"Fuck yeah," he said again.

"Miller?" Vaughn's voice went up a notch. "Where the hell are you?"

I put my hand over the mic. "Shh. Quiet, Caden. You shouldn't say that word."

"Miller?" Vaughn asked again.

"Fuck yeah. Fuck yeah. Fuck yeah." Caden's mouth split into a wide grin.

I climbed out of the truck and shut the door, leaving the kid inside to curse all he wanted. "Sorry about that. I must have driven through a dead zone."

"Do you have Jack with you?"

"No. He's at school. I'm in between appointments, that's all." I looked around the crowded parking lot, grateful we weren't on video.

"I'm going to try to reschedule that interview for tomorrow. I'd appreciate it if you'd do your best to be here for it."

"You got it, boss."

His low groan sounded over the background noise of downtown Chattanooga. "Cut the shit."

"I'll do my best to be there." Pushing Vaughn's buttons wasn't going to do me any good today. Besides, he was right. Hiring someone full-time, as soon as possible, was in everyone's best interest.

"Thanks." The line went dead.

Vaughn wasn't much for long goodbyes. I'd taken care of my twelve-thirty appointment. Now I needed to check in and let my boss know I'd be out of pocket for a few hours. Thankfully, he didn't care much about where I was or what I did as long as I delivered what I said I would when I said I'd do it. I sent an email to let him know something had come up that required me to be out of the office, then climbed back into the truck.

"That wasn't funny." I leaned over the seat to glare at Caden.

He smiled back, a glob of slobber running down his chin from between his toothy grin. "Fuck yeah."

Dammit. Amalie would skewer my balls and grill them over a bonfire if Caden spouted off his new favorite phrase when her mom got back in the truck.

"Let's play a new game, Caden. How about we sing together?" I tugged on my ears and started singing the song about ears hanging low that always used to make Jack laugh. Caden stared at me, a smile on his face. When I'd given it my all, I took a deep breath. "How was that?"

"Out?" His fingers fumbled with his car seat buckle.

"Not yet, little man. Amalie will be back in just a minute." Grateful that his short attention span had moved on to something else, I took a swig of my coffee. I missed so much when Jack was Caden's age. I'd been living with Vaughn to save money and get through school. Caden spent so much time at daycare during that time. I did the best I could, but I'd been stressed, sleep-deprived, and completely out of my comfort zone as a single dad.

Knowing what I knew now, I wouldn't mind going through that again. I'd appreciate it more this time. Thanks to my job, I had enough in my savings account that I wouldn't be stressed about money. The only thing missing was someone to share the experience with.

I'd done it alone and wasn't eager to sign up for that again. Amalie was great with kids. I wondered if she'd thought about having a family someday. Hell, I couldn't spend time thinking about that. She hadn't even graduated with her undergrad yet. I had no idea how many more years of school she had before she started student teaching.

It wasn't like she'd given me any indication she was interested in me beyond the way she'd responded to my kiss. It was a hell of a good kiss, though. Warmth flooded my system as I remembered how it felt to slide my hand up her neck, cradle the back of her head in my palm, and lower my mouth to hers.

My phone rang and pulled me out of my thoughts. I recognized my boss's number. Shit. I hoped he hadn't added a meeting to my calendar that I wouldn't be able to make. I grabbed it and checked the rear-view mirror to see if Caden had found something to keep himself busy. He held one of his cars in his hand and ran it over the window.

Satisfied he'd be okay for a minute or two, I answered. "Hello?"

"Miller, I'm glad I caught you. Just saw your email about needing to take care of a few things. I'll be out of the office tomorrow but wanted to talk to you about a few opportunities. Your name's been coming up in several conversations lately."

"Oh?" He had my attention, but Amalie would be coming out any minute, and I couldn't count on Caden to keep quiet for any length of time. "I'm in the middle of something right this second. Would it be possible to call you back later this afternoon?"

"I'll be on the road later. I can send you some information via email, then have my assistant set up a time for us to review on Monday if that works for you."

"That would be great." I'd bought myself a little bit of time. "Thanks, Karl."

"Thank you. I think you'll like what I'm sending over. There are some great opportunities ahead for all of us."

"I can't wait to check it out. Safe travels."

He disconnected, and I sat there looking at my phone. We must have won a new client or received a request for a proposal from someone on his target list. Either way, if he had me in mind to take the lead, that was good news.

"That was my boss, Caden. He's sending over some information for me to review. What do you think about that?" I reached back and tickled his bare foot.

Caden erupted in a fit of giggles, then sucked in a breath and let out a sneeze worthy of someone several times his size. Snot hung down his face in long streams.

"Jesus." I probably should have said "God bless you" instead, but the sheer amount of goop covering his face horrified and impressed me. "We'd better get you cleaned up before Amalie gets back."

He looked up at me, yellowy goop continuing to drip from his nose, and said, "Fuck yeah."

CHAPTER 18

Amalie

MY MOM LOOKED FRAIL, sitting on the exam table in the doctor's office during her appointment. She was only in her mid-fifties—way too young to think all her best years were behind her. We needed to find someone who could figure out what was going on with her and how to fix it.

"Well, that was a waste of time." Mom tugged her cardigan over her shoulders.

"It wasn't a waste. We've eliminated another path we needed to investigate in our search for answers." There were other providers we could talk to, including a functional medicine doctor specializing in complicated presentations.

"You need to start focusing on your future, honey." Mom patted my hand. "I'll be fine. I've got a good life here in Beaver Bluff with plenty of friends, good neighbors, and the best daughter a woman could ask for."

"Come on, Mom. You've still got a lot of life ahead of you."

She shook her head. "We'll see."

We stopped at the counter on our way out to pick up the prescription the doctor had written. That's all anyone seemed to want to do—treat her symptoms with drugs. I wanted to find someone to help us figure out why she was losing lung capacity instead of just continuing to try different prescriptions to see if they could make her more comfortable.

"Before we get back to the car, I have a question for you." She leaned against the railing in the elevator as I pushed the button to take us to the ground floor.

"What's that?" My stomach tightened. I'd been expecting an inquisition and couldn't believe it had taken her this long to get around to it.

"What's going on between you and Miller Bishop?" Her expression didn't give me any indication of what she might be thinking.

Inwardly, I groaned. Outwardly, I summoned a casual smile. "Nothing."

"Then why was he kissing you on the side of the highway?"

"You saw that?" The tightness in my gut spread to my lungs.

"Yes, I saw that. So did everyone else on Route 55."

I let out a loud sigh. "It was nothing."

"Your 'nothing' sure looked like something to me." The elevator door whooshed open, and my mother stepped out. "Be careful with that boy, Amalie. That's all I'm saying."

"He's not a boy anymore, Mom." I didn't know what I wanted from Miller, but I definitely didn't want my mother laying down any rules.

"The Bishops think they're better than everyone. Don't try to tell me you don't remember that day at the park. How old were you then? Nine?"

It was my tenth birthday party, but I wasn't about to remind her. "Something like that."

"You cried for days." Mom reached for my hand.

"He's changed, Mom." I couldn't tell which one of us I was trying to convince more—me or her.

"I hope so, honey."

I'd sent Miller a text to let him know we were on our way down. As we exited the clinic, he pulled into the circle drive and got out to walk around the truck.

"Everything go okay?" he asked as he opened the door for my mom.

"About as I expected," Mom said. She climbed into the back and reached out to Caden, who was picking fuzzy blue lint from between his toes. "What happened to your socks?"

"Socks bye-bye," Caden said.

"Amalie, can't you find him shoes he can't pull off? He can't go around barefoot. He'll catch a cold." Mom reached down and picked up the socks he'd pulled off his feet.

"Sorry. He took them off as soon as he woke up." Miller shut Mom's door behind her, then pulled the front door open for me.

"It's not your fault. He does it all the time at home, too. The kid wants to be barefoot," I said. "Do you mind if we stop somewhere for lunch on the way back? Caden probably needs to stretch his legs, and I should change him."

"I don't mind at all." Miller waited for me to get settled in the front seat then he closed my door for me.

"We're stopping on the way back for lunch. Is there anything you're craving, Mom?" I turned around to make eye contact.

She was counting Caden's toes and playing "This Little Piggy." "I'm not picky. Let Miller choose."

"There's a good burger place a few miles down the highway. How does that sound?" He grinned at Caden in the rearview mirror. "Are you hungry for lunch?"

Caden nodded.

"Okay then, it's settled." Miller focused on the road, and I used the opportunity to slide on my sunglasses and secretly focus on him.

What my mom said in the elevator kept running through my head. He wasn't the same person he'd been back then. Except for our initial argument at the Valentine's party, he'd been kind, courteous, and thoughtful. I wanted to hold onto the grudge I'd lived with for over a decade, but I was starting to think it might be time to move on.

"Miller, tell me what you do for a living," Mom piped up from the backseat. I half turned around, wondering why she felt the need to start grilling him.

"I told you, he's an accountant," I replied.

Mom glared at me like she didn't want me sabotaging her plan. "Well, what kind of an accountant?"

"I'm a consultant at the Kreigman Group. I help companies to be more efficient with their systems and processes," he said. "It's not super exciting, but I enjoy working with different businesses and seeing how they do things."

"Interesting." Mom nodded. "What made you want to become an accountant?"

I rolled my eyes. Listening to my mother interrogate Miller was going to get old quickly.

"Actually, I started my undergrad as an American Studies major." He lifted one of his shoulders and shrugged. "After Jack came along, I realized it would be better to work toward a degree I could put into practice right after graduation."

We were edging toward uncomfortable territory. Even though I was curious to learn more about Miller's history, I wasn't about to sit there while my mother asked about Jack's mom. "Hey, Mom, have you heard anything else about the new four-lane road they want to put in on your side of town?"

The way she tilted her head let me know she was well

aware of my intent to change the subject. "Nothing yet. We started a petition at Calm Waters, though."

"What's Calm Waters?" Miller asked.

Before my mother could tell him that was the name of the rundown mobile home park we'd lived in since my dad bailed on us, I blurted out a response. "It's the name of the neighborhood where she lives."

"And they're putting in a four-lane road?" Miller asked.

"All the way from Muster to Beaver Bluff." Mom looked out the window. "They're citing some law that gives them the right to kick people out of their homes and take their land."

"Eminent domain?" Miller asked.

"Eminent schminent," Mom said. "I don't know what it's called, but if they think they're getting me out of there, they'll have to haul me out themselves."

Miller looked over at me, his brow furrowed. "You can fight that, you know."

"Not in this case," I muttered. "Mom, it's not up to you."

"We'll see about that." Mom tickled Caden under his chin.

Caden cracked up and then lobbed one of his metal cars toward Miller's head. It bounced off and landed on the floorboard by my feet.

"He's going to cause a wreck one of these days." I turned back and pointed my finger at him. "We don't throw things, Caden."

"He is a handful, isn't he?" Mom bent close and tickled him again.

"Sorry about that. Are you okay?" I picked up the car and set it on my lap.

"He's got quite an arm for a two-year-old." Miller reached up and rubbed his head. "Believe me, I've had worse from Jack. He head-butted me with his two front teeth when he was about Caden's age. I still have the scar."

"Where?"

"Right here." He smoothed the hair at his right temple back a little.

Sure enough, I could see a faded scar about an inch long.

"Kind of makes you not want to have any more kids, doesn't it?" Mom asked from the backseat.

I glared at her again, but Miller just laughed.

"I'd love for Jack to have a brother or sister someday." He glanced in the rear-view mirror and met my mother's gaze. "But I'd need to find the right woman first."

A tall sign featuring an enormous cartoon burger drawing came into view. Grateful for a perfectly timed interruption, I thrust my finger toward the windshield. "Hey, is that the burger place?"

"Sure is." Miller turned on his blinker and got ready to exit.

Relieved to have changed the subject, I handed Caden's car back to my mother. At some point during our lunch stop, I needed to get her alone so I could tell her lay off the inquisition.

CHAPTER 19
Miller

AMALIE and her mom were quiet the rest of the way back to Beaver Bluff. While they'd been in the doctor's office, I'd called a tow truck to go pick up her car. I'd checked messages when we stopped to grab a quick bite for lunch and almost choked on my burger.

The guy at the garage said there was no telling how long she'd been driving around on bald tires, but all of them were below the legal limit for tread depth and needed to be replaced before they would allow her to pick up her car.

Knowing she'd never let me pay for them, I told the guy to say there was a sale running and to charge seventy-five percent of the cost to my card and let her pay the difference. We'd almost made it to the garage so she could pick up her car, but Caden was done being strapped into a car seat all day. I didn't blame him.

He'd removed his socks again and tossed them into the front seat. He'd also spit out the grapes Amalie had cut up for him as a snack… right onto my back window. Amalie was mortified and promised to vacuum out my truck and clean the windows when we returned.

I was more worried about her. It seemed like the stress of the past couple of weeks had been getting to her. The woman needed a break. With the Calbots coming home soon, I wanted to be the guy to give it to her.

She'd gone into the garage to pick up her keys, then came back to the truck to get the rest of her stuff while her mom went inside to use the restroom.

"I'm so sorry for ruining your day. If you knew what you were getting yourself in for, you probably would have driven on by when you saw me on the side of the road this morning."

"Hey,"—I reached for her hand—"I'm glad I could be here for you. You've got a lot going on."

She didn't pull away. Not even when I threaded my fingers through hers.

"You don't have to tell me anything you don't want to, but are things okay with your mom?" I didn't want to pry, but I couldn't shake the feeling the doctor had let her down.

"They're still trying to figure out what's going on. We didn't get the answers we were hoping for, that's for sure."

I wished I had the right words, but all I could come up with was, "I'm sorry."

"Everything will be okay. My mom's a tough cookie."

Like mother, like daughter. I wouldn't say it out loud, but after meeting Mrs. Rivers, I could tell where Amalie got her strength.

"Let me know if you need anything before the Calbots get back, okay?"

"I'm not taking advantage of you again. Thank you for today. I have no idea what you had to reschedule, but I appreciate it." Her voice broke at the end.

"I hope you don't take this the wrong way, but I enjoyed it."

She turned to face me. "You've got to be kidding. Hauling me, my mother, and a kid who was trying to single handedly ruin your backseat over a three-hundred-mile road trip is your idea of a good time?"

"Well, when you put it like that . . ." I grinned. Two weeks ago, if someone had told me I'd enjoy spending a day like this, I would have called them a liar. But it had become pretty damn clear over the past few days that it didn't seem to matter what I was doing as long as it involved spending time with Amalie.

"I feel like I owe you big time for today. What do you want? Homemade zoodles? A make-your-own-sundae bar delivered to your house? Whatever it is, you've got it."

I shot a quick look her way. "How about a date?"

"A date?" Her eyes went wide. "Like a boy-girl date?"

I rubbed my thumb over her palm. "Would that be so bad?"

"You really mean it?" Her voice filled with surprise, like she couldn't believe I'd want to ask her out.

"Of course, I really mean it. I like you, Amalie."

She didn't say anything for a long time. Long enough that sweat beaded along my brow line, and my pulse ticked up while I waited for some kind of response.

"The Calbots are supposed to be home tomorrow night." She didn't look at me but kept staring straight ahead.

"Is that a yes?"

"It's not a no." She finally turned toward me. "I don't know what this is, Miller."

"Do we have to know what it is? Can't we just go with it for a little while and see where it leads?" I wasn't looking for something long-term. Hell, I wasn't looking for anything at all. But with Amalie, it had found me.

"I'll have Saturday off." She pulled her hand away slowly.

"I have plenty of homework I need to do during the day, but if you want to do something together that night . . ."

"Yes." I didn't have any ideas about what we could do, but I wanted a chance to spend more time with her. Wanted to see if whatever this was between us would still be there if we spent an evening alone.

"Fine. It's a date." She grabbed her stuff from the front seat.

I leaned in to unbuckle Caden so I could move his car seat back to her vehicle. "What do you think? Should I take Amalie on a date on Saturday?"

He'd been sucking on his thumb for the past ten minutes, the only thing keeping him quiet. Now he tried to talk around it. "Frth ma."

Amalie reached for his wrist. "You can't talk while you're sucking your thumb. Try that again."

My stomach dropped. Even with his thumb in his mouth, it sounded like he was trying to repeat the phrase he'd overheard me say earlier. "That's okay. I got the general idea."

But Caden did what he was told for a change. He jerked his thumb from his mouth with a pop, looked at Amalie, and yelled at the top of his lungs, "Fuck yeah."

Her eyes went wide. "Caden Calbot, we don't say words like that. Your mother will tie your tongue in knots if you drop an f-bomb around her."

Fire raced across my cheeks. "Sorry, I was on the phone, and—"

"This is your fault?" She picked Caden up under the armpits and balanced him on her hip. "I trusted you with him."

"I'll fix this. I'll come up with something that sounds better, and he'll forget all about dropping f-bombs in front of his mom."

"I know you will."

"You do?"

"Absolutely. Because if you don't, I'll tie your tongue into knots too." She slung the strap of her tote bag over her shoulder and took off toward her car. "See you on Saturday, Miller."

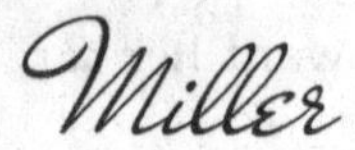

Miller

I STARED at the black words on the screen of my laptop. I'd read the email three times, and it still hadn't sunk in. The firm wanted me to start up a new office in Phoenix. We'd signed a new client. Not only did they want us to help at their central office, but they wanted us to take over their entire department and outsource everything for their regional and local branches, as well.

Phoenix.

Seventeen hundred miles away.

It may as well be Tokyo.

They'd requested me specifically. The job had a flexible start date, but they needed an answer as soon as possible. That's why my boss had been calling. And I hadn't been able to talk because I'd been helping Amalie.

I cradled my head in my hands. What was I going to do about Amalie? She was the first woman I'd been attracted to in seven years. I'd just found her. I couldn't leave. But this job was what I'd been waiting for. It was the chance of a lifetime. Short of starting my own firm, this opportunity would give me the freedom to do what I wanted.

It would also get me away from Beaver Bluff. Away from my dad's self-righteous judgement. Away from a town full of people who got their rocks off by making up stories about my son's mom. I could have put their lies to rest a long time long ago, but she'd asked me not to.

My cell rang, and my boss's name flashed on the screen. "Hey, Karl. I'm sorry I wasn't available yesterday when you called."

"I'm assuming you saw the email," he said.

"Yeah. That's quite an offer." The email outlined the terms: a VP title, a substantial raise, and tons of other perks I'd be a fool to pass up. I spun around in my chair and studied the pictures on the bookcase behind me. There was one of my parents holding a five-month-old Jack between them. Another one of me, Jack, and Evan standing by the pond behind mom and dad's house with fishing poles in our hands. Jack's first birthday cake that my mom made. Then one of Titus, licking Jack's face clean.

"I don't want to rush you, Miller, but they need an answer as soon as possible. If you're not interested, we'll need to find another candidate to present to them as our top pick."

"Of course. I need a day or two to think about it."

"It's a big move. The kind of move you've been waiting for," he added.

"It is. Can I take the weekend to think about it?"

"Absolutely. I'll talk to you then."

"Thanks." I hung up, feeling a nauseating mix of excitement and dread swirling around in my gut. There were just as many reasons to take the job as there were to turn it down. Maybe even more.

When I started with the firm, I mentioned a willingness to relocate. I'd been trying to get away from my past. Trying to prove, once and for all, to my dad that I wasn't the fuck up he always thought I was.

Becoming a Vice President of one of the biggest consulting agencies in Tennessee was the kind of thing that might finally have him thinking I'd made something out of myself. I should take it. If Amalie and I were meant to be, she'd understand. We could make it work long distance. I'd be making more money and could afford to fly her out as often as she could get away.

My gaze snagged on the most recent photo I'd put on my bookshelf. My sister Ruby had hired a professional photographer to come into the distillery a few months ago and take shots for the marketing assets for the anniversary celebration. We were all there— three generations of Bishops standing in front of the distillery that had been in our family for one-hundred-fifty years.

Could I take Jack away from everything and everyone he knew?

I wanted to call Amalie and talk it through with her, but I wasn't sure I could trust her to give me an unbiased opinion. Evan was usually my go-to guy. I picked up my phone and hit the button to call my brother. Maybe he'd be able to swing by for a drink later.

"Hey, what's up? Mom said she's watching Jack overnight tomorrow night. Can I assume you finally got your head out of your ass and asked the hot nanny out on a date?"

"I did."

"Congratulations. It's about fucking time." Evan covered the mic, and I heard him yelling something at someone in the background. He was at the distillery, probably bottling whiskey right now. Even though I didn't officially work there, I knew the production calendar by heart.

"Is now a bad time?" I asked.

"No. Vaughn's just being a dick about a small change on

the anniversary label, and Cole's freaking out that the blend isn't good enough. Wish you were here. They're arguing with each other over two different things."

I blew out a breath. It was best not to get between the twins when they were going head-to-head. Although, I'd been stuck in that position once, and the only thing that had snapped them out of it was to tell one of my dad's horrible, not-even-funny dad jokes.

"Oh, shit." Evan cleared his throat. "Vaughn just criticized the anniversary blend. This might come to blows, bro."

"Ask them what happened to the frog who parked illegally at the pond." I didn't remember many of the bad jokes my dad told over the years, but this one was a keeper.

Evan yelled out to my older brothers, and the arguing stopped. "Putting you on speaker, Miller."

Vaughn grumbled into the phone first. "He got toad, didn't he?"

"Why do you always have to ruin the punchline?" I laughed, picturing the scowl on his face. "Got you to stop your pissing contest, didn't it?"

"You think you get to tell bad dad jokes just because you have a kid?" Cole asked.

"Well, yeah," I admitted. "That's usually how it works. I'm glad you can appreciate it."

"You know what else I'd appreciate?" Vaughn asked.

"What's that?"

"You being here this afternoon for the final interview with the top candidate for the accounting job," Vaughn said. "If all goes well, and we have no reason to believe it won't since you put her through the wringer last time, then we'll offer her the job."

Knowing they were that close to replacing me stung a little.

It was my fault. It's what I'd told them to do. "I've got it on my calendar."

"Good. I need to call Ruby about the labels. Later, Miller," Vaughn said.

"I've got to get back to bottling before somebody messes up the line." Evan must have picked up the phone because his voice sounded closer than the others had. "Any words of wisdom for Cole before he implodes?"

"The anniversary blend is awesome. We all tried it and loved it. You need to relax, Cole." Ever since my brother had started working at the distillery, he'd been obsessed with trying to recreate the flavor profile our ancestors had perfected. Unfortunately, the proprietary mash bill had been lost or destroyed right around the time the feud between the two families started.

"It's close, but it's not quite there yet," Cole said.

"If anyone can figure it out, it will be you. In the meantime, everyone's going to go ballistic over the anniversary blend. Dad's going to be really proud of what you've put into it." As I said the words, I thought about how true they were. My dad had never been shy about telling my brothers what great things they were accomplishing at the distillery.

"We wouldn't be doing any of this if it weren't for you," Cole said. "I can't believe you're going to let Vaughn hire an outsider to take over for mom. She said you came up with a new way to track inventory and figured out how to save us fifteen percent on our overhead."

"I've got to get back to the line. If the two of you want to keep flinging sappy shit at each other, call on one of your own phones," Evan said.

"You know you love it when we get sappy," Cole joked. "Hey, Miller. Stop by when you come in this afternoon, okay? I've got a little something you can take home to Jack."

"Will do." The line went dead. Maybe it was best if I didn't use Evan as a sounding board. If I moved to Arizona, I wouldn't have my brother close by and would have to make decisions on my own.

I picked up a framed photo of Mom, Dad, my siblings, and me.

Family.

As much as my mom, brothers, and sister meant to me, my dad's attitude toward me tainted everything in Beaver Bluff. I didn't want Jack to grow up under his influence. Not when my father could turn on him at any moment.

That's what hurt the most. Now that I was a dad, I had a pretty good idea of what unconditional love entailed. I couldn't imagine Jack ever doing something so heinous, so awful, so unbearable that I'd turn my back on him and leave him to figure it out on his own.

That's what Dad had done to me.

Sure, he'd loosened up a bit. Time had dulled his memory of what went down between us, but I felt it like it happened yesterday. Mom tried to soften the blow, but our rift hurt her too. It was time to put all of us out of our misery.

That was the biggest reason I didn't want to take the job at the distillery. Working with my brothers and sister would be a dream come true. But family had the power to hurt you when you least expected it. I couldn't afford to take the risk.

CHAPTER 21

Amalie

SATURDAY MORNING, I woke up to bright blue skies and the sound of Mr. and Mrs. Calbot making pancakes with Bettina and Caden. They'd arrived home late last night, and I was officially off duty for the next forty-eight hours. I stretched my arms over my head and thought about my plans for the day.

I wanted to take my laptop to the library, grab a study room, and get caught up on as much of my coursework as I could. Then I had my date with Miller to look forward to.

Miller asking me out had been a surprise, especially after spending an entire day seeing me at my worst. I didn't like it when my plans got derailed, and last Thursday had been one major disappointment after another.

As I started to roll out of bed, my phone lit up with a text from Miller. He'd been checking in twice daily to see if Caden had uttered another "Fuck yeah." Thankfully, his suggestion to say something that sounded funny and then make a big deal out of pretending like I shouldn't have, had Caden moving on to saying, "Flipping flamingos." Since he hadn't lost his hint of a lisp, it came out more like "Fippin

Fingos." As long as it didn't involve any fucks, I was a-okay with that.

I relaxed against my pillow and couldn't help but smile as I read Miller's text.

> **Miller:** *Bosses got home last night?*
> **Me:** *Yep. I'm free.*
> **Miller:** *Caden still on a flamingo kick?*
> **Me:** *Fuck yeah!*
> **Miller:** *Not funny*
> **Me:** *Yes it was*
> **Miller:** *Tonight. 7pm. Wear something you don't mind getting dirty.*
> **Me:** *???*

What was that supposed to mean? I was finally going out with someone who made more than minimum wage, owned his house, and had an actual retirement fund already. Where could he be taking me that I'd be getting dirty?

> **Miller:** *It's a surprise*

Great. I flung the covers off and tugged on my leggings. I'd have time to come back and shower later. After filling a thermal mug with coffee and being talked into trying a few blueberry pancakes the kids had made with their parents, I left the house and headed into town.

Though I grew up in Muster, Beaver Bluff was the nearest big town. *Bigger* town, I should say. I'd spent plenty of time at the public library as a kid. It was my favorite place to go to catch my breath or sit with my thoughts. It had always been a refuge for me.

My favorite study room was empty, so I made myself

comfortable and spent the next five hours catching up. By the time my alarm went off to remind me to go home and get ready, I was satisfied with how much work I'd gotten done. Taking half the day off tomorrow was even a possibility. Feeling like a rebel, I headed back home to shower and change.

Not quite an hour later, I came out of my room and almost ran right into Mrs. Calbot.

"Are you going out tonight?" She didn't bother to try to hide the surprise in her voice.

"Yes. Just hanging out with a friend." She'd never asked much about my social life before. Hopefully, she wasn't about to start now.

"I need to talk to you about something, but it can wait until tomorrow. Have fun tonight, Amalie. You deserve it." She nodded, then turned to head back down the hall.

I didn't think anything of it. She probably wanted to adjust bedtime schedules or discuss introducing another food item into Caden's diet to see how he'd react. I didn't want Miller to come to the door and ring the bell, so I took a seat on the bench on the front porch and waited.

Miller had barely brought his truck to a stop before he hopped out. "Hey, you look fantastic. Are you ready to go?"

My gaze ran over the well-worn jeans that clung to his hips and the soft flannel plaid shirt he had tucked into his waistband. While it wasn't a tailored suit, he looked just as comfortable in jeans and flannel as he had in that form-fitting suit jacket the other day. It didn't seem to matter what he wore or what he said. Every time I saw him, I fell a little bit more.

"Are you going to tell me where we're going?" I took the hand he offered, eager for his touch. It had only been a couple of days since I'd last seen him, but I craved the way his hand felt in mine.

"We're going to the high school out in Bordent." He swung our hands between us on the way back to the car.

"The what?" Surely, he wasn't taking me to some high school dance.

"Bordent High. You know it?"

"Yeah, I know it. I'm just wondering why you're taking me to a high school on a date. It's not some missed high school dance fantasy you want to live out, is it?"

"No. Nothing like that."

I climbed into the cab of his truck and noticed he must have cleaned it out since he'd hauled us to Chattanooga. "Darn it, Miller. I said I'd clean up your truck for you after Caden trashed the backseat."

"Don't worry about it. I couldn't pick you up for our date with grapes stuck to the back window."

"He made me pick up the grape pieces." Jack leaned into the front seat. "Hi, Miss Amalie."

My eyebrows arched in surprise. I'd never dated a single dad before, but I'd assumed our first date might not involve bringing his kid along.

"My folks are watching Jack tonight. You were on the way, so I hope you don't mind if we stop by so I can drop him off." Miller slid into the front seat.

"Not at all."

Before he started the truck, the front door flew open. Bettina stood in the doorway, a wild grin on her face. "They're here! The chicks are here! Come see!"

"The chicks are here?" Jack unbuckled his seat belt and flung open the door. "Can I go look, Dad?"

Miller looked at me. "We have time if you don't mind."

"Of course not." I'd barely climbed out of the truck before Bettina grabbed hold of my arm and tugged me back to the house.

"Get your dad, Jack. Hurry, so we don't miss it." Bettina dragged me to the laundry room, where one of the chicks had pecked its way out of its egg. Its feathers were wet, and it looked like it had gotten a rough start.

"Is it a boy or a girl?" Bettina asked. She hopped up and down, shifting her weight from one foot to the other like she either had to go to the bathroom or was so excited she couldn't contain herself.

"Is Gruda here?" Jack came around the corner and joined Bettina in front of the egg-ubator.

Miller stopped in the doorway and peered in on us. "Is it just the one so far?"

"Yeah. They want to know if it's a boy or a girl so they can figure out who gets naming rights." I looked at him with clear expectations in my eyes.

"What makes you think I know how to tell?"

"You're the one who suggested Bettina could name the first chick if it was a girl and Jack could come up with a name if it was a boy. I figured that meant you'd know how to tell the difference."

He pulled his phone from his pocket. "Let me see how this works."

"Amalie, is that you?" Mrs. Calbot stopped by the open doorway. "I thought you left."

"Almost," I said. "Bettina caught me just in time. Mrs. Calbot, this is Miller and Jack Bishop. They're friends of mine."

"Mine too." Bettina put her hand on Jack's shoulder. "Best friends."

Jack grinned. "Yeah, best friends."

It warmed my heart to see them standing there together after all they'd been through.

"Well, name the chicken so Amalie can head out," Mrs.

Calbot said. "If you'll excuse me, I've got to go get Caden to bed."

"I enjoyed meeting you." Miller lifted his hand before she turned to head down the hall.

I turned toward him. "So? How do we tell?

His nose crinkled like he'd smelled something as foul as Caden's diaper. "It's called *venting*. We have to hold it upside down and wait for it to poop a little."

"Gross." Jack looked like he might throw up.

"Maybe we should wait for Mrs. Blessing to make the call when you get them back to school on Monday," Miller suggested.

"But then we'll have to vote on it with the whole class and everything," Bettina said.

Miller looked at me. I lifted a shoulder that was supposed to put the decision back in his court.

"Okay. But Amalie's got to help me," he said.

"How, exactly?" I eyed the tiny ball of feathers. I was afraid to touch it, much less squeeze it so it would poop.

Miller glanced around the pristine laundry room. "Do you have any rubber gloves?"

"You afraid of a little chicken poop?" I teased.

"Do you want to be the one to squeeze the poop out of the chicken?" he asked.

"Negative." I started pulling open drawers to see if I could find a pair of disposable gloves like the ones I'd seen Mrs. Calbot's housekeeper use for cleaning.

"I have some!" Bettina ran out of the laundry room and came back a minute later holding two pink and purple polka-dot rubber gloves.

I didn't bother trying to hide my grin. "Where did you get those?"

"They came with my cleaning cart." She looked so proud of herself for being able to help out.

Miller studied the gloves, probably trying to figure out if his big man paw would fit inside without shredding them. "I guess we can give these a try."

I took the phone he handed me and looked over the webpage he'd pulled up. "It says you just hold it upside down, and when it poops, you're supposed to look for a rudimentary male sex organ."

"A chicken penis?" Jack asked.

Bettina covered her mouth and giggled. Miller shot his son a look that could have silenced an entire drum line. I bit my lip and tried not to blurt out something equally inappropriate.

"Sorry," Jack said.

Miller tried sliding his hand into the glove but gave up when he realized he could only fit two fingers at a time.

"It was a good try, Bettina." I put my hand on her shoulder, and she smiled up at me.

Then the three of us watched Miller lift the top off the egg-ubator and reach in to wrap his massive hand around the tiny chick. It squawked and tried to hop away, but he gently circled it with his pointer finger and thumb.

"So now I just flip it over?" he asked.

"That's what it says. Do you want me to see if there's an instructional video?"

He shook his head, his brow furrowed in concentration. "No. We've got this, right, little chicky?"

Using both hands, he slowly turned the chick upside down. It must have startled at its whole world flipping because a burst of runny goop shot out of its bottom.

"Oooh, gross!" Jack ducked for cover, and Bettina slipped down the front of the cabinet in a heap of giggles.

"Do you see anything?" I asked.

"I don't know what I'm supposed to be looking for," Miller said.

Rising to my tiptoes, I leaned in, searching the tiny chick's rear features for any sign of its gender. "There's nothing sticking out."

"Must be a girl." Miller flipped the chicken back over and returned it to the egg-ubator.

"Why do you say that?" I asked.

"Because if it's supposed to be a guy, he's going to wish he was a girl. There's nothing there, not even a micro—"

"Okay, it's a girl. Bettina gets to name the first chicken." I stared at Miller over the top of the kids' heads, silently warning him not to say another word.

His laugh rumbled through his chest. "I'm going to wash my hands. I'll be right back."

"What do you want to name the chick, Bettina?" I made sure the top of the egg-ubator was secured while I waited for Bettina to announce her choice of names.

"Hmm." She put her finger to her lip.

Poor Jack looked like he was trying not to let his disappointment show.

"I was thinking about Elsa or Anna," Bettina said.

Jack groaned and rolled his eyes. When Bettina's head whipped around to face him, he pasted a smile on his face.

"Those are both good names." He nodded, trying to cover up his disappointment.

Bettina let out a dramatic sigh. "But I guess I'll go with Gruda."

Jack's forehead creased. "Gruda? But that's what I was going to pick."

"I know. And because we're best friends, I want the first chick to have the name you wanted."

"Really?" Jack asked.

My heart melted at the look on his face. Oh my goodness—to be six years old again. Not that I wanted to be. I wouldn't go back and do high school again if someone paid me a billion bucks. Well, maybe for a billion, but it would have to be at least that much to make it worth going through all that heartbreak and angst.

"What did I miss?" Miller came around the corner, wiping his hands on the front of his jeans.

"I'll fill you in later," I said. "Right now, we need to get going, and we should let Gruda get some rest before his first day of school on Monday."

"Gruda?" Miller's forehead wrinkled like his son's had a few minutes before.

"Like I said, I'll fill you in later." I spun Bettina around and herded her and Jack out of the laundry room.

Miller followed me, but before I cleared the doorway, he caught me around the waist. "Did the Ice Princess just give up her right to name the first chicken in her kingdom?"

"She's thawing. Rapidly," I added.

"Good." He rested his chin on my shoulder. It took every ounce of willpower I had not to flip around in his arms and press my entire length against him. "We should probably hit the road so we're not late for our date."

"Give me just a minute with Bettina?" I asked.

"I'll meet you on the driveway." He squeezed past me and called for Jack.

Bettina and I walked them to the door. I ran my hand over her silky soft hair. She was a good kid. She'd just been having some big feelings since her parents had been traveling so much. "That was a kind thing you did—naming the chick Gruda."

"He really wanted it to have that name." Bettina reached

out and took my hand. "I'm banking favors for when I want one from him."

"Where did you get the idea you have to bank favors?" If she'd come across that on the internet when she was supposed to be watching kid videos with her brother—I didn't know what I'd do.

"That's what Jack's dad said before. If you want someone to do stuff for you, you should do something for them first. Then they have to do what you say because they owe you."

"Oh, Bettina. It doesn't work that way." I suppose it did in some peoples' worlds, but that's not the outlook I wanted her to carry with her through life. "I think it's nice to do stuff for people just because you know it will make them happy."

"You do?"

"Sure. Did you see how happy Jack was when you told him you wanted to name the chick Gruda?"

"Yes." She gave me a wide grin.

"And how did it make you feel inside when he looked like that?"

"It made my heart smile." She nodded like she wanted to emphasize her point.

"Exactly. Wouldn't the world be a better place if we all went around with smiling hearts?"

"I suppose. But how will I get Jack to do things I want him to do then?"

I wasn't about to get into a deep discussion about why she shouldn't try manipulating her friends. "I've got to get going right now. We'll have to tackle that question tomorrow."

"Amalie?"

"Yeah, sweetie?"

"I love you."

I pulled her into a hug and wrapped my arms around her tiny

frame. Love wasn't a word I tossed around lightly. Despite the challenges that came with being a full-time nanny to someone else's kids, I loved Bettina and Caden more than I'd expected.

"I love you, too. Hearing you say that makes my heart smile." I pressed a kiss to the top of her head. "I'll see you tomorrow, okay?"

"Goodnight, Amalie. Have fun."

By the time the door clicked shut behind me, I was halfway down the sidewalk. We'd started our date with chicken poop. I could hardly wait to see how Miller planned to top that.

CHAPTER 22
Amalie

"I THOUGHT your parents were out of town." I'd never met Mr. and Mrs. Bishop, though I'd seen them around Beaver Bluff from time to time. Along with the Stewarts, they were the closest thing to royalty we had.

"They got back yesterday. When my mom heard I was looking for a sitter, she said I should bring Jack to their place. I think she went through a little Jack withdrawal while they were gone. He's the only grandkid so far."

"You must enjoy being close enough to spend time with your grandparents," I told Jack. I'd never met my mom's parents. They died when she was in high school, which was probably the main reason she'd ended up falling for my dad. I wondered what my life would have been like if my grandparents had never gotten in that car crash. Maybe my mom wouldn't have been so lonely. Maybe she wouldn't have hooked up with the first man who showed any interest in her. As much as I enjoyed playing the *maybe* game, it didn't matter because it didn't change anything.

"Are you close to yours?" Jack asked.

I didn't know how else to say it, so I told him the truth. "I never met my dad's parents, and my mom's parents died when she was in high school."

"I don't want Nana and Papa to die." Jack's brows knit together.

"Nana and Papa aren't going to die," Miller said. "I mean, they will eventually. We all will. But I'm sure you've got plenty of time left with them."

Great. Thanks to me and my big mouth, now Jack was probably going to have nightmares about his grandparents passing away. I was a real buzzkill to be around lately.

Miller pulled off the main road and started up a long drive. Tall oaks stretched their branches and formed a canopy over-head. The narrow lane wound through the trees, over a stream, and finally ended in front of a large, two-story brick house.

"Is this where you grew up?" I asked, trying to keep the awe from my voice.

"Yep. Do you want to come in, or would you rather wait for me in the car?" Miller asked.

"Oh, um…" Curiosity urged me to go in with him and take a peek. But I wasn't sure I'd feel welcome, especially since my mother was so pro-Stewarts.

"Come in, Ms. Amalie." Jack held out his hand. "I can show you where Nana keeps the M&Ms."

"Who doesn't love M&Ms?" I shrugged at Miller.

He walked to my side of the truck and held my door open. Apprehension rolled through me. I felt like the canary being sent down the mine chute to see if it would survive. Hopefully, I'd make my way back out again with my wings intact.

"They won't bite," Miller muttered against my ear. Feeling his warm breath sent a delicious chill racing down my arm.

"I'm not worried about meeting your parents. I just hope they don't—"

"Jack! I think you've grown two inches since I saw you last

month." A tall woman with a no-nonsense silver bob came down the stairs and headed straight toward Jack.

Miller reached for my hand. I appreciated the show of solidarity. "Mom, I want you to meet someone."

Mrs. Bishop let go of Jack's shoulders and turned toward me. She studied me with the same green eyes as Miller and Jack.

"Amalie Rivers, this is my mother, Rosalie Bishop."

I forced my lips into a nervous smile. "It's nice to meet you."

"Nice to meet you too. Miller told me the two of you are heading out for some fun tonight."

"That's right. I sure wish he'd tell me where we're going."

"He's always been a big fan of surprises," his mother confessed. "No doubt he's got something over the top planned for tonight."

Miller shook his head, but I caught the hint of a smile he gave his mom. "And this is my dad, Ronan."

I'd gotten the impression from our conversations about family that Miller and his dad weren't particularly close. There was an unmistakable resemblance, especially in the area around their eyes.

"Call me Ronan." Mr. Bishop took my hand in his. "It's nice to meet a friend of Miller's."

Friends… there was that word again. Were we just friends? Were we starting something new? I didn't know, and I'd spent way too many hours trying to figure it out. For tonight, I vowed to enjoy myself. It had been years since I'd been out with a man for something besides a college project.

"It's nice to meet both of you."

"Are you ready to have some fun tonight, Jack?" Mrs. Bishop asked. "I brought some sweets from the duty-free shop at the airport and thought we could spend the evening watching that new superhero movie."

"That sounds great, Mom. Thanks again for having him." Miller said. "We should probably get going."

"Miller, if you have a minute, I wanted to ask how the search for our head of accounting is going," Mr. Bishop said. "Vaughn told me your standards are too high, and you aren't happy with any of the candidates he's put forward."

"That's true. None of them have the right blend of expertise and experience." Miller shifted his weight from one foot to the other while he held his dad's gaze.

"The family's counting on you for this." Mr. Bishop sighed. Based on the weight of the tension in the air, I got the feeling that Miller and his dad had a somewhat strained relationship.

Mrs. Bishop wrung her hands together. "Amalie, would you like to join me in the kitchen for a glass of sweet tea?"

I shot a quick look at Miller, but he was still locked into a staring contest with his dad. Assuming her offer for a glass of tea was more about giving Miller and his dad some privacy, I took her up on it. "That would be great."

"Right this way." She led me through the foyer and into the kitchen.

I wasn't sure what I expected, but it wasn't the cozy, warm kitchen we entered. Exposed brick covered one wall, and family pictures hung on the others. There were black and white photos that looked like they were taken decades ago mixed in with images that couldn't have been more than a year or two old. I recognized some of the same photos from the reception area of the distillery.

"Don't mind the men. Miller and his dad haven't seen eye to eye in a long time." She pulled two glasses out of the cabinet, then grabbed a pitcher of tea from the refrigerator.

I heard tidbits of conversation from down the hall, but I

couldn't make out any of the words. Jack passed through the kitchen on his way to the family room. I'd barely taken a sip of my tea when Miller appeared in the doorway. His mouth was drawn into a tight line and a muscle ticked along his jaw.

"You ready to head out?" He held out his hand, obviously eager to get moving.

"Sure. Thank you for the tea. It was delicious." I offered an apologetic smile to Mrs. Bishop.

She waved us off. "My pleasure. Any friend of Miller's is always welcome here. You two have a good time tonight."

Jack came back to hug his dad, then Miller steered me toward the door. "Sorry, I need to get out of here."

"Did something happen with your dad?" I asked.

He twined his fingers with mine. "Nothing I want to talk about now. Come on. I don't want to be late."

With a million possibilities of where he might be taking me running through my head, I let him lead me out the front door.

CHAPTER 23
Miller

ARGUING with my dad had left me in a rotten mood. I tried to shake it off as we headed over to Bordent. Being around Amalie helped. When I was with her, my problems didn't seem as big. She had a calming effect on me, and I liked it. I wasn't sure how she would react to my big surprise for our date tonight. It seemed like a fun idea when I'd set it up, but now I doubted myself.

"Are you going to tell me what we're doing here?" she asked.

I held her hand as we walked toward the big gym. Light spilled out onto the sidewalk through the open doors. The sound of laughter and applause grew louder the closer we got.

"I thought we could do double duty. Check out some ideas for the carnival while getting you away from the kids for a while." I studied her face in the low light, gauging it for some sort of reaction.

"Oh, so this is research for the carnival." She bit down on her lower lip and loosened her grip on my hand.

I tugged her off the cement path and past the door to the gym. "Come here for a sec."

"What?"

Wrapping my arms around her waist, I pulled her tight against my chest and held her gaze. "This is a date first. Research second."

"Okay."

"If you want to skip the research part, we can. I wanted to take you out tonight and show you a good time. You've had so much going on lately, you deserve a little time to relax." I'd seen how much she'd been managing while the Calbots were off traipsing around the globe. Between putting herself through school, taking care of Bettina and Jack, managing her mom's health, and getting stuck with planning the school fundraiser, she was burning the candle at both ends. I wanted to help.

"What's so special about me? You've worked just as hard as I have, maybe more. You're a single dad trying to balance a full-time job with keeping the distillery running and finding a replacement for your mom. Maybe you're the one who needs to relax." She didn't melt into my arms, but she didn't pull away either.

I lifted my hand to brush her hair away from her cheek. "Maybe we both need a night out."

"Maybe we do." Her gaze settled on mine and a silent understanding passed between us.

If I was reading the signals right, she wanted a night out with me. But I was also picking up on a few things that went unsaid. Like she wasn't used to having someone do things for her and was reluctant to let me in. I hoped that after tonight, I'd be able to work my way past a few of her twalls. It seemed like she'd been doing things alone for so long. I wanted to ease that burden. Be there for her like my mom, brothers, and sister had rallied around me when I needed them most.

"What do you say? Do you want to go in, or should we

skip the entertainment and head straight to dinner?"

A loud cheer from the crowd came from inside. Amalie looked past me, though she wouldn't be able to see into the gym from where we stood.

"Now I'm curious. I think we need to go in so I can see the next over-the-top idea you want to propose."

I leaned down and pressed a kiss to her forehead. "What makes you think it's over the top?"

"Because everything you do is that way." She brought her hand up to grip mine, and we fell into step next to each other.

"Not everything," I said.

Amalie let out a soft laugh. "Our definition of over the top must be different."

"Well, if we go with the idea I'm sharing tonight, it might fall into the over-the-top category." I pulled out my wallet and handed the guy at the entrance a twenty. He passed back my change and held up a rubber stamp.

"Gotta stamp your hands if you want to go out and come back in," he said.

Amalie held out her hand, and we both received a bright purple donkey stamp on the back of our hands.

"Why is it a donkey?" Amalie asked as I led her down the hall toward the gym.

"You'll see."

Thirty seconds later, we stood in the doorway of the gym. Fans filled the bleachers on either side. The scoreboard showed we'd only missed a few minutes of the first period.

"What the heck is this?" Amalie turned to me. "Please tell me you're not seriously thinking about bringing donkey basketball to the spring carnival."

At that moment, a ball flew off the court and bounced against the wall next to her. A guy tugged on the reins of the donkey he was riding and headed our way.

I tossed the ball to him and looked at Amalie. Her jaw was slack, her mouth hanging open.

"You don't think this would be a ton of fun?" I bumped her shoulder with mine. "Imagine the teachers taking on the parents. The kids would love it."

One of the donkeys at center court let out a loud bray, then lifted its tail and dumped a pile of donkey doo on the polished wood floor.

Amalie looked up at me.

"They come with handlers." I gestured toward the middle of the court, where a teenager rushed out, scooped up the mess, and ran to the sideline.

"Oh, well, that makes everything better. It's a no-brainer. Bring on the jackasses." Amalie shook her head.

"Come on. It would be awesome. We could have kids and parents make donations to vote for the teachers or staff they'd most like to see on the court." I wished I could take credit for the idea, but my sister Ruby was the one who'd come up with it. She'd seen donkey basketball on social media, then looked it up and found a vendor just a few towns over.

"I don't know, Miller. I think you've lost your marbles with this idea."

"Do you want to sit and watch for a bit?"

"We may as well since you already paid for admission." Amalie wound her way through some other spectators standing around the gym's perimeter and found a narrow spot for two near the end of a row. "Is this okay?"

"Absolutely." There was no way we'd be able to sit side by side in the small space without touching. She sat first, and I squeezed in next to her, wrapping an arm around her shoulders so we'd both fit. Being this close to her—the scent of her shampoo tickled my nose, and the curve of her breast pushed into my chest.

Amalie watched the action on the court while I watched the emotions play over her face. I loved the way she pulled her bottom lip into her mouth before she smiled. Loved how her palm landed on my leg when either team got a shot up in the air. I couldn't wait to get her alone.

The game ended in a ten-to-ten tie. Neither team had been able to get their donkeys moving quickly. At least not until it was time to lead them outside and get them loaded up on the trailer that would take them back to the farm.

"Well?" I asked. No doubt Amalie had formed opinions about whether donkey basketball would work.

"I think it could be fun."

"I told you so."

"But,"—she put up her pointer finger—"we'd have to do tons of research on this. What kind of liability insurance does the company carry? We'd need a copy of the waiver they make people sign before they can participate. There's a lot that would have to go into this if you want to make it happen."

I wrapped my hand around her finger and pulled her into me. "Point taken. I'll look into it. As long as we're here, do you want to go see the donkeys?"

"Do you think they'll let us?"

"Come on, I'll introduce you to their handler." I led her to a long horse trailer where two guys were loading up the donkeys who had starred in the basketball game.

"Can I help you?" A man wearing a cowboy hat and a long duster jacket stopped on his way to the trailer. He held the lead to an animal in each hand.

"Hi, I'm Miller Bishop. I spoke to someone on the phone about booking a donkey basketball game for a school carnival in Beaver Bluff."

"Yeah, that was me. I'm glad you made it tonight. What did you think?" His grip on the leads relaxed.

"We thought it was great. Looks like fun," I said.

Amalie walked closer to the two donkeys. "Do you mind if I pet them?"

"I'll do you one better than that. Come over to the trailer with me, and you can give them their treat for playing so well." He offered Amalie one of the leads. "You want to walk her over?"

"Sure." Amalie gripped the lead of the donkey and started walking toward the trailer.

"That one's Jezebel, and this one here is her boyfriend, Maestro." The man stopped when he reached the trailer. "Wanna know why we call him Maestro?"

Amalie looked at me, her expression a mix of amusement and apprehension.

I let out a chuckle. "Of course, we want to know."

"Come on, Maestro. Sing for your carrot." He held a carrot about a foot above the donkey's head. Maestro's nose went up in the air, and his gums flapped around as he tried to nibble on it. "Sing, buddy."

The donkey flung his head back and let out a loud *Hee Haw*. Amalie's eyes went wide. Then Maestro tossed his head from side to side and brayed. It almost sounded like he was trying to hum some warped version of *Twinkle Twinkle Little Star*.

"That's it. Good job." The guy tossed the carrot up, and Maestro reared back on his hind legs and snagged it out of the air. "He's quite the performer, isn't he?"

"That was amazing." Amalie clapped her hands together. "Does he have an encore?"

I should have told her to be careful what she wished for. When I'd checked out the website, they had a video of Maestro on the home page.

"He loves to tango." The guy actually said it with a straight face. "Hey, Maestro. Would you like to tango with the pretty lady?"

"Oh, I don't know how to tango." Amalie shook her head, but the man had already reached into the trailer and held up a long-stemmed plastic rose.

Maestro took it between his giant teeth and carried it over to Amalie. She looked at me, then back to the donkey, and held out her hand.

He dropped the flower into her palm and nudged her around with his nose while the guy in the hat hummed some version of a tango. Amalie was a good sport until the donkey started nibbling on her sweater.

"That was great." I clapped my hands and stepped closer, trying to get Maestro to give Amalie some space.

"Bow to your partner, Maestro." With an exaggerated flourish, the handler signaled to the donkey.

Maestro put his front legs out straight and lowered his head toward Amalie.

"Wow, he's really something." She scratched the donkey between his ears and handed him the carrot the man tossed to her.

"Here, he performs solo at the Shellacky County Fairgrounds on the first Saturday night of the month." The man passed each of us a business card.

"We'll have to go check that out." I held out a hand to Amalie. She grabbed hold, her fingers squeezing mine tight enough to cut off the circulation. "I'll be in touch about our event."

"Sounds good." He tipped his hat before leading Maestro and the other donkey into the trailer.

"Can you believe that? He thinks that donkey can tango." Amalie snort-laughed as we walked through the parking lot.

"Hey, he made you look good. Isn't that what the male's

role is all about when doing those fancy dances?" I slung my arm around her shoulder and tucked her against me.

"Now I know why you told me to wear something I could get dirty. I feel like I have donkey slobber all over my clothes."

"I was afraid you might get pooped on at the basketball game," I said.

"My mother won't believe I danced with a donkey tonight."

I slid my phone out of my back pocket with my free hand. "She will if I show her pictures."

"You didn't!" Amalie reached for my phone, but I held it out of her reach.

"Maybe just one or two shots." I cracked up at the way she squeezed her eyes shut and shook her head. "And a short video."

"Miller Bishop, I'm going to wring your neck." She flipped around to face me and almost climbed my body like a jungle gym in her attempt to get my phone.

"Okay, I'll delete them. But don't you want to see them first?"

"Once. We can scroll through the pictures and watch the video one time. Then they go straight into your deleted items. Got it?" Her finger poked me right in the belly.

"Fine." I took her hand again. "Now, I have an important question for you."

"What kind of question?"

"Can I just ask it, or do you need me to tell you what it's about first?"

"I don't know. You've already caught me off guard tonight. Maybe you should give me a hint before you lay it on me." Her lips curved up on one side.

I enjoyed the easy way we could tease each other back and forth. It gave me a glimpse of what things could be like if we took our relationship a step or two beyond the friendship we'd started. "A hint about my question. Hmm, let me think about that. You could say it has to do with putting something in your mouth."

"Really? With this being a first date and all?" The way her eyes danced with humor let me know she was teasing. "There's no donkey required, right?"

"No donkey. I promise." My fingers squeezed hers. I'd been hesitant to date since I'd had Jack. First of all, there hadn't been time. Putting myself through school with a baby, then a toddler had taken all my time and energy. Second, women my age weren't interested in a guy with so much baggage. "I guess I'm out of practice. The last first date I had was over seven years ago."

Amalie's eyes widened. "Seven years. That's a long time."

"Yeah, it is." We'd reached the truck, and I stopped by the front wheel well. "Does that scare you at all?"

"What? Like maybe you've forgotten how to kiss or something?" she joked.

I stared into her eyes and brought my hands up to cup her cheeks. Then I leaned down and barely brushed my lips over hers. Her hands came up and covered mine. She tilted her head, and I took the kiss deeper.

Desire shot straight to my cock. Poor thing had been benched for years and was more than ready to get back into action. I didn't want to rush things and risk scaring her off. But damn, I wanted her.

Her lips parted. I slid my tongue inside her mouth. The lingering taste of peppermint greeted me. I lined my body up against hers, pressed my hips into her, and moved my hands to her back. Her breasts pushed against my chest, and my fingers itched to slip under her jacket.

I didn't want to rush things. Amalie was the first woman I

liked enough to pursue. I wasn't in this for just a night. She started to shiver, so I pulled back and wrapped my arms around her.

"Are you cold?" The temperature hovered in the low forties, which was unseasonably chilly for late February in this part of Tennessee.

"Are you offering to warm me up?" She looked up at me with such heat in her eyes that all thoughts of taking her out to dinner dissipated.

"Whatever you want. I'm at your service." We were tiptoeing around each other now, and I wasn't sure if she was still flirting or having the same thoughts as me—thoughts of getting tangled up together and letting our body heat chase the chill away.

"Well then, we'd better get going unless you plan on being at my service in the Bordent high school parking lot." Her eyebrows lifted like she was waiting for my next move.

"I don't want to get in trouble with the principal. We don't have time to plan another school fundraiser this spring." I kept hold of her hand and walked her around my truck so I could open the door for her. My heart pounded so loud she could probably hear it, but that didn't stop me from putting my hands on her hips and holding her back before she climbed inside the truck. "Hold up a sec, Amalie."

"What?" A smile lingered on her lips. She turned to me, a question in her eyes.

"I just wanted to look at you one more time."

Her arms went around my neck, and she pulled my mouth down to hers. I could have stood there kissing her all fucking night. But somebody drove by, honking and yelling out the window for us to get a room.

I laughed against her mouth. "Ready to go?"

She nodded.

CHAPTER 24

Amalie

I FELT ALIVE. Every cell in my body hummed with awareness. Miller had woken up some part of me that had been dormant for years. I didn't want to admit it, but I was falling for him. I didn't know when it had happened. Truth was, it didn't matter. All I could think about was his hands on my hips, his fingers brushing against my cheeks, his tongue sliding against mine.

I'd never been the kind of girl to lose her mind over a boy, especially a boy who'd treated me the way Miller had when I was just a kid. But he'd changed. He wasn't the same cocky jerk he'd been back then.

He held my hand on the drive back to Beaver Bluff. We didn't talk, just enjoyed the low music coming from the local country station and the anticipation building between us.

When we reached the town limits, he squeezed my hand. "I got a little distracted before and didn't have a chance to ask, but do you want to grab a bite to eat?"

"Are you hungry?" I didn't care what we did next as long as he didn't take me home. I wasn't ready for our time together to end.

"I could eat." He glanced over, and his lips curved up into a smile. "But then again, I can always eat. We could swing by Jackie Jay's, or if you're not that hungry, I can make us something back at my place."

"You can cook?" The only thing I'd seen him do so far was pick up a pizza. A man who kissed like him shouldn't get to have talent in the kitchen too. He was too good at too many things. If he kept revealing hidden talents, I might just want to keep him.

"Do I look like I've missed many meals?" He looked down at his stomach, but all I saw was the promise of a six-pack of abs I'd been dying to skim my palms over.

"What's your specialty then?" I expected him to say something easy like scrambled eggs or pancakes.

"If I tell you, you'll laugh."

"No, I won't."

He shook his head. "You will."

"Try me."

"All right. My specialty is something I like to call Beaver Bluff Three Way." He bit back a smile while he checked my reaction.

My mind went wild with possibilities. "You are talking about something you serve in the kitchen, not the bedroom, right?"

"Geez, Amalie, get your mind out of the gutter." He set our joined hands on his thigh as we passed through town.

"What am I supposed to think?" When he didn't slow down in front of Jackie Jay's, my stomach twisted. Looked like we were headed back to his place, though I wasn't sure if I was game for a Beaver Bluff Three Way.

"Have you heard of a Cincinnati Three Way?"

"No. I guess I haven't traveled enough to be wise to the

ways of the big wide world." That was something I planned to change as soon as I had the chance.

"It's a dish they serve in Cincinnati. They dump a bunch of chili on top of spaghetti noodles, then pile it with cheese. You eat it like a casserole." He shook his head. "It's good to know what a dirty mind you have."

"Really? And why's that?" He'd stopped the truck in front of a cute little one-story house with a big wraparound front porch.

"Because it might come in handy later."

Heat shot to my core, and a deep ache pulsed between my legs. Tension between us had been ratcheting up since the day I met him in the hallway at Bettina's school. What was going to happen between us tonight seemed like a foregone conclusion. My need was like a keg of gunpowder, waiting for a spark to set it off. I wondered how long it would take once we got inside.

Miller helped me down from the truck and led me to the front door. "I want you to know you're the first woman I've brought home with me since I found out about Jack."

The impact of what we were doing hit me then. This wasn't just a fling or a one-night stand. Miller was a dad. Being with him would mean tying myself to Beaver Bluff. I wasn't sure I was ready for that kind of responsibility. But when I walked through the front door, all of my worries didn't hold nearly as much weight as my intense desire to alleviate the desperate need between us.

Before I had a chance to look around, he'd captured my mouth with his. His fingers tugged the zipper on my jacket down, and I slid my arms out of the sleeves. He backed me into the room until my legs hit something low. I tumbled onto a couch.

Miller knelt in front of me and untied the laces on my

boots. His movements were quick and sure, like he'd done this a thousand times before. He helped me kick off my boots, then he climbed onto the couch and pushed me back against the cushions. His weight pinned me in place, but I didn't mind, especially when his thick thigh nestled between my legs.

"Sorry, I don't want to hurt you." He mumbled the apology against my lips and set his hand on the ground to give himself a little leverage.

I wanted to feel him against me, wanted to be pinned in place, wanted to grind my hips against him as he plunged his tongue into my mouth and reminded me what it was like to feel.

"You're not hurting me at all." I slipped my hand between us and worked the buttons on his shirt front free. I'd been imagining running my hand over his abs for too long. Tonight I wanted to know what it really felt like.

He slid his shirt from his shoulders, then reached behind his head and pulled off the t-shirt he had on underneath. My first glimpse of his chest made me choke on my breath. The man was flawless. His pecs looked like they'd been sculpted out of marble. The definition of his abs had me sucking in my stomach.

"What's wrong?" He'd slipped his hands under the hem of my sweater, but I scooted out from under him on the couch.

"We can't." I shook my head back and forth. "Not with all that."

"All what?" He was on all fours, crawling across the couch to get to me.

"All that." I pointed at his chest, his abs, the perfect "v" formed by the muscles on the sides of his waist that pointed toward the bulge in his jeans like a freaking road sign. It might as well have read, "Get your orgasms here."

He glanced down like he was completely unaware he had

the body of a professional athlete. "You want me to put my shirt back on?"

"Yes. I mean, no. I mean, I don't know." I should have known this wouldn't go well.

"Why don't you let me take yours off?" He bent and kissed my neck. Goosebumps raced down my chest and pebbled my skin. "Then we'll be even."

I squirmed under him, but all that did was create beautiful, bittersweet friction between my hips and his waist.

"Just a peek?" His warm breath brushed over my skin, weakening my resolve. "I want to see you, Amalie. You taste so good. I want to kiss every inch of your skin."

I wanted him to kiss every inch of my skin too. Although, I'd rather he did it with his eyes closed. "Can we turn off the light?"

He pulled back and sat up. His thighs straddled my hips, and he towered over me. "Then I wouldn't be able to see you."

"I realize that. It's kind of the whole point." I'd never felt so self-conscious. I believed in body positivity, owning the skin I was in, and projecting confidence. But all of that fell by the wayside now that I was faced with his glaringly gorgeous physique.

"I wish you could see yourself through my eyes. You're beautiful." He leaned over and kissed my neck. "Stunning. Breathtaking. One of a kind. I think I should start calling you Sugar because you taste sweeter than any dessert I've ever had."

My inhibitions faded, and my desire grew as he continued to trail kisses over my skin.

"You can stop me anytime. We won't do anything you don't want to, okay?" He reached for the hem of my sweater.

Nodding, I put my hands on his and eased my sweater over my head.

He held my gaze while his fingers traced a path down my shoulders and between my breasts. "You're so fucking perfect."

My nerve endings overloaded. Every kiss, every flash of his warm breath, every whisper added fuel to the fire inside me. He moved on to work on the button at my waist. Impatient now, I pushed his hands away and shed my jeans. Standing there in my mismatched bra and panties, I was grateful he couldn't tell what a shivering bundle of aching need he'd turned me into.

"Come to bed with me, Amalie." He reached up and took my glasses from my face. After he set them down on a side table, he skimmed his hand down my arm until he twined his fingers with mine. Then he tugged me toward the bedroom.

At that moment, I gave up worrying about anything else except what would be going on inside the four walls of his room.

CHAPTER 25

I WAS A MOTH, and she was the flame. My body was drawn to hers by some invisible force that had me desperate to claim her. She might not realize it yet, but she was meant to be mine, and if things went my way, I was about to ruin her for anyone else.

I couldn't see her well in the dim light of my room, but my hands were doing a pretty damn good job of exploring her curves. She was a little self-conscious, and I was more than willing to do what it would take to make her feel comfortable. For now. Once she knew what kind of power she held over me and how good we would be together, we'd never make love in the dark again. I wanted to see the look in her eyes when I made her come.

With her on her back and me on my side, my fingers were free to roam over her skin. I couldn't decide which part of her to explore first. I skimmed my palm over her belly and past the waistband of her panties while I scraped my teeth over the cup of her bra. The little moans she made urged me on. I wanted her to lose control, shed her inhibitions, and give in to the blazing inferno that threatened to burn us up.

"You like that, Amalie?" I brushed my finger across her clit, then slid it between her folds to find out if she was as wet as I hoped.

Her knees bent, and her hips bucked against my hand. "Yes."

"How about this?" I slipped the tip of my finger inside her wet heat. The scent of her arousal flooded my nose, making my mouth water. I couldn't wait to taste her. Later. For now I resisted the need to sandwich my cheeks between her thighs and plunge my tongue deep into her sweet pussy.

"Oh. Yes, that too." She arched toward me, trying to take me deeper.

"Patience, sugar." My cock was so hard I wasn't sure I could hold off on sinking into her. I pulled my hand away and shifted so I could feel around in my nightstand drawer. Please let me have a condom. I should have checked earlier, but I didn't want to jinx myself. Until I'd seen her tonight, I thought maybe I'd been overestimating the heat between us. As soon as I saw her, I knew I hadn't exaggerated my need.

My fingers closed around a square packet. Thank fuck.

"Everything okay?" she asked.

"Just making sure I've got the protection covered. Are you sure this is what you want?" If she said no, I wasn't sure what I'd have to do to find relief, but I needed her to want this as much as I did. "It's okay if it's not. Just talk to me."

Her palms cupped my cheeks. "Yes, I want this. I want you."

Hearing her say it unleashed something inside me. "Good."

She shifted beneath me. I fisted my cock and pumped a few times to make sure I was nice and hard for her. Then I unrolled the condom and hovered over her. Her panties had to go, so I hooked my finger around the waistband and jerked them free.

Her hands skimmed my ribs as she tried to get a grip on my sides. "Come here, Miller."

Hearing my name come out of her mouth, all throaty and sexy, had me poised at her entrance. I eased the tip of my cock into her slick heat. My cock was ready to blow, and I was less than an inch in. I propped myself up on my arms and sank into her a millimeter at a time.

"Goddammit, Amalie. You feel so fucking good." I wanted her to know exactly how amazing she made me feel.

"You feel pretty fantastic, too." Her chest heaved, and her tits brushed my pecs.

I had to feel her skin on skin, so I shifted my weight to one arm and slid a hand behind her to unclasp her bra. She pulled her arms out of the straps, and I lowered my mouth to take one of her hard nipples into my mouth.

"Ohhhhh." She sounded surprised. Then a low moan rumbled through her chest. "Oh my god."

I sucked on her nipple, swirling my tongue around the hardened bud, taking as much of her tit into my mouth as possible.

The walls of her pussy clenched around me. She was close. I didn't want her to come yet. I didn't want our first time to end so soon, so I pulled out and lifted my head. "What do you want?"

"I want you." Her nails scraped over my shoulders as she tried to pull me back into her.

"What do you want me to do?" I needed to hear her say it. Needed to hear her tell me I was the one she wanted. Because I didn't just want her, I craved her. I hadn't even come inside her yet, but I knew I'd never be as out of my mind for a woman as I was for her.

"I want you inside me, Miller."

"I want that too."

"Then stop teasing me." Her breath came out in short, rushed puffs.

"Is that what I'm doing?" I pushed back into her and swiveled my hips, grazing her g-spot with my cock.

"You know you are."

Bending over her, I licked the length of her neck. She tasted like the perfect mix of salty and sweet. My cock throbbed as I imagined what she'd taste like when I sandwiched my head between her thighs and licked her creamy slit.

"I'm going to make you feel good, sugar."

"Yes, please."

"Then I'm going to turn on the lights and do it again. And again. And again. You got that?"

"Yes."

"Good." I pulled my hips back and then pushed into her until my balls rested against her dripping pussy. Then I did it again, easing in and out of her slowly.

She lifted her legs and clasped her ankles over my ass. The shift in angle let me sink even deeper into her. Fuck, I was going to come. I needed her to lose control first, so I reached between us and circled her clit.

"Mmmm." She bit down on her lip.

"Let go. Come for me, Amalie." I whispered, urging her on. "I've got you, sugar."

Her hips collided with mine then she stopped moving underneath me.

"That's it, just like that," I growled into her ear and put pressure on her clit.

She gasped. "So good."

Knowing she was riding the wave of her release made me want to join her. I bent down, sucked hard on her nipple, and pumped in and out of her slick channel. My fingers dug into her hip. I couldn't get close enough to her. Couldn't get deep enough. Couldn't go fast enough.

I exploded into her. With her tight pussy clenched around me, my release rocketed through me. Then I collapsed on top of her, careful not to crush her under my weight.

CHAPTER 26
Amalie

I COULDN'T COMPREHEND what had just happened between us. The orgasm, I understood. But there was something else. Something that touched on some sacred part of me deep down inside that I'd never been aware of before. Knowing he had access to that part of me scared the crap out of me. It also made me hope for things I'd never considered.

"I need to get us both cleaned up." Miller sprawled over me, his leg hooked over my belly, his arm draped over my breasts.

"Stay for a minute." Though neither of us had moved for at least five full minutes, my pulse still thundered through my ears, and my heart still careened around in my chest.

His lips brushed the side of my breast. "Anything for you."

I had no doubt he meant it. Even though I couldn't see his face, I pictured the smile on his lips. I still felt those lips on my ear, whispering all the deliciously naughty things he would do to me later.

Later.

Later implied there might be a round two. Or a round

three. My thighs quivered at the thought. I already knew I'd be sore. How lame would a round two or three render me?

Whatever happened, it would be worth it.

I'd always thought the kind of stuff that just happened between us was an urban legend. Women in books had toe-curling orgasms, not average women like me. But it had happened. Despite maybe leaving my body for a few seconds, I'd experienced it myself. And now that I had, I wasn't sure I could ever go backward.

"Are you hungry?" Miller's whiskers scraped against my chest. "I've got the stuff for a Beaver Bluff Three Way in the fridge."

"A three-way, huh? Are you tired of me already?" I teased.

"Hell no. But I want to make sure you eat something so you have enough stamina for what comes next."

I wasn't ready to talk about what might happen when we left the safety and security of these four walls. "You're worried I might not be able to keep up with you?"

"No. What I have planned for dessert doesn't require you to do anything more than lie there and enjoy yourself."

Goosebumps pebbled my skin. If what he had planned matched what I thought he had planned, I was already looking forward to it.

The bed shifted as he rolled off. "I'll be back in a second."

"Okay." I stayed there, inhaling the scent of his shampoo from his pillow. With his heat gone, I climbed under the covers to keep myself warm. Being there, knowing I was the only woman who'd ever been inside his personal space, made me feel invincible.

While I waited for him to return, I sorted through possibilities in my head of where we might go from here. What would my mother say when I told her I'd completely fallen for a

Bishop? Would the Calbots be okay with that? Would his family? The stupid feud complicated everything, even things that didn't have anything to do with it.

Miller came out of the bathroom but left the light on. I squinted against the bright light and held my hand up to shield my eyes.

"If you're not ready for a three-way, how about an omelet?" He picked up his button-down shirt from the floor and held it out to me. "You can put this on if you don't want to walk around my kitchen naked."

"I don't know. I've always wanted to dine in the buff."

Miller chuckled. "If you sit down at my kitchen table like that, the only thing I'm going to want to eat is you."

As much as that image appealed to me, my stomach grumbled in disagreement. "How about real food first?"

"Sounds like a plan." He helped me into the shirt, and I turned around and started to button it up the front.

With him in a clean pair of gray sweats and me swallowed up by his long, plaid flannel shirt, we headed into the kitchen.

"Okay. Let's see what kind of skills you've mastered in this room of the house," I teased.

His eyes lit up. "Is that how this is going to play out tonight? We'll visit each room in my house so you can see what tricks I've got up my sleeves?"

I ran my hand over his corded forearm. "You don't appear to be wearing any sleeves. That must mean you don't have any tricks to share."

His mouth curved into a wicked grin. Then he put his hands on my hips and hoisted me onto the granite kitchen island. The countertop felt cool under my naked ass, and I gasped.

Miller crouched down in front of me and used his hands to

slide my knees apart. "Challenge accepted. Now spread those legs so I can taste you. There's going to be a slight delay in me making your dinner."

CHAPTER 27
Miller

WHEN I CRACKED open an eyelid the next morning, sunlight streamed through the slit in my bedroom curtains. Amalie sprawled over me, her arm flung over my chest, her pelvis aligned with my hip. Last night, with her hair pulled back and her face made up to bring out her features, she'd looked gorgeous. But this morning, with her hair spilling onto my chest and her lashes fanned against her cheek, she took my breath away.

I could have stayed there all day with her nestled against me, but our time together was limited, and I wanted to make the most of it. So, I eased out from under her and searched for my sweats.

By the time she entered the kitchen, I'd brewed a pot of coffee and had almost finished scrambling the eggs. She must have pulled a t-shirt from one of my drawers. It hung loose on her shoulders and left her legs exposed. My cock twitched at the sight of her full, swollen lips. It had only been a couple of hours since I last had her, but I'd never get enough.

"How did you sleep?" I turned from the stove and grabbed an empty mug out of the cabinet.

"Mmm. Better than I have in a long time."

"Coffee?" I asked.

"Yes, please. How about you? Are you tired this morning?"

"Tired, yes. Too tired to try to wring as much as we can out of the time we have left? No." I handed her a steaming mug of the dark brew. "Do you take cream or sugar?"

"No. Black is fine." She closed her eyes and took a small sip. "Thanks. I'm a total crab without my coffee."

"Good to know. What other things do I need to know about you?" I scooped some eggs onto a plate with a strip of bacon.

"Um, let's see. I'm a dog lover." She reached down and scratched Titus between the ears.

"Don't give him any love this morning. He's already helped himself to half the bacon." I glared at the wicked beast as I carried my plate and coffee over to the table.

"You can't blame him. This smells delicious." She joined me, tucking her leg underneath her as she took the seat to my left.

I pictured the three of us at my kitchen table. . . Jack, Amalie, and me. I'd never been able to see a woman in my future before now. Not until her. The possibility threw me, especially when I'd set a plan in motion to move away.

"Do you need to get back by a certain time? I was hoping we might be able to spend the day together before I have to pick up Jack. My mom bought tickets for some space expo thing in Nashville, so they'll be gone most of the day."

"I have homework, but I can finish it later. Is there more research you want to do for the carnival?" She held a piece of bacon between her fingers and nibbled on the end.

All that did was draw my attention to her lips. Lips that had been wrapped around my cock a few hours ago. Blood surged to my dick, and I reached down to adjust myself under the table.

"You okay?" She glanced at my lap, the look in her eyes telling me she knew exactly what was going on in my sweats.

"For now." I slid a bite of eggs into my mouth. Though we'd spent time together since we met, not much of that had been alone. I wanted to get to know her better and find out what plans she had for her future. "So, tell me what made you want to become a teacher."

Her nose crinkled. "You want to talk about serious stuff so early in the morning?"

I laughed and glanced at the clock on the microwave. "Early? It's after ten already, well past the time of day when it's appropriate to start asking serious questions."

"Okay." She exhaled slowly while she poked around her eggs with her fork. "When I was in second grade, we read a book about amazing women in history. I can't remember exactly who all of them were, but they were women like Marie Curie and Amelia Earhart. You know, women who make a girl think she can be anything she wants."

I nodded, encouraging her to keep going.

"Well, up until that point, I'd only ever seen women do things like clean and work the checkout at the grocery store. My mom worked two jobs to support us." She lifted her head and jutted her chin out just a bit. "My teacher was the one who told me I could be whatever I wanted when I grew up. The only thing holding me back was myself."

"Sounds like a really good teacher."

"She was. I want to inspire kids the same way she inspired me." Her shoulder lifted in a lopsided shrug. "I've got one more semester of classes before I start student teaching."

"You'll be an amazing teacher, Amalie."

She pointed her fork at me. "You can bet I won't allow dads to bring ice cream in for parties, no matter how hot they are."

"You think I'm hot?" I teased.

"We're not doing this again." She shook her head as a smile spread over her lips.

"What do you want to do when you're finished with school? Are you planning on sticking around Beaver Bluff?"

"I hope not. I've always wanted to travel. That's one of the reasons I took the job with the Calbots. Mr. Calbot works for an international investment firm, and they're always taking off somewhere that requires a passport. As the nanny, I get to go with them."

"Where have you been so far?" I felt like I'd gotten to know her body inside and out, but I wanted to know everything about her.

"We went to Paris a few summers ago, then spent the winter at a condo they rented in Antigua. That was before they had Caden. Since then, they've limited taking the kids with them, especially with Bettina in school. I thought we were going to get to go to Switzerland with them since it was a shorter trip, but they decided not to take the kids at the last minute." She sighed, like jet-setting around the world was as natural to her as eating a plate of scrambled eggs in my kitchen.

"So, have you ever been to Switzerland?" I'd gone on a solo adventure after high school.

"No, but it's at the top of my list of places I want to go."

"It's gorgeous." Though not as beautiful as the sight of her sitting next to me. "Maybe we can go someday."

Her cheeks flushed the cutest shade of pink, and she snapped off a bite of bacon to hand to Titus. "I'd like that."

My heart grew wings and seemed to soar out of my chest. Amalie made me wish for things I never thought possible. "So, what do you want to do today?"

"What are our options?"

I sat back from the table. "I could make a run to the gas

station to fill up on necessities, and we could spend the day in my bed."

The suggestion brought on another blush. "You don't think you'll get sick of me?"

I didn't mean my laugh to come out as loud as it did, but what did she expect when she asked such a ridiculous question? "Never."

"This. . . this. . . thing between us." Her gaze bounced from my chest to the table. "What exactly is it that you're looking for?"

I scooted my chair closer to hers. "Hey, look at me, sugar."

She lifted her chin and met my gaze. Her armor was gone. I saw beyond the front that she'd propped up to protect herself. At that moment, I felt her vulnerability and need for assurance.

"I wasn't looking for anything." My hand covered hers where it rested on the table. "But then I met you."

"And now?" Her lower lip trembled. "I don't want to push, but you're a dad, and there's a kid involved, and—"

I silenced her with a kiss. Though I wanted to scoop her up in my arms and flip her over my shoulder, caveman style, I kept it sweet and gentle. My palm cupped her cheek, and I pulled back enough to look into her eyes.

"Now? I don't know." She deserved a hell of a lot. Most importantly, she deserved my honesty. "But I do know that I want you in my life, Amalie. Yes, I've got a kid, and he has to be my top priority. He got a raw deal when he ended up stuck with me for his dad, but I'm doing the best I can."

She lifted her hand to cup my shoulder. "What happened with Jack's mom, Miller?"

If we were going to give this a shot, she needed to know everything about me—the good and the bad. "Come here."

This wasn't the kind of conversation I wanted to have over

a plate of eggs. I held her hand and led her into the family room.

"We may as well get comfortable. This may take a few minutes." I sat in the corner of the sectional and tugged her down next to me. My arm went around her back, and she flung her legs over one of mine so they hung down between my thighs.

"You don't have to tell me anything you don't want to." Her cheek nestled against my collarbone, and I breathed in her scent.

"I want you to know. But you've got to promise to keep it to yourself. What I'm about to tell you, I haven't told anyone. Not my parents, not my siblings, not Jack. No matter what happens between us, you've got to protect him."

Her forehead creased, and she reached for my hand. "I promise."

I took in a shaky breath. "It was a one-night stand my freshman year of college. I was eighteen. She was a visiting professor from Syria, though she wasn't that much older than me. Hearing her talk about what was going on over there moved me, and I went up after her presentation to ask a few questions. One thing led to another, and we ended up spending the night together. Eighteen months later, she showed up, handed me Jack, and said she was moving back to Syria to help fellow refugees get out."

"Oh my gosh." Amalie squeezed my hand. "What happened to her? Is she okay?"

"No. She died a couple of months later. I got a telegram from a non-profit she'd been working for."

"I'm so sorry. That must have been such a difficult time."

Relief flooded through me. I'd been carrying my secret for so long. I didn't have words to describe how it felt to finally share it with someone.

"It was. My dad was used to me fucking up, but fathering a kid was the final straw. He told me if I didn't find Jack's mom and marry her, he'd cut me off. I tried to tell him a version of the truth that wouldn't get her in trouble and me expelled for having sex with a faculty member. In the end, it didn't matter. He pretty much disowned me, and I grew up real fucking fast."

"I didn't know." All those years of listening to people bad-talk Miller piled up, threatening to bury me under their weight. "People said all kinds of things."

"Yeah, I know. I'd rather them talk bad about me than drag her name through the mud. I barely knew her, but from what I did know, she deserves to be remembered for what she did for the women she tried to help, not for the one-night stand she had with a college kid."

"So why not tell your parents the truth now? Don't you think enough time has passed that they'd understand?"

"You don't know my dad." My shoulders tensed as I thought about the few times I'd tried to bring it up.

"And what does Jack know about his mom?"

"That she loved him very much but had to move away and couldn't take him with her. He hasn't asked more than that yet. If he did, I'm not sure what I would tell him." I brushed a hunk of hair away from her face, caught off guard by the understanding in her eyes. "Eventually, I'll tell him the truth. When he's old enough to understand."

"You might be surprised at how much he understands now. When I was about Jack's age, I found out my mom had been lying to me for years about my dad."

Her eyes grew big and took on a haunted look. I rested my hand on her arm, encouraging her to go on.

"She always said he'd died when I was a baby. Then I found out he didn't die. He just left us. He lives in Reno now with a wife and three sons." She looked at me, the past hurt still visible in her eyes. I reached for her hand, sensing this wasn't something she typically shared. "It took years to forgive my mom for lying to me about it. She thought she was protecting me, but she almost ruined our relationship over it."

"Thanks for telling me that." I squeezed her hand.

She scooted her bare ass onto my leg and stretched to kiss my cheek. "You've shared a secret with me. Now I feel like I should share one with you. What would you say to taking a drive this afternoon?" Her hand slipped down my stomach to rest on the growing bulge in the front of my pants.

"How soon would we need to leave?"

She flipped around to straddle me. Her bare pussy brushed against my belly. "How long will it take for you to run to the gas station and back?"

"I have a better idea." I flipped her on her back and slid down her body to blow my hot breath over her clit. "Why don't we get cleaned up, then go on a drive and pick up necessities while we're out."

My shirt rode up her torso, leaving her bottom half exposed. "Are you sure you wouldn't rather run out now?"

I slid my hand under her ass and angled her hips up so I could slide my tongue along the seam of her slit. "I've got everything I need right here in front of me."

Then I bent down and showed her with my tongue, my fingers, and my lips, exactly what I'd been fantasizing about doing to her since I woke up with her in my bed.

CHAPTER 28
Amalie

HE WAS INSATIABLE, and I was in heaven. I couldn't remember a time when I'd been so full of happiness and felt so light. It was like he'd driven all my stress and worries out of me overnight. My muscles ached in that so-good way from being twisted and turned and satisfied all night long, and I'd never felt better. It was all due to him.

I turned to glance at Miller. He drummed his fingers along the steering wheel to the beat of the fast-paced country song on the radio. Scruff covered his cheeks, and he looked like he hadn't slept in days. Then he turned his head and smiled at me. Not the teasing smirk he'd been giving me for the past couple of weeks, but a genuine, heartfelt grin that summed up everything that had happened between us.

"What are you thinking?" He lifted our joined hands to his mouth and pressed a kiss to the inside of my wrist.

"Nothing much," I lied. The truth would freak him the hell out. There was no way I would admit to wondering where he'd rather go on a honeymoon—the beach or the mountains.

"I don't believe you." His brows arched, challenging me to tell the truth.

"Fine. Don't believe me." We were on our way to check on my mom. It had been my Sunday ritual for a few years. I'd work all week with the Calbots, then pick up something for Sunday night dinner and take it to her place. She'd stopped going out since she had such a hard time getting around.

After Miller confided in me, I wanted to do something to show him I trusted him. He'd already met my mom, but he hadn't seen where I'd grown up. I didn't want to hide who I was or where I came from. If there was any chance of a future between us, he needed to know and accept all of me, and I needed to know he'd changed.

"Are you sure you want to tell your mom you're officially dating a Bishop?" He'd been all-in until we exited the highway. "Maybe we should give it some time. Let her get to know me better before we tell her."

"Nope. I don't keep secrets from my mother. If we don't tell her now and she finds out later,"—I shook my head—"trust me, taking the fallout now is a million times better than telling her the truth a few months down the line."

"I can't believe I let you talk me into this." Miller's phone rang. The name "Boss" appeared on the small screen on his dash.

"Do you need to get that?" I asked, wondering why his boss would call him on a Sunday afternoon.

"Nope. I'm off the clock. Whatever he needs to talk to me about can wait." He rubbed his thumb over my knuckles. "I've got priorities."

My belly warmed at the thought of being one of his priorities. "What should we pick up for dinner? Are you craving anything?"

He set our joined hands on his thigh. "Just you."

"I meant food-wise. You can have me anytime you want me."

"Unfortunately, that's not entirely true." He glanced over, his mouth set in a hard line. "As much as I've enjoyed our time together and would love to spend every waking moment buried inside you, I've got to be a dad first."

I knew he'd feel that way. That was one of the reasons I was attracted to him. He put his kid first, so unlike my father, who'd abandoned his responsibilities. "Of course. We'll just have to get creative on spending time together."

"You're really up for this?" he asked.

"Up for what?" I had a feeling I knew what he meant, but I wanted to hear him say it. Wanted to make sure we were on the same page with expectations.

"Up for taking on Jack and me. We're a package deal." He'd pulled into the parking lot of the small hometown grocery store. Despite superstores setting up shop in the bigger surrounding towns, Muster still only rated a locally owned mom-and-pop shop.

"If we're going to start talking about your package, we might never make it to my mom's for dinner," I teased.

He smiled but held my gaze. "I'm serious, Amalie. I really like you. If you want to keep this casual, we can. But if it's up to me, I want more."

My mouth went dry at the same time my chest tightened. He was saying all the right things. Judging by the sureness on his face, he meant it.

"How much more?" I asked.

"All of it." He cut the engine and leaned over the armrest. "I want all of you. Can you handle that? If not, I'd understand."

"Come here." I fisted my hand in his shirt and pulled him toward me, a sureness settling in my heart. Then I tilted my head and kissed him.

"Is that a yes?" he whispered.

"Yes, it's a yes."

We kissed in the parking lot of the Muster Family Market until the windows steamed up. Miller came up for air first.

"We'd better get dinner over to your mom's place before she gives up on us." He gently took my hands from where they clasped around his neck. "I'm already starting off on the wrong foot. What if I made dinner instead of just picking up something store-bought?"

"Like what? Are you going to impress her with your Beaver Bluff Three Way?" I might have been teasing, but it wasn't a bad idea. "I think you should do it. What do we need to get inside?"

"Ideally, I'd make the chili from scratch, but since we're in a hurry, I can probably doctor up something from a can."

"All right, let's go."

I tucked my hand in the crook of his arm as we walked across the parking lot and entered the store. I'd never been grocery shopping with a man before. Miller grabbed a cart from the corral and pushed it toward me.

"Do you want to drive the cart, or would you rather be the one who snatches stuff off the shelves?" he asked.

"You're the one who knows what we need, so you'd better do the snatching." I swapped spots with him and wrapped my hands around the handle of the metal cart.

"Okay then. We need pasta." He searched the signs hanging from the ceiling for the pasta aisle. "Come on, Amalie. Try to keep up."

I laughed and stayed on his tail as he gathered spaghetti, canned chili, shredded cheese, and a handful of spices. Seeing him study the labels of canned chili was kind of a turn-on. Either my standards had eroded over the years, or Miller could make anything look sexy. Based on what he'd done to me last night . . . and this morning . . . and this afternoon . . . I was leaning toward the latter.

He looked at me as he put the last ingredient for his infamous Beaver Bluff Three Way in the cart. "Should we get something for dessert?"

I usually skipped it or had a piece of fruit, but picking up something sweet and sugary would be a treat. "That's not a bad idea."

"What do you want? Ice cream?"

"After what happened at the Valentine's Day party?" There was no way he could misinterpret my smirk.

He wrapped his arms around me from behind and tucked his hands into the front pocket of my jeans. "If it hadn't been for that party, we wouldn't be standing here together right now."

"You don't think so?" I leaned back against his chest.

He kissed along my jawline, his whiskers scratching my cheek. "I'd like to think we would have found our way to each other without getting sent to the principal's office."

Tempted to turn around in his arms and make out in the condiment aisle, I settled for tilting my head and pressing my lips to his cheek.

"If not ice cream, then what?" Miller asked.

I thought about what my mom said about a man like Miller being unable to change. Everything he'd said and done led me to believe he had. But still, there was a little nagging feeling that I might be overestimating him. "Do you like cake?"

"What kind? Carrot cake? Red velvet?" He reluctantly pulled his hands out of my pockets. "Do they have a bakery?"

"It's at the front of the store. It doesn't look like much, but they make everything from scratch. When I was younger, all I ever wanted for my birthday was a store-bought cake from here."

"Did you ever get one?" Miller took over steering the cart. I led us to the front of the store.

I was treading on dangerous ground now. Before I could be with Miller, really give him my entire heart and soul, I needed to know if he remembered that afternoon at the park. "Once. The woman who used to run the bakery made a rainbow surprise cake that had candy and sprinkles inside."

"Well, let's get one of those for dessert." Miller looked over the cakes in the refrigerated case. "What color frosting does it have?"

"White buttercream with rainbow sprinkles. They won't have it, though. She retired and took her recipe with her when she did." Thinking about it now, the heartbreak I experienced that day came rushing back. I had to grab hold of the bakery case to steady myself.

"How about cupcakes instead? These have rainbow and chocolate sprinkles." Miller held up a plastic container of white cupcakes with chocolate frosting and sprinkles.

The smile that stretched across his face was too big, too bright. He didn't remember. Why would he? For him, that day was all about hanging with his friends and playing football. For me, it meant so much more.

I swallowed the prickly lump in my throat. "Sounds good. We'd better get going before Mom thinks I forgot about her."

We got to the checkout and worked together to set all our items on the conveyor belt. Miller insisted on paying for the groceries despite my repeated protests.

"Save your cash to pay off those tires." He held my hand while he slid his credit card into the slot. "Tonight's my treat. When we get to your mom's place, I want you to sit down and relax while I do all the work."

"Are you for real?" I shook off the apprehension that had grabbed hold of my heart. So what if we were from two different worlds? We could still make it work. I was overreacting, looking for reasons to shut things down before they got started.

I grabbed the bag holding the cupcakes while he picked up the two brown paper bags full of our other groceries.

"This is for real, Amalie. You and me. It's as real as it gets."

Swoon. He constantly surprised me, this man I'd always looked at as some spoiled rich kid with his head in the clouds, whose feet never touched the ground. Until a few weeks ago, I thought he was an entitled frat boy whose family had paid off his baby mama. My cheeks burned as I thought about how wrong I'd been about him.

People always made incorrect assumptions about me, and I got so mad when they did. I shouldn't have let my mom get into my head about Miller. She was wrong about him, and tonight I'd prove it to her.

"Are you ready to see my mom again?" Once we told her we were officially dating, word would spread quickly among the Stewarts. There was only one thing that traveled faster than the speed of light, and that was the speed of gossip through a town the size of Beaver Bluff.

Miller laced our fingers together. "Let's do it."

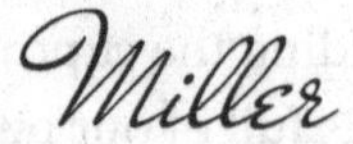

CHAPTER 29

"IS THIS IT?" I asked as the robotic voice on my GPS told me to take a right into the Calm Waters mobile home park.

"Yep." Amalie sucked her lips into her mouth and bit down like she was trying not to let her nerves get the best of her. She'd already picked at the cuticle on her pointer finger until it bled.

I turned my head, sweeping my gaze from one side of the road to the other. "This is where you grew up?"

"Yep." She gave me a tight grin and turned to look out the window.

I drove deeper into the mobile home park. Now that I knew more about her, I put the pieces of the puzzle of her past together. After her dad left, her mom probably had limited options. She'd probably been lucky to find a place to call home. Based on what Amalie said, it was supposed to be temporary. I might not have grown up in a neighborhood like hers, but I knew what was like to feel stuck.

I tried to picture Amalie as a little girl, coming home to an empty trailer while her mom held down multiple jobs. That could have been Jack's life if his mom hadn't brought him to me. Though I wished things could have turned out differently for her, I'd always be grateful that she had the courage to return to Knoxville with him. Maybe Amalie was right about me telling Jack the truth sooner rather than later. His mom deserved to have her story told.

But first, I needed to win over Amalie's mom if I wanted a chance at a future with her. I'd tried to pick up a bouquet on the way out of the grocery store. All they had left was an ivy plant with a blue plastic bear holding a "Congratulations on your baby boy" sign sticking up from the middle. Amalie said it wasn't necessary, but I didn't want to show up without some sort of gift. She said I could pull the bear out after we bought it, but I didn't realize the damn thing was part of the container.

Amalie entered the trailer first. "Hey, Mom, we're here."

I followed, carting the groceries and the plant. Her mom sat in one of the two chairs in the front room. She got up as we entered and hugged Amalie.

"I told you to keep the door locked when you're home alone," Amalie said.

"You think someone's going to try to come in and take advantage of an old bird like me?" Her mother nodded to me. "Hi again. Are the two of you still pretending to be just friends?"

"Mom!" A pink rash swept across Amalie's cheeks, and she shot me a look full of apology.

"Anyone can see it on your face, Amalie. You're positively smitten."

I bit back a grin. Hearing her mom call her out on liking me was a big boost to my ego. My chest puffed out a little more, and I avoided Amalie's gaze.

"Should I get started on dinner right away, or do you want me to put the food in the refrigerator until it's closer to time to eat?" Though I'd volunteered to make dinner, I wasn't sure what their Sunday evening routine typically consisted of.

"We can get started. I know you need to get back so you're there to put Jack to bed." Amalie pulled the groceries out, set them on the counter, then folded the empty brown paper bags and tucked them under the kitchen sink.

"Jack must be your son?" Her mom asked. One eyebrow arched so high it disappeared behind her wavy brown bangs.

"That's right. He's in first grade with Bettina. That's how Amalie and I met." Thankfully my nerves didn't come through in my voice.

"I see." Mrs. Rivers glanced over at the ivy plant with the baby blue bear.

"Oh, this is for you. I wanted to get flowers, but they didn't have much of a selection." My voice bobbled a little, but I thought I recovered fairly well.

"Well, isn't that sweet of you?" Mrs. Rivers nudged Amalie's arm. "Did you see what your boyfriend brought me?"

Amalie's eyes widened, and she opened her mouth like she was about to correct her mom for making the wrong assumption. But then she took a deep breath and put her hand on my arm. Her possessive touch took the edge off my nerves.

"I did. Isn't he a keeper?" Amalie rose to her tiptoes and kissed me on the lips.

I fought the urge to cup her ass and pull her into me. It felt good to be claimed as her boyfriend. I hadn't held that title since high school. Even then, what I had with the girl I thought was my first love didn't compare to what I felt for Amalie.

"Are we going to eat, or am I going to have a front seat to watching the two of you struggle to keep your hands off each other all night?" Mrs. Rivers tsked and brushed past us toward the counter.

I kissed Amalie one more time, then pulled back so I could start dinner. "Why don't the two of you relax, and I'll get dinner going."

Mrs. Rivers narrowed her eyes. "Are you a chef?"

"No, Mom. He just likes to cook and has been promising me he'd make one of his favorite meals. Do you want a glass of wine or something while we wait?" She put her arm behind my back and gave me a side hug while I washed my hands under the kitchen faucet.

"Sure. I'll take a glass of wine. I hope you brought some since you know I don't keep that stuff around." She took slow steps toward the club chair where she'd been sitting when we came in.

Amalie found a corkscrew in one of the drawers. I opened the bottle of cabernet we'd picked up on the way over.

I filled a stockpot with water to get the pasta going while Amalie carried two glasses of wine to her mom. Then she took the chair opposite and held out her glass for a toast.

"What are we toasting to?" Her mom asked.

"How about Miller?" Amalie smiled at me.

My heart swelled a few sizes at the attention.

Her mom clinked her glass against Amalie's. "To Miller, making us a dinner we won't soon forget," her mom added.

I inclined my head toward the two of them. "Thanks. I'll try to not mess it up."

"So, Mom . . ." Amalie set her glass down on the small table between them. "There's something I wanted to talk to you about."

"What about?" Her mom took a small sip of wine. She didn't look the least bit curious. I kept stealing glances at the two of them as I used the manual can opener to pop open cans of chili.

Amalie's gaze shifted to me, then back to her mother. "It's

about your lease. I looked into that letter you received from your landlord, and he has every right to terminate your agreement since the government is claiming eminent domain."

Amalie didn't ask me for help, but I'd been involved in a case like that with one of our clients. "You can still fight it."

Mrs. Rivers looked up. "I can stop them from taking my house?"

"You don't know all the details." Amalie's lips stretched into a grim line. "I looked into it, Mom. There's nothing we can do."

"That's what they want you to think." I took a few steps toward where they sat by the table.

Amalie sat back, her expression unreadable.

"All you need is a good attorney to sort through it for you."

"And how much would that cost me?" Mrs. Rivers asked.

"I'm not sure. Probably a couple grand as a retainer until they can dig into things and get a good idea of what the case involves." I didn't want to start spouting off numbers since the only attorneys I'd worked with were from corporate firms.

"A couple grand?" Mrs. Rivers rolled her eyes. "What did I tell you, Amalie? Mr. Bishop must think I have a money tree out back."

I looked at Amalie, not understanding the faux pas I'd just committed. "Sorry. I was just trying to help."

Mrs. Rivers got up from the table to pour herself another glass of wine.

"Mom, let me get that for you." Amalie reached for the bottle and added more to her mother's empty glass. "It's a little more complicated than that, Miller. My mom owns the trailer but not the land. If her landlord makes a deal with the government, as long as he's given her proper notice, he doesn't owe her a thing. She's welcome to pick up and move this somewhere else, but—"

"I don't know that this place would survive a move," Mrs. Rivers said.

I looked around the interior. With fake wood paneling on the walls, it was difficult to tell what kind of shape it was in. There were a few stains on the ceiling, probably from water leaks that went too long before a repair. One window was covered in thick plastic like it had been broken but not yet replaced. It was difficult to picture Amalie growing up in a place like this.

"We'll figure something out, Mom. We always do." Amalie set the bottle back on the island and rested her hand on top of her mother's. "And here I thought we'd spend all night talking about Miller."

"What about Miller?" her mom asked.

My gut clenched. I didn't know how strong Amalie's mom's ties were to the Stewart family, but I hoped they didn't go so deep that they could threaten to tear us apart before our relationship got going.

"I know you've got strong feelings about the Bishop-Stewart feud," Amalie started.

Mrs. Rivers let out a laugh. "Honey, everyone within a hundred miles has strong feelings about that."

"I'm hoping you won't let any preconceived ideas about his family history cloud your judgment." Amalie held her mom's gaze, her spine straight, her voice calm and steady.

"I'll do my best. I got at least five phone calls from people who saw you canoodling around the market before you got here. If this town could run on gossip, we wouldn't have to worry about getting swallowed up as a suburb of Beaver Bluff." She sighed and took another long sip of wine.

Amalie glanced from her mother to me to back to her mom again before taking a deep breath through her nose. I wasn't sure if I should abandon dinner prep and go to her or keep watching for the first bubble to boil in the pot of salted water. The salty water won.

"And?" Amalie leaned forward, her forearms resting on her thighs.

"And what? Am I happy that the first man you decide to date is part of the Bishop clan? What do you think?"

Sensing it might be a good time to join the conversation, I reluctantly left my food prep station and pulled a chair over to sit by Amalie.

"Mrs. Rivers, with all due respect, I hope you'll form your own opinions about me based on our interactions and how I treat your daughter and not rely on a generations-old feud." I didn't know how much influence her mother's opinion of me held, but I hoped Amalie had gotten to know enough about me to see what kind of man I was.

"Call me Janna." Mrs. Rivers glanced up and met my gaze for a brief moment. "Amalie, I thought I raised you to make up your own mind about things and not let others influence you."

"You did, Mom. That's why Miller and I are sitting here. I just hope you feel the same way." Amalie reached for my hand and squeezed it.

"I trust your judgment, sweetheart. If you say Miller Bishop is a good person, then I believe you. I just wish I could say the same about his grandfather and the rest of his family."

My gut wrenched at the dig against my family. "Do you mind if I ask what happened to make you feel that way?"

Janna tapped her nails on the table. "How much time do you have?"

Amalie cast a nervous glance between the two of us. I shifted my leg close enough to touch hers, hoping that would settle her nerves. I wanted to know if my family had done something worthy of criticism.

"I've got however long it takes," I told her.

"Well then, I'd better start at the beginning."

Janna told me how her dad had worked at the distillery when my grandfather was in charge. The feud had been going on for years, and the division between the Bishop and Stewart families had never been so deep. Just like Amalie, she'd been an only child and often walked to the distillery after school since her parents didn't want her to go home to an empty house.

She'd take her schoolwork into one of the barrel houses where the warehouse workers put up barrels and find a quiet spot to do her homework. One day my great uncle Amos who was just a few years older than her, talked her into playing hide and seek with some of the other boys. She'd seen them duck in and out of a trapdoor on the bottom floor of the warehouse, so she decided that's where she was going to hide. While she was down there, the men working in the rick house moved a rack of barrels on top of the door.

She ended up trapped there for two days while her dad and everyone else searched high and low for her. It wasn't until Amos confessed that he'd seen her go down in the cellar that they found her. Since then, she'd held a grudge against my family and if ever forced to pick a side as most folks in Beaver Bluff had to do from time to time, she always sided with the Stewarts.

"Mom, I had no idea that happened. Why did you never tell me?" Amalie held onto her mother's hand.

"It never came up. Karma took care of Amos, and I just wanted to put it behind me."

"That's why you never took a job at the distillery." Amalie glanced over at me. "I always wondered why she'd skip over the better-paying jobs at Devil's Dance to work two different jobs for the same amount."

"I didn't want to be anywhere near there." A visible shudder ran through her, and she shivered.

I felt like shit. Knowing that someone I was related to had been responsible for putting another human being through that kind of trauma made me see red. If Uncle Amos hadn't passed when I was a kid, I would have had a few choice words for him.

"On behalf of my family, I'm incredibly sorry for what you experienced." I offered Janna my hand. "I don't know how to make it up to you."

"It's in the past." Janna gave me a weak smile.

"Well, I know one thing you can do." Amalie got up, pressed a kiss to her mother's temple, and nudged her chin toward the kitchen. "We can get dinner going so we're not eating at midnight."

"I'd be happy to." I resumed my post at the kitchen counter with a heaviness in my heart that wasn't there before.

CHAPTER 30
Amalie

WE DIDN'T LEAVE my mom's until we'd eaten every bite of Miller's amazing Beaver Bluff Three Way. He promised it was even better with homemade chili, but my mom and I thought it was delicious just how he'd served it. I started to believe that anything Miller did would automatically rate higher on my internal scale. He'd made an impression on me, and I couldn't stop smiling whenever I thought about how things were between us.

I wasn't ready to end our date, but he had to pick up Jack, and I still had homework I'd been putting off to spend time with him. We'd cleaned up my mom's kitchen and stood on the stoop to say our goodbyes.

"Thanks for having me for dinner," Miller offered his hand for my mom to shake, but she pulled him into a loose hug. He hugged back and headed down the steps. "I'll go warm up the truck while you say goodbye to your mom."

I nodded and waited until he got into the truck before I looked back to my mom. "Well? What did you think?"

"He seems nice enough."

"But?" I prompted. There was definitely a "but" coming. I

could tell by the way she toyed with the heart pendant I'd given her a few years ago for Mother's Day and wouldn't make eye contact.

"A leopard can't change its spots, honey."

"What's that supposed to mean?"

"It means that men like him like women like us for one reason. Once he gets it, he's not going to stick around."

"Miller isn't Dad." Based on what my mom said about my dad, he claimed to be in love until she found out she was pregnant. Then he told her his parents wouldn't let him marry someone they disapproved of and gave her money to get an abortion. When she refused, he left. Cut her out of his life and moved on, leaving her to support herself and me. Miller would never do that.

"He's not rich?" she asked.

"Just because he's rich doesn't mean he's an automatic asshole."

"No, but has he owned up to that day at the park?" She brushed the lapel of my coat with her fingers. "Does he even remember it?"

"I've got to go, Mom. I'll figure out something about the trailer, okay?" I pulled her in for a quick hug, then scrambled down the steps.

The whole way back to Beaver Bluff, her words rang in my ears. I didn't think Miller was just after me for a good time. But what if he hadn't changed? He'd said a few things while we were at my mom's that made me realize how different our two worlds were. What if, deep down, he still held onto some of those beliefs?

There was one way to find out. As he turned into his parents' drive to pick up Jack, I twisted to face him.

"Hey, can I ask you something?"

"Sure. What is it?" He tightened his grip on my hand.

"You know that cake I was talking about earlier?"

His smile almost glowed in the dark. "Yeah, rainbow layers with white frosting and sprinkles and candy inside. What about it?"

My breath stalled somewhere between my mouth and my lungs. I forced it down so I could continue. "I did have one of those cakes once. It was my tenth birthday. My mom saved for months so I could have a party at the park."

"Was it as good as you thought it would be?" He didn't give any indication that he remembered.

It was a long time ago, and there's no way it could have held the same impact on him as it did on me. I couldn't base the future of a promising relationship on an incident that took place over fifteen years ago. Yet, I continued.

"I never got to try it. Some boys were playing football close by."

"Oh yeah?"

"They threw the football at my cake then took off when it got ruined." Thinking about it brought back the same feelings I'd experienced then.

He cleared his throat. "What park did you say that was?"

"I didn't say yet. It was Beaver Trail Park, the area with the picnic shelter and the playground."

"That was you?" He tugged his hand from mine and wiped his palm on the leg of his jeans.

I nodded as he stopped in front of his parents' garage. "Yep."

He shifted his gaze from the driveway to my face. "Oh hell, Amalie. It was an accident. My friends and I were tossing the ball around, and one of them pointed out that cake. I bet him that he didn't have the power to toss the ball that far. He said he could take out that cake in one throw." Miller cut the engine and turned to me. "I never thought he'd do it."

"But he did." The disappointment I'd felt that day came racing back. I'd been on one of the swings, pumping my legs to send myself flying higher and higher. I saw the boy pull his arm back, the football gripped tightly in his hand. Then it flew forward, sailing through the air in a perfect arc.

"Is that what's got you down, sugar?" He reached up and brushed my hair away from my cheek. "It was just a cake."

My mom was right. He didn't understand. "It's not about the cake, Miller."

"Then what's it about?" A deep crease appeared between his brows.

"It's about you not thinking anything about ruining a girl's birthday party. The only birthday party I ever had. The only real cake I ever had."

"I said I was sorry. I'll buy you another cake. Just tell me what kind you want."

"That's the problem." I nodded. "You still think you can fix everything by pulling out your wallet, don't you?"

"That's not what I said at all." He tightened his hands on the steering wheel. "What brought this on? Did the guy at the tire store say something to you?"

The bottom dropped out of my stomach. "The guy at the tire store? Why? What did you do?"

Miller didn't respond.

"Why would you ask me about the guy at the tire shop?" The realization of what he'd done felt like a slap in the face. "You paid for my tires, didn't you?"

"Not all of them." Miller stared straight ahead.

"You may as well have. I thought the price he gave me seemed too good to be true." My chest hurt. Like someone had shoved a dull knife into my heart and was twisting it around and around.

"I was just trying to help."

"I don't want your help. Not like that."

A muscle ticked along his jaw. "I don't get you, Amalie. Maybe we need to take a step back from this. Maybe I should just take that job in Phoenix to give you some space."

"What job in Phoenix?"

"My company wants me to set up a satellite office."

"And you didn't think that was worth mentioning before?"

"Before what? I just found out about it yesterday, and Phoenix is only a few hours away. There's a non-stop flight from Knoxville."

"I can't believe you." I wanted my mom to be wrong about him, wanted him to be the man I thought he was instead of the man he'd always been. Her words rang in my ears . . . *Men like him like women like us for one reason.* I couldn't handle this right now. "It's late, and I've got studying to do. Can you take me home, please?"

He glanced up at the front door. His mom stood in the doorway, waving. "We need to talk about this, but I've got to go in and get Jack. Do you want to come with me?"

I crossed my arms over my waist. "I'll wait here."

He stood by his side of the truck with the door open. His gaze pressed down on me like a fifty-pound weight sitting on my chest. I fought the urge to look at him.

"I'll be back in a few minutes." Then he closed the door and made his way up the sidewalk, leaving me behind.

CHAPTER 31
Miller

I COULDN'T STAND KNOWING Amalie was sitting in the truck, pissed as hell at me, so I told my mom I needed to run her home first, and then I'd be back to pick up Jack. He was watching a basketball game with my dad and was more than happy to spend extra time with his grandparents.

Amalie didn't say anything the whole way back to the Calbots. I walked her to the door, still unsure what I needed to say to fix things. As much as I wanted whatever was going on between us to work out, I didn't know how it could.

"I'm sorry." We stood by the Calbot's front door. She had one hand on the doorknob. I sensed her desperation to get inside like it was a living, breathing thing.

"Yeah, me too." She tipped her chin up. The outdoor light reflected off her glasses.

I wanted to reach up and pull them from her face. Wanted to see her look at me the way she had last night, when everything felt possible.

"Goodbye, Miller." Her bottom lip trembled. She disappeared through the doorway.

The custom-carved door shut behind her with a thud. I

guessed that's what *The End* sounded like. A desperate laugh bubbled up inside. How could we have an end when we'd barely had a beginning?

Jack was curled up on the family room couch when I returned to my parents' place. My mom took one look at me and steered me into the kitchen.

"Let me make you some hot tea." She had me sit down at the table while she put the kettle on the burner.

I didn't even like tea, but I didn't want to be alone. Not now. Not when I'd been rejected by the only woman I'd ever fully opened my heart up to.

"How did your date go?" Dad came into the kitchen and set his empty glass in the sink.

"Fine." He was only trying to make conversation since my mom was there. When we were alone, he never acknowledged me.

He leaned against the counter and crossed his arms over his chest. "Amalie seems like a fine woman."

"She is." I wasn't about to tell him she would continue being a fine woman without me. It still hurt too much to think about, much less admit to my dad that I'd somehow managed to fuck up something else.

"Good. I'm glad to see you've found someone after…" He paused like he wasn't sure how to finish his thought.

"After what, Dad?" Maybe I shouldn't have pushed it, but I wasn't really acting like myself. Could have had something to do with being gutted. I was angry and looking for an outlet. And my dad stood directly in my line of fire.

"Look, son . . ."

"Son? That's rich. I was under the impression you didn't think of me as your son anymore. Not after . . ." I let the words trail off, intentionally copying his choice of words.

"Miller." Mom stood by the sink, halfway between us.

"What?" I didn't want her to get caught in the middle. Not again. Mom hated conflict, especially within her own family. She'd been trying to get the two of us to reconcile for years.

"That's a horrible thing to say." She pulled a tissue from the box on the counter and dabbed at her eyes.

"It is, isn't it?" I glared at my dad, waiting for him to deny it, to say something that would minimize what I'd been going through for the past six years.

"Ronan?" Mom's entire face crumpled. Her mouth turned down, her brows pulled together, and her eyes squished closed.

Dad scrubbed a hand over his chin and tilted his head back. "I've never understood you, Miller, but that doesn't mean I don't think of you as my son. You're a dad now. You should know a father's love is unconditional."

I got up from the table, my hands clenched into fists. "Don't you dare bring Jack into this. Despite you thinking every move I make is an epic fuck up, that my whole life has been one marathon fuck up, he's the best thing that's ever happened to me. And I'm going to make sure he knows every single day of his life how much I love him. My love for my son truly is unconditional."

Dad's cheeks flushed a faint shade of pink. "I've never thought that about you. Yes, you've made mistakes, but we all have. Over the past few years, you've turned things around."

"That's right, I have." I tapped my hand on my chest. "I've done that. You know people actually think I'm pretty good at stuff? I even got a job offer . . . a great job offer. They want me to set up a satellite location in Phoenix, and I'm going to take it."

"Phoenix?" Mom clutched her hands to her chest. "But that's so far away."

My jaw softened as I looked at my mom. This wasn't how

I'd planned on breaking the news. "We'll come back as often as possible, and I hope you'll want to come out to see us too."

She tossed her tissue in the trash and grabbed my father's hand. "This has gone on long enough. I won't have my family ripped apart because you're too stubborn to admit when you're wrong, Ronan Bishop."

Dad closed his eyes for a long blink. When he opened them, he nodded and held my mom's hands to his lips. "Can you excuse us for a few minutes, sweetheart? I need to talk to Miller alone."

Mom glanced back and forth between us and nodded before leaving the room.

I didn't know what to think. I'd never seen this side of my father before.

"Walk with me?" he asked.

"Fine."

I followed him down the hall, stopping while he pulled on his fleece-lined jacket. We stepped out into the yard. I wasn't sure I could feel anything, but the crisp night air sent a jolt through my nervous system. Memories of trotting along dad's side while he made the rounds of the property washed over me. He'd always preferred walking over talking. He wasn't a man who bared his heart and soul easily. I wondered how much I was going to get out of him tonight.

He shoved his hands in his pockets. "Don't move to Phoenix, Miller."

Anger bubbled up inside like a pot of water about to boil over. "I'm a grown man. You can't tell me what I can and can't do anymore."

He stopped by the side of the barn. "I'm not trying to tell you. I'm begging you not to."

There was something different in his voice. Something that

tugged at me and made me want to hear him out. "Mom can come visit, and I'll bring Jack back—"

He pulled his hand out of his pocket and reached for my arm. "Don't do this, please. I've made mistakes . . . so many damn mistakes, but I never meant to hurt you."

"You told me you didn't think of me as your son anymore. How was that not supposed to hurt?" I wanted to jerk my arm away, yet part of me needed closure from him.

Dad turned to face me. The light that hung from the corner of the barn illuminated the lines on his face, making him look much older than his fifty-plus years. "I'm sorry. I should never have said that. You were such a difficult kid to parent. It felt like you looked for ways to disobey me and challenge me."

I thought back to my teen years. "Hell, I probably did. It was impossible to follow in the footsteps of Vaughn, Cole, and Evan, so I didn't even try."

"There was a lot of pressure on you." Dad nodded. "It wasn't fair. Didn't mean you had to go to such extremes to make sure no one saddled you with the same expectations."

That was true. I'd put my parents through a lot trying to figure out who I was and where I fit into the family dynamic. "I'm sorry I wasn't a better son to you and mom."

His grip on my arm tightened. "I'm sorry I didn't set a better example."

We stood like that for a few long moments. Then Dad loosened his grip again.

"When you told us about Jack, I just wanted you to do the right thing. I couldn't understand why you wouldn't go after her. Why you didn't want to give that boy a mother."

It was time to come clean. Time to stop protecting a ghost and honoring the woman who'd given me my son. "I couldn't go after her because she died."

"What?" Dad's jaw dropped. "Why didn't you tell us?"

I took a deep breath, steeling myself to finally tell the truth. "She was a visiting professor from Syria. We had a one-night stand, and eighteen months later, she showed up with Jack. I was a sophomore in college who had no idea what I wanted to do with my life. She was knee-deep in working with women refugees in Syria and begged me to take him."

"Why didn't you tell us?"

"She asked me not to tell anyone. I didn't want to risk her losing her job and putting Jack in the center of some scandal. She wanted to go back and continue her work. I tried to convince her to stay. Told her we could work something out, that it was too risky to go back, and I didn't want my son to grow up without a mother."

His shoulders shook. He pulled his hand away from my arm and swiped at his cheeks. I'd never seen my dad cry. Not when my grandpa and grandma died, not when he had his leg crushed under a pallet of grain, and not when he and my mom renewed their wedding vows a few years ago.

"You should have told us. I thought . . . dammit . . . I thought you'd knocked up some coed who didn't want to take responsibility for her actions. We should have been there for you."

"Mom was. Vaughn, Cole, Evan, and Ruby too. The only one who wasn't there, Dad, was you." I knew it would hurt for him to hear that truth, but it had to be said.

"I'm sorry. I've been a foolish old man. Please tell me it's not too late. Give me another chance to be the father you've always needed. I never thought you'd want to leave. Everything I've done, everything my father did and his father before him... everything's been for you and your siblings and the ones who will come after."

The kind of peace I'd always wished for settled in my soul.

I still didn't agree with how my dad treated me, but it was time for me to take some responsibility for my actions.

"I suppose if I moved to Phoenix, I'd miss this."

"What? The smell of cow manure coming from the neighbor's fields?" Dad chuckled.

"Well, yeah, I guess. And seeing my breath in the cold air."

"It's too damn hot in Phoenix. Like living in the outer ring of hell, son."

Son. For the first time in too fucking long, I wanted to hear him call me that. "I'd probably melt."

"You'd go through whiskey withdrawal for sure."

The mood lightened. I didn't want to move to Phoenix anymore. I wanted to sit down at my parents' kitchen table and have a glass of whiskey with my dad.

"Hey, I've got a bottle of the anniversary blend in my truck if you want to try it." I held out my hand, hoping my dad would take that as the olive branch I intended.

He took my hand in his. "I think this calls for something even more special than that. I've been waiting to open my last bottle of Devil's Dance Distinct. Want to join me?"

My mom once told me people had different love languages. Some valued physical touch. Others drew more meaning from acts of service or spending quality time together. My dad's love language was whiskey.

Knowing he wanted to open his last bottle of his most valuable whiskey to share with me was the simplest yet grandest gesture he could have made.

"I'd love that, Dad."

"Good. Do you mind if I ask your mother to join us? I think she'd love to hear the truth about Jack's mom."

"Sure." I drew back and met my dad's gaze.

He opened his arms, and I pulled him in for a hug. The last

time I'd hugged my dad he still had a few inches on me. Now I towered over him.

Today had been full of ups and downs. I felt like I'd lost Amalie before I even had her. But I'd also gained something too. She'd told me family was the most important thing. I was man enough to admit she was right. Hopefully, I'd just found my way back to mine.

CHAPTER 32

Amalie

EVEN THOUGH MY heart felt like it had been surgically removed, no one seemed to notice as I made my way through the Monday morning routine at the Calbot household. Since Mrs. Calbot was home, I didn't have to take Caden along when I drove Bettina to school. Navigating the halls while taking the egg-ubator back to the classroom was challenging enough.

The kids couldn't wait to see if any eggs had hatched, and Bettina had taken great pleasure in telling them she'd decided to call the first one Gruda. Thankfully, neither she nor Jack went into detail about how we'd determined if the chick was male or female. No doubt, info about that endeavor would dribble out over the next few days during recess.

I'd driven through the coffee hut in town before I headed back to the house, but not even the combination of caffeine and sugar from my raspberry latte was able to lift my mood. I still couldn't get over my argument with Miller last night. It seemed like we'd made so much progress. Knowing he hadn't changed at all slayed me.

As I pulled the door from the garage to the laundry room

closed behind me, I caught sight of Mrs. Calbot standing in the hallway like she'd been waiting for me.

"Amalie, I'm glad you're back. Do you have a moment?"

"Of course." Caden and I didn't need to leave for his music class for another thirty minutes.

"Why don't we go into the kitchen?" She led the way, and I followed.

Caden sat in his highchair at the table. Mr. Calbot was trying to get him to hold some sort of hat on top of his head long enough to snap a photo.

"Caden, look over here." I whistled to distract him for the few seconds Mr. Calbot needed to get his picture.

"Thanks, Amalie." Mr. Calbot pulled up the photo and flipped his phone around so we could see it. "What do you think? We'll get a picture of him next to Bettina in that skirt and apron we brought her when she gets home from school, then we can send out our announcement."

I felt like I'd walked in on a conversation in progress. "What announcement?"

"That's what I wanted to talk to you about," Mrs. Calbot said. "We're moving to Switzerland, and we want you to come with us."

"Excuse me?" I heard what she said. I just couldn't process the information.

"Dave's been asked to spearhead the European division. That's why we stayed a few extra days. We found a charming little villa on a lake outside of Geneva. It's got the most gorgeous views." She unbuckled Caden from his highchair and picked him up while she told me about their new villa. "Of course, we'll rent at first to make sure we like it there, but honestly, what's not to like about Switzerland?"

Caden reached for me. Without thinking, I held out my arms. That's when I realized the outfit he had on was a pair of toddler-sized lederhosen with an embroidery-edged shirt. He looked like he was ready to take a stab at the Matterhorn.

"But I've got school, and my mom's here. I can't leave her behind." The reality of what she was saying started to sink in. They were moving the whole family across the ocean. I'd been with them since Bettina was a baby. Besides my mom, they were the only family I had.

"The villa's more of a chateau," Mr. Calbot said. "There's a separate wing with its own kitchen, bedroom, and living room. We'd never expect you to leave your mother behind. She'd be very comfortable there, and there's a clinic where they can do some advanced breathing treatments that might help her feel better."

"You could continue school online, couldn't you?" Mrs. Calbot asked.

"Um, I don't know. I think so, at least up until it's time for me to do my student teaching."

"By then, who knows? You might decide you'd rather teach overseas." Mrs. Calbot smiled like it was settled, but I still had a million questions flying around in my head.

"What about Bettina's school? When are you planning on moving?" The stark white kitchen walls felt like they were closing in on me.

"Dave needs to get over there right away. I thought the rest of us could follow in a couple of weeks. We'll hire someone to keep up with the house here until we decide whether we're coming back. Bettina only has a couple more months before school lets out for the summer, and she's already way ahead of the other children." She waved a hand in the air like she was dismissing every single one of my concerns. "We'll call it a long summer break, which should give you plenty of time to get out and explore the new surroundings."

"Um. I need to think about this."

Mrs. Calbot put a hand on my shoulder. "Of course you do. I hope you'll come with us. We consider you part of the family, Amalie. And your mother too. It wouldn't be the same without you."

My initial impulse was to wrap my arms around her and hug her tight. She was handing me a one-way ticket out of Beaver Bluff. For good. I'd always wanted the opportunity to travel but could never see myself leaving my mother behind.

With Mom about to lose her house, this was the perfect solution. If she were willing to come with us, I wouldn't have any reason to say no. Miller was willing to leave me behind and move halfway across the country. He'd made it perfectly clear where his priorities fell. He'd also made it perfectly clear he hadn't changed a bit.

Maybe I was the one who'd changed, and it was for the better. Maybe my time with him hadn't been a waste after all. Not if I'd learned it was time to start putting myself first. Moving to Switzerland would be the first step.

CHAPTER 33
Miller

I'D NEVER BEEN SO proud and so fucking miserable at the same time. Everyone kept coming up to me to tell me how fantastic the carnival was. Even Frannie was impressed. She'd stopped by the pop-up shelter I'd set up as our carnival HQ to tell me I'd exceeded her expectations. Either she didn't know me as well as she thought she did, or her expectations had to have been pretty damn low to begin with.

Over the past two days, I'd lost count of how many times I had to smile and nod and pretend like everything was fine. Amalie should have been here with me. Then I wouldn't have had to pretend. If she were standing by my side, everything would have been okay. Instead, she'd moved to Switzerland.

Switzerland!

She didn't even have the guts to tell me or say goodbye. I found out when a note came home from Jack's teacher. Mrs. Blessing wanted each kid to make a card for Bettina so she'd have one to open every few days to remind her of home.

Now I was nursing a broken heart and trying to hold my shit together so I could make it through the spring carnival I'd insisted on planning. Karma sure could be a bitch.

"Can I go on the big slide again?" Jack stopped by the tent with a couple of boys from his class to check in. Since Bettina moved, he'd fallen into a slump. I'd forced him to come to the carnival and was grateful he'd found a few friends to hang out with.

"Yeah. Here, take some tickets to share with your friends." I pulled the wad of tickets I'd bought out of my pocket and handed him half. The carnival would wrap up tonight. Then I had to make sure everything got cleaned up before heading over to help at the anniversary celebration at the distillery tomorrow.

I wondered what Amalie was doing right now. I'd found my thoughts drifting to her more and more over the past week. Since the last night I saw her, we hadn't talked, emailed, or even messaged each other. We'd only been together a split second in the grand scheme of things, although it had been the best split second of my entire life. The hole she'd left in my heart was big enough to park a pickup truck in. Maybe even a pick-up parked on top of a trailer, attached to a semi.

"Hey, Dad. Can I hang out with Spencer at the distillery tomorrow?" Jack hiked his thumb over his shoulder at Spencer Stewart, who stood just outside the shade cast by the tent.

My gut prickled at the idea of my son having a Stewart as a friend. But then I thought about what Amalie might say. Maybe this next generation wouldn't be burdened with battling the feud. If that was going to happen, it was up to my brothers, my sister, and me.

"Yeah, sure. Here, give Spencer some tickets too." I ripped another handful of tickets from the roll and tucked it back into my pocket.

"Thanks, Mr. Bishop." Spencer folded them and grinned at Jack. "Hey, let's go get a slushy first. Then we can see how many rides it takes down the big slide to get us to puke."

I opened my mouth to tell them what a horrible idea that would be but then snapped it closed. I'd done much stupider shit than that when I was his age. Usually, it was prompted by something one of my brothers said, but Jack was much smarter than I ever was as a first grader. He'd find his way.

Speaking of brothers, I spotted Evan's head bobbing through the crowd. At six-foot-four, he usually towered over everyone else.

"Hey, how does it feel to be the man of the hour?" Evan tugged off his Devil's Dance baseball cap as he stepped into the shade.

"When I find the man of the hour, I'll ask him," I said.

"Good to see you haven't lost your sense of humor." Evan slid onto a plastic chair.

I sat down on the other side of a fold-up table. "Yeah, my comedy game is strong right now. Might even go into stand-up."

"How are you really doing?" Evan held my gaze.

"Work's fine. The carnival's fine. Everything's fine." I stared right back at him, hoping he couldn't see through my lies.

"But . . ." Evan prompted.

"But what? She's gone. I let her walk away."

"You had to, Miller."

I glared at him through narrowed lids. "And why's that exactly? I should have told her how I feel. Had a big fucking heart with our initials in it written in the sky. Spelled out *I love you* with chocolate chips on a cookie as big as a Volkswagen."

"You think that would have changed her mind?"

"Maybe." I was pouting like someone half Jack's age.

Evan whacked me with his baseball cap. "All that might have done was delay the inevitable. If things are meant to be between the two of you, they'll work out."

"Work out how? She's gone." I spread my arms wide. She'd made her choice, and I had to live with the aftermath. When I heard through the Beaver Bluff grapevine the Calbots had invited her and her mom to live with them in Switzerland, I knew she'd leave. She'd told me that family was the most important thing in the world. How could I expect her to let them go without her?

"If it's meant to be, it'll be."

"That's some psychological woo-woo shit people came up with to make themselves feel better." I shook my head.

"Miller. Can you spare a moment?" My dad stepped under the shelter. I'd been so focused on moping that I hadn't seen him coming.

"Sure." I got up from the chair I'd been slouching in and reached into the cooler. "Want a cold bottled water?"

"Yes, please." Dad held out his hand to take the bottle I offered, then leaned against the table, putting his back to Evan. "You've done a great job on the carnival, son. The inflatables seem to be very popular with the kids."

"Jack's been down that damn slide at least a dozen times." I nudged my chin to the edge of the field where all the inflatables had been set up. The slide sat next to the big obstacle course—the one I'd been in when I'd lost my race against Amalie. I would have gladly let her win every other contest between us if she'd stuck around.

"You're doing a great job at the distillery too." Dad unscrewed the cap from his water bottle and took a long sip. "I know I don't say it often enough, but I'm really proud of you, Miller."

"Thanks, Dad." We were still navigating the boundaries of this new easiness between us, but hearing him say it, especially in front of one of my brothers, made my heart expand.

"I'm glad you decided to stay and work at the distillery.

You're the only one who can run interference between Vaughn and Cole without major collateral damage." He squeezed my shoulder before letting his hand fall back to his side. "And you're doing a great job with Jack. You're a much better father to him than I ever was to you."

"That's not true at all," I said. "Our past doesn't need to define us. It's what we do differently once we realize the mistakes we made in the past that matters."

"Well, I suppose retirement will give me the chance to do many things differently. I was thinking about getting Jack his own fishing pole for his birthday, if that would be all right with you. We had good times down at that fishing hole, didn't we?"

I thought of the picture of Dad, Jack, and me that used to sit on the bookshelf in my old office. "We sure did. I think Jack would like a pole of his own. Maybe the three of us could spend some time on the dock sometime soon."

"I'd like that, Miller." Dad held out his hand like he expected me to take it.

Instead, I pulled him into a tight hug.

He squeezed me back just as hard as I squeezed him. Amalie had been right. Family was the most important thing. And as far as I was concerned, she was just as much a part of my family as my brothers and parents. She didn't have to go to Switzerland to follow her family when she had one right here in Beaver Bluff.

I needed to find a way—a non-over-the-top way—to make sure she knew just that. It was time to let her know I'd finally learned from my mistakes. Time to own up to my past and not be afraid to fight for the future I knew I wanted.

CHAPTER 34

Amalie

"AMALIE, YOU'VE GOT A DELIVERY." My mom said something else I couldn't make out, then the outside door to our suite of rooms clicked closed. A few moments later, she nudged the door to my bedroom open and stood in the doorway with a white box in her hands. It was about sixteen inches tall and had bright pink writing across the side.

"What is it?"

"I don't know. Maybe you should get up and find out." She turned to carry it back to the kitchen, and I followed.

I'd been having a difficult time since we'd been in Switzerland. It was like my mom and I had traded places. She was thriving—the fresh mountain air had worked wonders on her lungs—and I'd taken over her grumpy attitude and then some.

I knew what was at the root of my mood change. It was Miller.

Despite my big speech about how family should come first, I hadn't been able to get him out of my mind. I woke up every day wondering what he might be doing... if Jack was having a hard time with Bettina being gone...what household item Titus had chewed up overnight.

Switzerland was incredible, but me in Switzerland? I was barely getting by. Something needed to change.

"Aren't you going to peek inside?" Mom stood next to the table, her hand planted on her hip.

"Did you order something?" I eyed the box. It looked like a bakery box, but my birthday wasn't until next week.

"No, but it smells delicious. If you don't get over here and open it, I'll do it myself."

I shuffled to the table and slid my finger under the tab holding the lid closed. The smell of vanilla and sugar drifted up from the table. My stomach rumbled in response. I flipped the lid back and stared down at a tall cake with white frosting.

Mom peered over my shoulder. "Is there a note or something?"

"I don't see anything."

"There." She pointed out the edge of an envelope taped to the bottom of the box.

I slipped my finger under the seal and pulled a small square card out of the envelope.

Dear Amalie,

I get it now. It wasn't just a cake. Even though I can't turn back time and do things differently, I want you to know I've changed. I didn't take that job in Phoenix. Running away from things that scare me won't solve anything. So, I'm here. Willing to fight for you. Willing to wait for you. The cake is in your court.

Yours,

M

Tension spread through my chest. It felt like my heart was being stretched out tight like a rubber band. I couldn't breathe.

"Who's it from?" Mom asked.

I snapped out of it, though my veins felt like they were full of something thick and cold. "Miller. The spring carnival is this weekend, and I guess he just wanted to say thanks."

Mom picked up the cake box and took it over to the counter. "I wonder how he found a bakery to deliver a cake. I bet Bettina and Caden will enjoy it. Maybe they can have a slice after we visit the park this morning."

"Yeah, that sounds good." I needed some space. Needed to get away from that cake. I'd just turned to head back to the bedroom when Bettina barreled through the door of our wing.

"Good morning, Amalie. Good morning, JaJa." Despite her mother's instructions to knock before entering, she never did.

"How did you sleep, sweetheart?" Mom asked.

"Great." She walked straight into my mom's open arms for her morning hug, then noticed the cake box on the counter. "What's that?"

"Jack's dad sent a cake since you can't be at the carnival this weekend," Mom said.

"Oh, cool. Can we have some for breakfast?" She rubbed her hands together and made a beeline for the box.

"Not so fast." Mom intercepted her before she reached it. She really had been getting better. I hadn't seen her move that fast in decades.

"Please, JaJa?" Bettina's brow furrowed, and she stuck out her bottom lip. That kind of move had never worked on my mom. She'd be better off sneaking in later and cutting a big piece for herself when my mother wasn't watching.

"What do you think, Amalie? Is cake for breakfast a bad idea?" Mom smiled at me.

"Are you kidding? She can't have cake for breakfast. Her mom absolutely wouldn't be okay with that." My mother was caught up in Bettina's web. We needed to talk about that soon.

"It's okay. I already ate breakfast." Bettina swiped a finger along the top of the cake, then popped the glob of frosting into her mouth. "This can be a morning snack."

"I like the way you think." Mom tapped the top of Bettina's head, then pulled a plate from the cabinet.

I didn't have enough energy to argue. Not when Miller had just ripped open the wound in my chest that hadn't even healed. I'd been down since we left Beaver Bluff, but knowing he'd been thinking about me, knowing he still wanted to try to make things work . . . this was a new level of pain.

I'd already been feeling like crap and letting my mom take the lead with the kids. She said she didn't have anything else to do and enjoyed spending time with them. They'd always looked at her like a grandma figure—a young grandma figure, according to my mother.

"Do you want a piece too, Amalie?" Bettina asked.

"No, that's okay. I'm going to get dressed so we can head out. Don't cut such a big piece, Mom. She'll be bouncing off the walls for hours."

"I don't bounce. I skip," Bettina called out.

Skip, bounce, what was the difference? Anything faster than a slow shuffle required more energy than I was willing to exert.

"If you don't want me to cut too big of a piece, then why don't you come do it?" Mom asked.

"Fine." I turned back and pulled a knife from the drawer.

Bettina rested her chin in her hands while she waited.

The knife slid through the cake, and I lifted a thin slice onto a plate.

Bettina gasped and looked up at me with wonder in her eyes. "It's a rainbow cake, and there's rainbow sprinkles inside."

It looked just like the cake I'd always coveted as a kid. But where had Miller found a rainbow sprinkle cake? The last time I'd seen one was at the Muster Family Market before their grandma had retired.

"How did he know?" I stared at the colorful layers of rainbow cake. It was just how I remembered.

"I bet he thinks you're the one who got away." Bettina slid her fork into her mouth and then licked it clean.

"Miller Bishop?" Mom looked from me to the cake to Bettina and back to me again.

My mom didn't get it... didn't get me. But somehow, Miller did.

"Yep." Bettina reached over to swipe some extra frosting from the edge of the cake round with her finger. "They were in love."

I glared at her. "That's a leap. We were barely even dating when we moved."

"Doesn't matter. The heart wants what it wants."

"Are you seriously quoting a Selena Gomez song to me?" I clamped my hands to my hips.

Bettina didn't look up, jut poked her fork into the next layer of cake.

Mom faced me, concern evident in the crinkles around her eyes. "Is that true, Amalie? Were things that serious between the two of you?"

I thought about lying, brushing off the question, or even laughing at the ridiculous idea that I could be in love with Miller Bishop. I cared about him. I still thought about him all the time. I missed him like I'd left a piece of myself behind in Beaver Bluff, Tennessee. The realization dawned on me slowly at first. Then it seemed to knock me over the head.

I was in love with Miller Bishop. The kind of love I'd wished for and assumed would always be out of my reach.

Tears started to well up in my eyes. "I think so."

"Told you." Bettina's lips curved into a smug, knowing smile. "He loves you too."

"What makes you think that?" Hope fluttered in my chest.

"Because Jack and I told him you were his LOML, and he didn't deny it." She looked so proud of herself.

"What does LOML mean?" Mom asked.

Bettina rolled her eyes. "It means love of my life, JaJa."

"Well, it doesn't matter if he does." Miller probably had no idea what LOML even meant. I swiped the back of my hand over my cheek. "Because I'm here and he's there and there's nothing either of us can do about it now."

Mom and Bettina wore the same expression: bright eyes, lips curved upward like they were about to start laughing.

"What?" I asked.

Mom glanced at my phone sitting on the counter. "You've heard of a phone, haven't you? Why don't you call him?"

"You've heard of a plane, haven't you? Why don't you go tell him?" Bettina mimicked my mother's stance and put one hand on her hip.

The possibility of seeing him made my heart feel like it had wings. Then I looked at the two of them. I couldn't leave Bettina, and I couldn't ask my mom to come back to Tennessee with me, not when she was feeling better than she had in years.

"I can't. Not when I'm needed here." I took in a shaky breath.

"Needed by who?" Mom asked. "You've been in a slump since the day we got here. I've been doing most of the work with the kids."

I was about to call her out for telling lies, but then I thought about what I'd been doing since we arrived in Switzerland. She was right. While I'd been wallowing in self-pity, she'd been pulling most of the weight when it came to caring for Bettina and Caden.

"I'm sorry, Mom. You're right. I don't know what's gotten into me lately."

"I do." Bettina left her empty plate on the counter and climbed off the stool. "You love him. You'd better go back and tell him."

"What about you and Caden?" I asked.

"JaJa can take care of us." Bettina snuggled into my mom's side.

"But—"

"But nothing," Mom said. "I feel better than I have in years. I don't want to go back to Tennessee. There's something about the air here… it's fresher, cleaner, and better for my lungs. I'll stay and take over with Bettina and Caden. It will feel good to start earning a living again. Especially when I'm going to need money for airfare so I can come visit every once in a while."

"What if he doesn't want me there? What if he's moved on? What if he's so hurt that I left that he'll never be able to forgive me?"

"The man went to the trouble of sending you a cake from halfway around the world. He's clearly not over you yet," Mom said.

"A really good cake," Bettina added.

"You think?" I wanted to believe them. I wanted to think that Miller had been pining away for me since the moment I'd left Beaver Bluff like I'd been pining away for him.

"Doesn't he have that anniversary party for the distillery coming up?" Mom asked.

My breath froze in my lungs. "It's tomorrow."

"Weren't you supposed to go with him?" She tilted her head forward and peered at me over the rim of her bifocals.

"Well, yeah, but that was before we moved, and he's probably found someone else to take by now. Besides, I'd never make it in time."

"There's a flight at four o'clock that would get you into Nashville tomorrow afternoon." Mom looked up from her phone.

"That would cost a fortune."

"It's not as bad as I thought." Mom glanced at the ceiling like she was running numbers in her head. Then she typed something into her phone. "There. Done deal. We'd better get you packed and to the airport in time."

"Mom! You can't just buy me a plane ticket like that."

"I just did." She held out her phone, showing a one-way ticket booked in my name.

I slid my fingers into my hair and grabbed two fistfuls. "What's gotten into you? The money you got from the sale of the trailer was supposed to be for you."

"It's for us. Let me do this for you, Amalie. You've been paying your way since you were old enough to get a job. I've never had more than two nickels to rub together and could never help you. It's my choice what I want to do with this money, and I'm choosing to spend it on you." She set her phone down on the counter and cut a thick slice of cake. "Now, let's eat some of this delicious cake for a morning snack, and then Bettina and I will help you get ready to go."

"Mom, I don't know what to say."

"I know what you can say," Bettina offered.

"What's that?"

"You can say I can have another piece of cake." She clapped her hands together and glanced back and forth between my mom and me.

"I think you'd better ask JaJa about that. Seems like she's going to be in charge of you from now on."

CHAPTER 35
Miller

MY PHONE PINGED as I walked through the gates of the area we'd marked off for the anniversary celebration. I didn't expect to hear anything from Amalie, but my heart gave a little jump every time I got a notification. This one was the bakery I'd found outside of Geneva, letting me know that the cake had been delivered yesterday afternoon. At least I knew she'd received it. I'd only had the description she'd given me to go by. Hopefully, I'd paid enough attention that whatever they delivered was close to the cake she remembered.

I wasn't looking forward to the party, especially coming on the heels of the carnival at Jack's school. Two major events in the space of three days was a lot to pack in. At least I wasn't in charge of the anniversary celebration. Ruby was the one trying to juggle all the to-do's today.

"Miller, you're here." She met me by the table that we'd set up to collect tickets. "I thought you and Jack could keep an eye on the root beer stand."

"You sure that's a wise choice?" I asked.

"What do you mean?"

"I mean, we might drink more of the inventory than we

sell." Cole might not have recreated the original Devil's Dance mash bill, but he'd come up with a winner in the form of a new Devil's Dance craft root beer. We'd debuted it at the school carnival two days ago, and the distillery had already sold out of everything except for the kegs we'd set aside for the party today.

Ruby waved away my concern. "We're not doing an official launch on that for another month or two. I can only handle one new product at a time."

"Where are all your helpers?" I hadn't seen any of the Stewarts on site yet. As much as I wished we could put the damn feud behind us, when they pulled shit like not showing up for our joint anniversary party, it made me want to find a way to squeeze them out of the business.

"Evan's inside doing a final inventory so we know how much product we have on hand. Vaughn's probably popping antacid pills to ward off any ulcers. I haven't seen Cole and Danica yet. No telling what they've been up to." She pursed her lips in annoyance. "How long is the honeymoon period supposed to last?"

"Seeing as how they're not even married yet, I think we've got a ways to go." As the youngest in the family with four older brothers, Ruby hadn't been exposed to a bunch of lovey-dovey stuff growing up. We'd always thought of her as one of the guys since she was the only girl. Now that I'd had my heart shredded, it seemed like we'd done her a favor.

"Well, if they're not here in the next fifteen minutes, I might need you to go rustle them up." She stole a quick look at a piece of paper secured to the clipboard in her hand. "Before you start on the root beer, can you make sure Mr. Shepler has everything he needs before he takes the stage?"

"You bet." I looked around for Jack. He couldn't have gone too far since we'd just arrived.

"I'll check in with you later. Keep your phone on you in case I have to send out an SOS."

"Everything's going to be fine, Ruby." I set my hand on her shoulder, hoping it would provide some comfort. People had been telling me the same thing for the past several weeks. Everything was going to be fine. But in my case, everything wasn't going to be fine. It would probably never be fine again. Since Amalie left, the only thing getting me through was knowing that I had to take care of Jack.

At least for Ruby, once she got through the day, it would be over, and she wouldn't have to live through it again. For me, every day without Amalie was the same as before. At least I'd sent the cake. Knowing I'd owned up to my past mistakes and told her how I felt was the first step in moving on.

"Hey, Jack. Come on. We need to check backstage." I motioned for him to head my way and took off toward the temporary grandstand we'd set up at the far end of the property.

Ruby wanted the stage set up between two of our oldest barrelhouses. She said it would look good in all the pictures people would post of the event. All I cared about was how much it was costing us. It would have been cheaper to set up closer to the building so we didn't have to run so many power cords. Now that I was working full-time at the distillery, my siblings had better get used to me having stronger opinions about things.

I poked around backstage, wincing as I peeked into the temporary green room we'd set up for the performers. Ruby had given me a copy of the band's rider when I told her I'd booked Knox Shepler for the event, but seeing the spread in person made me realize how much it was costing us. Amalie had been right about that too. I did tend to do things over the top. Since she left, I'd been keeping that in check, trying to tell myself it wasn't what I did but how I made people feel that was important.

My chest ached as I thought about her. It was Sunday night in Geneva. She was probably feeding Bettina and Caden dinner before starting their bedtime routine.

"Hey, Dad. Can Spencer and I hang out backstage while the band warms up?" Jack asked.

I turned to a guy dressed in cowboy boots and a black felt cowboy hat who'd introduced himself as the band's manager. "Are you all set? Need anything?"

"We're good. The kids are welcome to watch from back here as long as they stay out of the way." He nodded toward me and took off to the other side of the stage.

"You hear that, Jack? Stay out of the way."

Jack gave me a thumbs-up before he and Spencer disappeared behind a cluster of speakers.

Maybe it was time to let my kid teach me a lesson. He'd moved on. Though he'd never fully replace the hole Bettina left in his life, he wasn't sitting around and moping about it. He'd made new friends. He'd put himself out there. I needed to stop punishing myself. Tonight would be the last time I'd let myself think about Amalie. I'd send her off with a toast of Devil's Dance anniversary blend, then shut down that part of my brain and heart for good.

Unfortunately, making that decision didn't ease any of my pain. I traced my steps back to the root beer stand and was ready when Ruby opened the gates.

The next few hours flew by. It was good to have something to do. Being busy helped pass the time, and I was surprised when Evan showed up with Frannie to take over.

"We're supposed to take it from here." He stepped behind the table and moved over so Frannie could follow.

"Where do I need to go next?" Ruby told me to plan on

spending the entire day helping out, so I was sure she expected me to rotate to another station.

"The boss said you're done for the day." Evan slipped one of the Devil's Dance Distillery aprons over his head, then handed one to Frannie. "Knox is supposed to take the stage soon. Why don't you go enjoy yourself for a little while?"

"I've got work to catch up on. If you see Jack around, tell him to find me in my office." I tossed the apron I'd had on under the table.

Evan stopped me with a hand on my arm. "It's been over a month, man. Don't you think it's time to move on?"

"Move on?" I slowly turned to face the two of them. "What do you think I've been trying to do?"

He glanced down at his feet, his hand still on my arm. "I shouldn't have talked you out of making a splash."

"Hell, is that what this is about? You feel guilty because you think me taking out a full page ad in the Times or having an airplane write our initials in the sky would have changed her mind?" I stepped back so that Evan's hand fell away.

"Maybe." He shrugged, then lifted his chin to meet my gaze.

"All that would have done was to delay the inevitable and put her on the spot." Amalie made it clear she wasn't a fan of my over-the-top gestures. Even sending the cake had probably been too much.

The band had just taken the stage, and the crowd started clapping to the beat of the music. Evan said something, but I couldn't hear him over the bass wailing from the massive speaker a few feet away.

"What did you say?" I yelled.

He lifted his arm and pointed up. "Was this one of your ideas?"

I looked at the sky and saw a hot air balloon in the

distance. It looked beautiful against the backdrop of the late afternoon sky. I shook my head. "Nope, this wasn't me. Just good timing and good luck, I guess."

"Hey, everyone. Look up." Knox clapped his hands on stage and directed everyone's attention to the balloon heading our way. "As most of you know, the first single I released was about how falling in love made it feel like my heart had grown wings. I don't usually play that song during my set, but I've had a special request to perform it tonight."

Jack suddenly appeared at my elbow. "Did you really bring a balloon in, Dad?"

I put my hand on his shoulder. "This wasn't me."

"Do you think it's going to land here?" Jack pointed up as the balloon got closer. It did seem like it was drifting a little lower in the sky than it had been a few moments ago.

The first bars of the song came through the speakers. Knox started singing about how it felt to fall in love, and I couldn't take another fucking moment.

"I'm going to head inside." I pulled the rest of the tickets out of my pocket and tried to hand them to Jack. "Here, use these up, then come and get me when you want to go home."

Jack didn't take them. He was too busy holding a hand over his eyes and squinting into the sun.

"Hey,"—I pressed the tickets into his stomach—"do you want these or not?"

I needed to get away. The combination of the music, the damn balloon, the ache in my chest, and the knowledge that I should have done more to stop Amalie from moving halfway across the world threatened to smother me.

"Wait." Jack grabbed my hand along with the tickets. "Is that Amalie?"

The mention of her name turned me inside out. "Where?"

"Up there." Jack pointed to the basket hanging down from the balloon.

It was definitely getting lower. Low enough that I could just make out two women inside the big wicker basket. One was blonde, and the other had on a hat or something that covered up her hair. Convinced that wishful thinking had me seeing things, I shifted my gaze to my son's face.

"Jack, I know you're sad Bettina moved, but we've got to stop hoping she and Amalie will come back." If it was this hard for him to process a friend moving away, I was glad I'd decided to stay in Beaver Bluff so he didn't have to start over in a new place.

"But she *is* coming back." He dragged his gaze away from the sky and looked into my eyes. "That's her, Dad."

Why did he have to make this so hard? I rested my palm on his shoulder, prepared to let him down easy. Then I glanced up one more time. One of the women in the basket unrolled something. She lifted it over the edge, trying to flatten it against the side.

I love you, Miller.

My heart stopped beating.

What the fuck?

Jack started jumping up and down and even landed on my foot a couple of times. I barely felt it. Every part of me was too focused on the hot air balloon preparing to touch down about a hundred yards away.

"Come on." Jack grabbed my hand and tugged me toward it. Toward the woman in the basket. Toward Amalie.

CHAPTER 36

Amalie

I'D HAD a hard time finding Miller in the crowd at first. Based on the hundreds, if not thousands, of people scurrying around like ants on the distillery grounds below, they'd had an impressive turnout for the anniversary party. It seemed not everyone was averse to his over-the-top ideas.

As the balloon drifted closer to the party, I started to make out clusters of people in the crowd. I recognized a few of the Stewarts. Then I saw Miller's parents standing by the patio they'd built off the back of the tasting room. Gigantic buildings where they stored the whiskey barrels dotted the landscape, and the band took the stage that had been set up between two of them.

It was colder than I expected, floating hundreds of feet above the ground, but also so peaceful. I'd tugged a knit beanie over my ears when we started to climb into the sky. Hopefully, Miller would still recognize me when it came time to hold out the sign I'd made.

"Are you ready to start our descent?" The balloon operator I'd hired out of Nashville assured me she'd be able to land this thing on the distillery grounds. Then all I needed to do was grab Miller and tell him what a huge mistake I'd made by leaving him behind.

With my heart pounding triple time in my chest, I nodded.

The balloon slowly drifted down. The ants on the ground became bigger and bigger. Soon, I picked out Miller's brothers and sister.

Then I saw him.

Miller.

He and Jack stood halfway between the stage where Knox was singing the song I'd requested and the distillery offices. Jack pointed up at me, but Miller didn't appear to be looking. I unrolled the sign I'd made and held it over the side.

That's when he looked up. We were still too high for me to get a read on his expression, but Jack started jumping up and down. Seeing his excitement made my nerves spike. This was so unlike anything I'd ever done. I was way out of my comfort zone. About a hundred yards above my comfort zone.

As the balloon got closer and closer to touching down, Jack and Miller ran across the grounds. I couldn't wait to get my hands on both of them. I wanted to pull them into a hug and never let go. How the hell had I convinced myself I could move so far away and be okay?

Miller must have seen the sign pressed against the basket. He cupped his hands around his mouth and yelled something. The breeze garbled his words and made it sound like Caden trying to talk when he had something in his mouth.

"What?" I yelled back.

Jack ran off, but my attention stayed on Miller. He tried again, but the wind carried his words away before I could hear him.

"I'm going to set down right over there if that's okay with you?" The balloon operator pointed to a clearing another fifty yards away.

I turned back to look over the edge of the basket just in time to see Jack hand Miller a bullhorn. A high-pitched noise pierced through the distance between us. Miller did something to the handle, then held it up to his lips.

"I love you, Amalie." His words came out loud and clear.

My heart felt like it was doing cartwheels, back flips, and round-offs, all at the same time. The ground was getting closer and closer. I leaned over the side of the basket and cupped my hands around my mouth. The wind ripped the sign away, and it floated to the ground.

"I love you, too, Miller," I yelled.

Jack ran toward where the sign blew across the grass. Miller reached for the weight the pilot had lowered over the side and caught hold of one of the ropes. The basket touched down.

Before I could climb out, Miller wrapped his arms around me and tugged me over the side.

"I thought I'd lost you," he mumbled against my ear.

"I'm sorry I put us through this." I slid my hands under his jacket, needing to feel his solid chest. Needing to make sure this was real.

"I'm sorry I let you go." His nose slid along mine. "Don't worry. It's not going to happen again."

"Good. I was so blind, Miller. I'm sorry I couldn't see what was right here in front of me. When I told you that family came first, I only thought about the family I belonged to. Not the one I wanted to make. I thought if you were so willing to leave your family behind, you might do the same to me someday."

He brought his hands up to cup my cheeks. "I'd never leave you. I wanted to come after you, but I was afraid you'd turn me down. I've changed, Amalie. I'm not afraid of putting myself out there anymore. Being around you, I learned how to be a better man. I want to be the man you need me to be, and I'm going to be the man who deserves you if you'll let me."

My knees went weak. He was saying all the right things, offering me everything I've ever wanted. "You're already the man I need, Miller."

He held my gaze. The love in his eyes said it all.

"Oh, I almost forgot." I took his hand and tugged him toward the basket where I'd left my bag. "I brought you something."

"I don't need anything but you, Amalie." He tried to nuzzle his lips against my neck, but I ducked out of the way.

"You might not say that after you've tried this cake." I pulled a small box out of the bag.

"You brought me cake all the way from Switzerland?"

"No. I brought you and Jack cake all the way from Switzerland."

"Let me get this straight. You're not a fan of my over-the-top gestures, but it's okay for you to show up in a hot air balloon, declare your love for me in front of half the county, and bring cake from the other side of the world?" His smile let me know he was teasing, but there was still some truth to his words.

"I love you for who you are, not what you do," I said. "You don't have to do stuff like that for me to appreciate you."

"But you liked the cake?"

"I loved the cake." My arms went up to circle his neck. "Maybe sending me a cake from time to time would be okay."

"We'll work on that." He closed the narrow distance between us and slanted his mouth over mine. While the music played around us and he claimed me with his kiss, my heart grew lighter and lighter until it felt like it was flying.

Jack crashed into us, wrapping his arms around both of our

waists and squirming his way between us. "Can we have a family hug?"

"A family hug, huh?" I kept one hand on Miller's shoulder and moved the other to pull Jack in close. "I like the sound of that. What if we take our family hug up in a hot air balloon?"

"Can we, Dad?" Jack's eyes burned bright with excitement.

"We sure can. We've got a lot to celebrate since Principal Masterson just told me we raised enough money at the carnival to pay for the new playground equipment."

"We did? That's amazing." In that moment, I vowed to never doubt him again.

"I've got to warn you, Jack. When we go up in the balloon, there's going to be kissing." Miller eyed me over the top of his son's head. "Do you think you can handle that?"

"Can you keep it to a minimum?" Jack asked.

I held Miller's gaze as I led them both to the basket. "No promises, but we'll try."

We took off again, slowly floating up into the air while Miller's family gathered below us and waved. With one arm around Miller and one around his son, I felt like I was finally where I was supposed to be. Finally, where I wanted to be. I was home.

Epilogue

MILLER

IT HAD BEEN a couple of months since Amalie decided to come back to Beaver Bluff. No matter how long it had been since we'd gotten together, I was always eager to get my hands on her. Based on the way she'd been grinding her backside against my front since we showed up to taste the next batch of Cole's special release, she felt the same way.

"What if we ducked inside the barrel house for a few minutes?" I suggested. Jack had been super clingy lately which had cut into our time between the sheets.

"Have I told you lately what a brilliant mind you have?" she mumbled against my ear.

No one would miss us for a few minutes—or a half hour, if things went as well as they always did between us.

I grabbed hold of her hands and jogged toward the door of the big building. The sooner we got inside, the sooner I could be inside her.

I'd barely locked the door behind us when I pinned her against the wall and pressed my lips to hers. Here, in the semi-darkness of the old barrel house, we could hold the rest of the world at bay. It was just me and her and a bunch of bottled-up need. She must have felt the same way because her knees almost buckled when I slid my foot between hers and ground my pelvis against the apex of her thighs.

Her hands went to the button at my waist. I might have gone years without sex before I'd met Amalie, but that was before I knew what I was missing. Sex with her wasn't just sex. It was sex on steroids. The kind of sex people wrote epic poems about. How did I ever think I'd be able to live without it? Without her?

I shifted my lips to her ear, ran my tongue down her neck, and pressed kisses against her collarbone while I worked my jeans down my hips.

"There's no rush," she whispered.

"Yes, there is, sugar."

Her soft laugh sent goosebumps racing over my skin. "Why are you in such a hurry?"

I pulled back enough to look her straight in the eye. "The sooner I come inside you, the sooner we can do it again."

"I can't argue with that solid logic." She hiked her skirt up her thighs and helped me wriggle her panties down her hips.

Within moments of entering the building, she was sliding onto my cock, her back up against the wall, my chest pressed against hers.

"This. This is what I've missed." She sighed as she stretched around me. "Good god, Miller. Did it feel this good the last time we did this? It's been so long I can't remember."

I chuckled. It had been less than a week, but we were insatiable together. "It always feels this good with you, Amalie."

Despite the need building inside me, I made love to her slowly, rocking my hips into her gently, pressing deeper and deeper each time.

Her legs tightened around my waist. Then her whole body trembled. I continued to ease in and out, over and over and over again, until her nails dug into my shoulders, and she went limp against the wall. One more piston of my hips, and I spilled into her. I couldn't wait to get some time with her alone so I could make love to her properly. We'd had to sneak around lately, but I planned on taking her away for the weekend after school got out for the summer.

She'd barely rested her feet on the floor when the door opened on the other side of the barrel house. Like hell I was going to let someone catch us with my ass hanging out and her panties on the ground.

I grabbed her hand and crouched down, feeling around with my other hand for where we'd tossed the clothes we'd removed.

Amalie stifled a giggle.

"Shh," I whispered. Low voices came from the entrance of the warehouse. Probably some kids messing around while their parents finished up their shift, just like I used to run through the rick houses when I was their age. I wasn't going to confront them with my cock hanging down between my thighs. Our best bet was to avoid them until they got tired of fumbling around in the dark.

A bright beam of light bounced off one of the barrel racks. Shit, they were using a flashlight.

My fingers brushed against a handle of some sort—dirt and hay and who the hell knew what else packed around it. I didn't know what it was, but I was going to find out. Finally, I touched the edge of something that felt like what was left of Amalie's panties. I wadded them up and shoved them in my pocket.

Thank fuck, my jeans were nearby. I let go of Amalie's hand just long enough to pull them on, then pressed her against the wall.

"Stay here. I'm going to get rid of them," I whispered.

She nodded.

The best defense was to go on the offense, so I took a deep breath and ran my hand along the rough wall until I found the light switch.

"What the hell's going on in here?" My voice bounced off the barrels, making it sound bigger and louder than I'd intended.

The intruders shrieked, laughed, and ran out the same way they'd come in. Just kids. Next time I wanted some alone time with my girl, I'd be more selective.

Amalie walked over, her skirt in place and no evidence of what had just happened between us except for the flush on her cheeks.

"Sorry about that." I took her hand and ran my foot along the dirt floor, searching for whatever I'd touched earlier. There it was. The edge of something metal poked up from where it was encased in dirt.

I let Amalie's hand go and knelt to take a closer look. "Well, I'll be damned."

"What is it?" She crouched next to me.

"It's a handle. There's something under here." No one had ever mentioned there being something under the barrel houses. I wondered if Vaughn or Cole knew about it. I brushed the dirt away with my hand, then stood and used my foot to make faster progress.

"Do you think . . ." Amalie stared at the ground as the shape of a wooden door appeared on the floor. "Do you think this is where my mom got trapped all those years ago?"

"That's what I'm wondering. Help me clear it off?"

We focused on brushing the dirt away until we'd revealed a piece of wood measuring about two feet by two feet.

"What do you think it is?" Amalie asked.

"I don't know, but we'll find out." I yanked the metal ring.

Slowly, the door cracked open. It smelled cool and dank and musty. I turned on my flashlight app and directed the beam to point down into the hole.

"Do you see anything?" Amalie asked.

"It's deep." I looked at the opening, wondering if there was any way in hell I could squeeze my hips through. This was the point where I should get my brothers. We could grab a few shovels, plug in some shop lights, and figure out if there was anything worthwhile in the hole we'd uncovered. But I didn't want to leave. If this was where Amalie's mom had been trapped, I wanted to make sure there wasn't anything bad inside before I brought in the others.

"Hold the light?" I asked.

She took my phone and waited until I bent over and lowered the top half of my body into the hole. "Can you pass it to me?"

Her fingers brushed mine as she handed me the light.

The beam ran over dark dirt walls. Thick roots grew through the sides of the hole, and there were enough spider-webs down there to make a grown man shiver.

"What's down there?" she asked.

"Nothing." I swept the light around in a circle, my hope of finding something disappearing. Then the light picked up something shiny. "Hold on. There's something down here."

"Can you tell what it is?" Amalie squeezed my leg.

I shifted the light and pointed it at the far corner of the hole. Two barrels and three ceramic jugs sat up against the wall.

A rush of adrenaline made my hand shake. "Holy shit."

"What?"

I couldn't make out the letters stamped on the barrels, but I recognized the emblem burned into the side. "It's Devil's Dance. We've got to get Cole. I think we might have found the secret to figuring out how to replicate that old mash bill."

Thanks for picking up this copy of **Tasting Temptation**! For an exclusive bonus scene with Miller and Amalie, subscribe to Dylann's newsletter: https://dylanncrush.com/tasting-tempta tion-bonus-scene/.

And to pre-order the next book in the series, Sipping Seduc-tion: https://dylanncrush.com/sipping-seduction/.

Also By Dylann Crush

WHISKEY WARS SERIES

Drinking Deep

Tasting Temptation

Sipping Seduction

TYING THE KNOT IN TEXAS SERIES

The Cowboy Says I Do

Her Kind of Cowboy

Crazy About a Cowboy

LOVEBIRD CAFÉ SERIES

Lemon Tarts & Stolen Hearts

Sweet Tea & Second Chances

Mud Pies & Family Ties

Hot Fudge & a Heartthrob

HOLIDAY, TEXAS SERIES

All-American Cowboy

Cowboy Christmas Jubilee

Cowboy Charming

THE LOVE VIXEN SERIES

Getting Lucky in Love

STANDALONE ROMANCES

All I Wanna Do Is You

About the Author

USA Today bestselling author Dylann Crush writes contemporary romance with sizzle, sass, heart and humor. A true romantic, she loves her heroines spunky and her heroes super sexy. When she's not dreaming up steamy storylines, she can be found sipping a margarita and searching for the best Tex-Mex food in the Upper Midwest.

Dylann co-hosts Romance Happy Hour (https://www.romancehappyhour.com/) with live episodes every 2nd and 4th Thursday of each month and is the founder of Book Box Babe (https://www.BookBoxBabe.com) where readers can find hand-curated, romance novel themed subscription boxes, and specialty items.

Although she grew up in Texas, she currently lives in a suburb of Minneapolis/St. Paul with her unflappable husband, three energetic kids, a clumsy Great Dane, a lovable rescue mutt, a very chill cat, and a crazy kitten. She loves to connect with readers, other authors and fans of tequila.

You can find her at www.dylanncrush.com.

www.ingramcontent.com/pod-product-compliance
Lightning Source LLC
Chambersburg PA
CBHW011200190726
48286CB00009B/2851